A Few Drops of Bitters

G.A. McKEVETT

Kensington Publishing Corp.
www.kensingtonbooks.com

KENSINGTON BOOKS are published by

Kensington Publishing Corp.
119 West 40th Street
New York, NY 10018

First Kensington Hardcover Edition: August 2021

First Printing: October 2022
ISBN: 978-1-4967-2017-7

ISBN: 978-1-4967-2018-4 (ebook)

10 9 8 7 6 5 4 3 2 1

Printed in the United States of America

PRAISE FOR G.A. MCKEVETT AND THE SAVANNAH REID MYSTERIES

AND THE KILLER IS . . .

"McKevett tempers coldhearted murder with heart-warming relationships as she highlights serious social issues. Cozy fans will rejoice."

—*Publishers Weekly* (Starred Review)

BITTER BREW

"This long-running cozy series again injects plenty of humor into the mystery and heightens interest with the frame story concerning rare genetic diseases. And, of course, the larger-than-life Savannah continues to delight."

—*Booklist*

"Clever banter adds levity to an emotionally taxing mystery, and Savannah's Granny Reid offers her earthy wisdom and a shoulder to cry on. Fans of darker cozies will be well satisfied."

—*Publishers Weekly*

BURIED IN BUTTERCREAM

"A wonderful edition to the series."

—*Suspense Magazine*

CORPSE SUZETTE

"Savannah's as feisty as ever."

—*Kirkus Reviews*

MURDER A LA MODE

"Added to a well-plotted mystery, the very funny depiction of a different side of reality television makes *Murder á la Mode* a delight."

—*Mystery Scene*

PEACHES AND SCREAMS

"A luscious heroine, humor, and down-home characters."

—*Library Journal*

Books by G.A. McKevett

Savannah Reid Mysteries

JUST DESSERTS
BITTER SWEETS
KILLER CALORIES
COOKED GOOSE
SUGAR AND SPITE
SOUR GRAPES
PEACHES AND SCREAMS
DEATH BY CHOCOLATE
CEREAL KILLER
MURDER A` LA MODE
CORPSE SUZETTE
FAT FREE AND FATAL
POISONED TARTS
A BODY TO DIE FOR
WICKED CRAVING
A DECADENT WAY TO DIE
BURIED IN BUTTERCREAM
KILLER HONEYMOON
KILLER PHYSIQUE
KILLER GOURMET
KILLER REUNION
EVERY BODY ON DECK
HIDE AND SNEAK
BITTER BREW
AND THE KILLER IS . . .
A FEW DROPS OF BITTERS

Granny Reid Mysteries

MURDER IN HER STOCKING
MURDER IN THE CORN MAZE
MURDER AT MABEL'S MOTEL
MURDER MOST GRAVE

Published by Kensington Publishing Corp.

For my grandangels,
Antonette,
Michael,
Eve,
Kris,
and Lillyan

When I look into your eyes,
I bless every road I've traveled,
rocky and smooth,
that led to you.

Acknowledgments

I'd like to extend a very special thank-you to a lovely lady, dear friend, and chef extraordinaire, Dany Foster, for "catering" the wedding dinner. As a private chef to the rich, famous, and vacationing visitors in the beautiful area of Tahoe, Incline Village, and Truckee, Dany is a gifted magician, conjuring amazing food and wonderful memories for those fortunate enough to sit at her table. https://www.chefdanyfoster.com/

Thank you, Leslie Connell, my faithful copy editor, whose friendship and contributions to this series will never, never be forgotten.

I wish to thank all the fans who write to me, sharing their thoughts and offering endless encouragement. Your stories touch my heart, and I enjoy your letters more than you know. I can be reached at:

sonja@sonjamassie.com
and
facebook.com/gwendolynnarden.mckevett

Chapter 1

"You better live in fear, Savannah girl. Look over your shoulder in the daytime and sleep with one eye open ever' night," Granny Reid called out as she watched the shenanigans in the backyard through her granddaughter's laundry room window. "That boy you've taken in . . . he's a handful and a half!"

"You're telling me?" Savannah Reid called from the adjacent kitchen, where she stood at the stove, preparing breakfast for her household, which seemed to be growing by the day. "I found a spider nearly the size of my hand in my lingerie drawer two mornings ago. Fortunately, it was fake. But before I realized that, I nearly had myself a heart attack."

Savannah chuckled at the memory as she removed the sizzling, crispy strips of bacon from her cast iron skillet and turned off the heat. Her grandmother had given her that beloved utensil, which had been used by Granny, her mother before her, and no one was sure how many generations before that. It had seen a lot of bacon, fried eggs, and cream gravy in its day and had even been pressed into service as a weapon on more than one occasion.

The Reid gals were renowned, originally in Georgia and now in Southern California, for their ability and willingness to administer a serious skillet smackin' when sufficiently roused.

Leaving the bacon to drain on a platter covered by paper towels, Savannah stepped out into the laundry room to join her grandmother and see what her newly acquired foster son, "Mr. Brody Greyson," as he liked to call himself, was doing at the moment.

Trying to find a frog for her shower? Earthworms for the cats' dishes?

No, she thought. *He'd never play a trick, even a harmless one, on a pet.*

Brody loved animals fiercely. It was people he liked to mess with, not innocent "critters," as he liked to call them with his Southern drawl that was as thick as Savannah's and Granny's.

Savannah walked over to stand next to Gran and slipped her arm around the older woman's shoulders. "What's the little rug rat up to now?" she asked, peering out the window into her backyard.

"I'm not sure," Granny replied, "but it appears to me he might be playin' hide-'n'-seek with the Colonel."

"He probably is. Brody's been working on teaching him that. Dr. Carolyn told him it was a good way to bond with his new buddy."

"Dr. Carolyn?"

"His veterinarian friend."

"Oh, right. I remember him sayin' somethin' about her. Seems to think highly of her."

"He does, and so do I. She's scary smart, funny, and down-to-earth."

Granny looked up at Savannah, a loving grin on her face. "Sounds a lot like somebody else I know and love. I'm not surprised you two get along so good."

Savannah gave her grandmother a sideways hug, then turned her attention to her backyard. She spotted the small boy with tousled blond hair and a pixie face, which was flushed from the exertion of play on a warm, Southern California day, running from one potential hiding spot to another.

Bare feet and tanned skinny legs flying, he darted behind the garage, then out again, over to the gazebo and through her flower garden.

She winced when he came perilously close to her prized Lady in Red peonies, but he deftly maneuvered past them and leapt over a bed of Martha Washington geraniums, landing squarely on one of her mosaic-adorned stepping-stones.

"He's a spry one," Granny remarked. "Thank goodness, or those pretty blooms of yours would be lyin', flat as a flitter, on the ground."

"I know. I told him once how much my garden means to me, and he's been careful ever since. Though he does visit the strawberries more often than I'd like. I don't think I'll have enough left to make jam this year."

Granny chuckled. "Somethin' tells me you'd rather see strawberries on that youngster's face than in a jar any day."

"That's true. I don't think there was a lot of fresh

food available where he came from, judging from the way he gobbles up every bite he gets his hands on. Obviously, his little body needs it. I'm just happy I can provide it."

"You and Dirk have done wonders with him already. He's blessed to be with the likes of you two. Good people who care about him. Really care."

"We're the ones who're blessed. Other than a fake spider and some short sheeting, and the occasional and unexpected, cold and refreshing squirt from a water pistol, he's a joy."

Savannah grinned as she watched the boy head for the utility shed near the back of the property and the alley. "This particular round of the game is about to come to a happy ending," she said.

"Yeah, I believe you're right. Do you see what I see?"

"I do. A long, copper-colored tail sticking out from behind that shed, wagging up a storm."

"The Colonel's never been worth a hoot at hiding. He always forgets about his backside."

They watched as Brody raced toward the shed and the waving appendage that wagged even faster as the boy approached.

"I see you! I see you, Mr. Colonel Beauregard!" Brody shouted as he, too, disappeared momentarily behind the shed.

"Here comes the tussle," Granny said.

"The tussle's what it's all about." Savannah laughed as, true to her grandmother's prophecy, Brody and his quarry reappeared, the child dragging the 100-pound bloodhound from his hiding place.

As the boy, who was less than half the dog's size, tackled the Colonel and forced him to the grass, the hound's loud, plaintive baying suggested he was suffering greatly. But he always sounded the same, whether he had just received the bite of steak he had been begging for from the barbecue grill or was being denied the opportunity to chase Savannah's cats.

Savannah could swear she saw something akin to a grin on the droopy, sad-sack face as Brody and the dog grabbed each other in an eyeball-to-eyeball wrestling embrace, then rolled together across the yard.

Brody squealed with delight, and the Colonel howled with equal joy.

"I'm so glad there's a boy around to keep that mangy mutt occupied," Granny said, laughing. "I'm too old to roughhouse with 'im that way. When he's been over here for the day, he goes home and sleeps like he's a hibernating grizzly."

"Brody tends to wear everybody around him to a frazzle," Savannah agreed, "including Dirk and me. But we wouldn't have it any other way," she added as she saw her rough-and-tumble foster son plant a quick kiss on the hound's wrinkle-furrowed brow.

Savannah glanced at her watch. "I'm going to have to call a halt to the wrestling match out there if he's going to get to school on time."

"I'll walk him to school, if you want me to. I don't mind one bit," Granny offered so sweetly that Savannah was sorry to have to decline.

"Dirk already said he wants to take him, so I reckon he's got dibs. You have to get your reservation for Brody time in early."

"I could pick him up when he gets outta school," Granny was quick to suggest. "The Colonel and me, we could walk over together, then the three of us could stop at the drugstore and get ice cream cones on the way back. The Colonel loves it when I give him the last bite of my cone. I'd get him one of his own, but it gives him so much gas, he ain't fit to be around man nor beast."

Savannah leaned over and kissed the top of her grandmother's hair, noticing how it glistened silver bright in the morning sunlight coming through the window. "That sounds nice. Brody'll love it. You share the Colonel with us, it's only fair we share the boy with you."

"Colonel Beauregard's as fine a pooch as ever there was, but I'm still gettin' the best of that deal."

"You are," Savannah told her. "You might have to sweeten the pot with one of your carrot cakes sometime soon."

"Be glad to."

"One thing about the ice cream business, though. He promised Dr. Carolyn he'd go to her clinic at four and help her clean some kennels for an hour or so. Seems she's got a busy day today and needs some help."

"'Help' her exercise some kittens or puppies is more like it. We both know it ain't the kennel cleanin' he's interested in."

"Can't blame him much. I'd love to have a job playing with kittens and puppies. It'd beat what I do for a living anytime . . . or don't do at the moment," Savannah added when she recalled that she hadn't had any sort of private detecting for profit in a long while.

Even Dirk's cases had been quite mundane. A break-in here. A drug bust there.

All in all, the sleepy little coastal town of San Carmelita, California, had been quiet—even on weekends when their beaches were inundated with hordes of visitors from Los Angeles.

Savannah was happy for her fellow townsfolk that they hadn't been committing any serious crimes against each other lately. But she held the strong opinion that "quiet" was a second cousin to "boring."

As boring as a house could get with a six-year-old boy, a bloodhound, frequent visits from a feisty grandmother, and Savannah's little sister, Alma, planning an extravagant wedding to a world-renowned movie star.

There was plenty of activity at all times in the household, but lately, none of it had anything to do with catching bad guys or gals, and that translated to yawns for Savannah.

With all of her newly acquired parental responsibilities and her determination to help Alma have her dream wedding, Savannah had a lot to do. But not anything that got her blood pumping and her brain spinning, and she missed the "action."

Granny nodded toward the kitchen. "I hear your man up and about in there. He'll be hollerin' for his breakfast in a minute."

"Van?" a deep voice called out from the kitchen. "Where are you, darlin'?"

"Out here with Granny."

"I smell bacon and coffee."

Savannah chuckled. "Gran, it's scary how accurately you can predict human nature."

"You do somethin' over eighty years, you're bound to git good at it," she replied with a sly grin. "I'll go start the eggs, while you round up that young'un."

"Thank you, Gran. Be sure to throw a bunch in the skillet while you're at it. Don't hold back. The boy eats as much as Dirk, and I never thought I'd say that about anybody."

As Granny retreated to the kitchen, Savannah stepped to the back door and opened it. "Yoo-hoo," she called out. "Brody boy, stop that wallowing around on the ground, getting mud and dog slobber all over you, and come wash up for breakfast."

Brody froze in midwrestle, then with a great effort, rolled his opponent off him. Even the hound looked surprised at the sudden change of events.

"Sure!" the boy yelled back. "Be right there!"

With exceptional speed and enthusiasm, even for one as vivacious as Mr. Brody Greyson, the child raced inside, the dog at his heels. Savannah had to step aside to keep from being knocked over like a spare bowling pin.

"Wow! You must be plumb starved!" Savannah declared as he streaked by, followed by the baying Colonel.

"Yep" was the curt reply as he ducked into the half bath, gave his hands a quick rinse, then took off for the kitchen.

But it wasn't hunger on the kid's face that gave Savannah cause for concern.

No, it was the smirk.

Savannah had been raised with six sisters and two brothers, one named Waycross. He spent much of his childhood time and energy playing various pranks on his family, his schoolmates, and the tiny, rural town of McGill, Georgia, where Granny had raised them.

Much to his family's embarrassment, the community's general opinion of the child was: That Reid kid's got a lotta nerve just bein' a redhead, let alone a hooligan on top of it.

So, Savannah knew more than her share about mischievous boys and what a sneaky grin and a twinkle in the eye meant, when worn by a male six-year-old.

Something was up. As Granny had predicted, she would have to look over her shoulder and sleep with one eye open until she knew what.

Chapter 2

Detective Sergeant Dirk Coulter had worked late the night before on a fruitless drug house stakeout. He had arrived home after midnight, cranky and too tired to eat much more than a sandwich. So, Savannah wasn't surprised when her husband asked if he could have a bowl of cereal while the eggs were frying and the biscuits baking.

Brody jumped up from the table and raced to the cupboard where the boxes of assorted flakes, crisps, and crunches were stored. He returned almost immediately with a box of granola in one hand and the toothsome grin even broader across his face.

There it is again, Savannah thought. *Something wicked this way comes for sure.*

Fetching cereal might be helpful, but the task seldom caused a child to smile, and Brody was grinning like a kid who'd just been asked if he wanted to go to Disneyland for the day.

Savannah glanced at Granny, who had just taken a chair at the table, and saw that her grandmother was also watching the boy closely, one eyebrow slightly quirked.

Dirk, on the other hand, had just crawled out of bed. Without a sufficient infusion of caffeine-laden coffee, his detective skills were dull at best. He was barely conscious.

But, since they now had a child in the home and Granny was visiting, he had at least deigned to upgrade his usual breakfast table attire from his boxers to pajama bottoms and a T-shirt.

Never let it be said he doesn't give a hoot about his looks, Savannah thought when she saw him run his fingers once through his hair.

Normally, he would have given her at least a moderately lusty good morning hug and kiss when he came downstairs, but after Brody gagging quite loudly upon seeing anything even remotely resembling "gross, mushy junk," they were limiting their displays of affection to their bedroom.

Gone were the days of impromptu romantic encounters on the sofa, beneath the kitchen table, or on the staircase.

Aww, the price of "parenthood."

But, as Savannah took over for Granny, flipping the eggs, one by one, onto the platter with the bacon, she glanced Dirk's way and saw that he was watching her with a somewhat wistful look in his eyes.

No, things hadn't been quite the same in the romance department since they had become foster parents, but she knew the desire was still ever-present, and she had always found that to be one of the most satisfying benefits of having a love life.

Knowing you were wanted.

As though reading her thoughts, he gave her a wink and an ever-so-slight air kiss, which she returned.

She nodded toward the bowl in front of him. "You best chow down that bowl of cereal before it gets soggy and these eggs get cold," she said, setting the platter between him and Granny.

"Yeah, I had a few bites of it already," he said, grimacing down at the bowl. "I'm not crazy about this new stuff you got."

"It's organic, high-protein granola," Savannah said. "Tammy swears it's better for you than that puffy, sugary stuff you like."

"Yeah, well, shows you what *she* knows, health nut that she is." He grimaced. "This stuff tastes like sh—" He looked at Granny, then Brody. "Garbage. Tastes worse than garbage, in fact."

"You sound like an expert. You been eatin' a lotta garbage lately?" Brody asked, suppressing a giggle.

"No, he has not," Granny interjected. "Mostly he eats my granddaughter's good down-home cookin', and that's some of the best food to be had on God's green earth."

"That's for sure!" Brody said. "But she didn't cook this here new cereal, and Dirk don't like it one itty-bitty bit." Brody reached over and poked one of the pieces floating in the milk. "What does it taste like, really?" he asked with what looked to Savannah like a mock serious expression on his face.

"Like a combination of dirty socks and a stale tuna sandwich."

"Ah, come on now . . . it cain't be all *that* bad." Granny reached over and slid the bowl to her side of the table. "Lemme have a bite."

"No!"

Everyone jumped and turned to look at Brody, who had practically hurled himself across the table to grab the bowl away from Granny. He pulled it against his chest and wrapped his arms around it.

"What the heck, young man?" Dirk said. "You don't snatch food outta anybody's hand, let alone from *hers!* Around here, we show respect to our elders!"

Savannah would have joined her husband in his admonition, but she could see he was doing fine on his own . . . besides, a light bulb had flipped on in her brain.

"I'm sorry, Granny," Brody said, looking rattled and more than a little remorseful. "It's just that, well, he said it didn't taste good, and I didn't want you to put something icky in your mouth, 'cause, you know, you're our most elderest elder."

Savannah walked over to Brody, put her hand on his shoulder, and squeezed, a tad harder than usual. With the other hand, she reached around him and took the bowl from him.

She studied the assorted bits and pieces floating in the milk, poking a few with her fingertip.

"Hm-m," she said. "Some of these pieces are green." She held the bowl up to her nose and took a sniff. "Smells sorta strange, too. Even for Tammy's oddball, healthy stuff."

"Lemme go flush it down the toilet," Brody offered,

far too eagerly. "I mean, if it's bad, we don't want anybody else eat-in' it."

Savannah picked up one of the green bits, looked it over, then put it to her nose and sniffed it. "Well, well. I think we're gonna need to have a talk with that Tammy about her recommending this cereal to us. These green pieces *do* smell like gym socks and a week-old tuna sandwich, and I suspect there's a good reason why that's true."

"Maybe it's past its expiration date," Brody said, grabbing the box and making a big show of looking for the stamp. "You gotta watch out for that. Especially with cereal. Ain't nothin' worse for you than expired cereal!"

Savannah walked over to the cabinet and took out a different box. "I hope the cats enjoy their new, healthy, organic food that their aunt Tammy recommended I get, too."

Brody looked alarmed as she headed for the cat dishes in the corner. "No!" he said. "I wouldn't give them that! It might not be good for them! Dr. Carolyn says you gotta be careful what you give your pets. They can't eat everything we do."

Savannah pointed to the writing on the box. "It doesn't expire for several months yet, and it's all wholesome ingredients that cats enjoy."

"Like tuna?" Granny asked with a twinkle in her eye.

Savannah read the fine print on the end of the box. "Hey, exactly like tuna. It's the number one ingredient, in fact."

A second later, the room seemed to explode.

Dirk jumped up so fast that he overturned his chair. Brody dove under the table, crawled to the other side, where he scrambled to his feet, and ran for the back door with Dirk in pursuit.

"Boy, when I get my hands on you," he roared, "you are gonna wish that you—"

Brody escaped through the door half a second before Dirk reached him.

But the cop who had come up empty-handed during his surveillance the night before seemed determined not to lose his quarry, even if it meant apprehending the culprit in his own backyard, in full view of any nosy neighbors, while still wearing his pajamas.

Colonel Beauregard raced after them, slipping and sliding on Savannah's freshly waxed floor, his ears and jowls flapping, filling the house with his full-throated baying.

Savannah and Granny casually walked to the utility room window and watched as man, boy, and dog met in the middle of the yard—thankfully nowhere near Savannah's peonies or geraniums—in a writhing, howling, laughing heap of testosterone-fueled manliness.

"I ain't ever eatin' nothin' in your house again that didn't just come outta a sealed can or jar," Granny said.

"You don't need to worry," Savannah told her. "Brody would never let you or the kitties eat something they weren't supposed to."

"Just Dirk," Granny said, watching her grandson-in-law apply a knuckle-noogie to Brody's head as the child squealed with laughter.

The Colonel grabbed Dirk's fist in his big, wet mouth and fake growled until the rubbing stopped.

"Getting one up on another fella, it's a guy thing. So is taking revenge on the guy who gotcha," Savannah said.

Granny laughed. "Apparently so. Let's leave them to it, while you and me go tie into them eggs and biscuits before they get cold."

As they headed back toward the kitchen, Granny added, "You've got plenty of peach preserves, right?"

"Of course. Apple butter, too."

"That's a *girl* thing."

"It sure is!"

Chapter 3

"Are you absolutely, positively sure that we were invited to this party, Brody?" Savannah asked the boy for the third time since he had come home from the veterinary clinic, after so proudly announcing their impromptu plans for the evening.

"Dr. Carolyn said she wants us to come to a party at her house tonight!" he had proclaimed as Savannah was driving him home from his backbreaking labor of playing fetch with the clinic's mascot, an ancient golden retriever named Maggie Malone. "It's a birthday party! It'll be so much fun. I can't wait!"

Savannah had voiced her concerns that maybe she should call the good doctor and confirm the invitation only to be told, "Why? Don't you trust me? I wouldn't lie about a thing like a birthday party!"

After half an hour of questioning the youngster, Savannah had gleaned precious few facts to connect the dots. Apparently, the birthday "boy" was Dr. Carolyn's husband, Stephen, and no, they weren't expected to bring a present, since it was such short notice, and no, they didn't need to dress up. Dr. Carolyn didn't care about such things. Brody insisted she had said so while offering the invitation.

As a result, Dirk, Savannah, and Brody were riding along in Dirk's vintage Buick Skylark, heading north on the Pacific Coast Highway. It was a lovely drive with gently sloping, California-beige hills to their right, pristine beaches to their left, and the mighty ocean in all its grandeur filling the western horizon. The sun hung low in the turquoise sky, setting the clouds ablaze with shades of golden and coral.

As pleasant as the trip had been so far, they were hoping to arrive soon at the small community of Joya del Mar, jewel of the sea. While officially part of San Carmelita, an expanse of undeveloped beach separated it from the rest of the town.

Few people even knew about Joya del Mar, and that was how the residents wanted it.

The exclusive enclave seldom, if ever, experienced any sort of crime, so neither Savannah nor Dirk had answered any calls there. Before tonight, they had never socialized within its boundaries before. So this was a new and interesting experience for them both.

It was fun to see how the "other" social set lived and to enjoy that privileged, alien world firsthand. Even for just one night.

Dirk claimed to know its exact location, but since he often boasted of knowledge he possessed in only limited amounts, Savannah was holding her phone in her hand, its GPS activated.

According to the ever-repositioning arrow, they were drawing close.

"It's right up there," Brody said, leaning forward as far as his seat belt would allow and pointing to an unremarkable road ahead on their right. It had cracked paving and no sign at all to inform drivers of its significance.

The female voice on Savannah's phone agreed with Brody by instructing Dirk to, "Turn right in five hundred feet."

"Ain't much of a road," Dirk said, stating the obvious, as he pulled into the right lane and slowed to make the turn. "I've seen dirt-bike trails paved better than that."

"It might not be much of a road," Brody protested, "but it's a supercool place! You guys are in for a treat!"

"You sound pretty sure there, buddy," Dirk said as he guided the Buick around a sharp right U-turn that led them into a short tunnel and under the highway. "Have you been here before?"

"Oh, yeah! Lotsa times!" Brody paused, reconsidered, and added, "Well, twice."

"What did you like about it?" Savannah asked.

Brody snickered. "You'll see."

They emerged from the tunnel and continued on toward the neighborhood, which appeared to be only one block deep and three or four blocks long.

But the houses were magnificent.

Mansions all, sitting side by side, they had glorious views of the ocean, including the beautiful Channel Islands, floating on a bed of sea mist in the distance.

Unlike the beachfront properties in San Carmelita, these estates were built on large lots with plenty of room between them and even had fully landscaped yards, instead of the standard, tiny patches of sand that separated the town's beachfront properties.

"Wow!" Savannah said, taking it all in. "Dr. Carolyn is so laid-back, so casual and unassuming there in her clinic. I never expected her to live in a place like this."

"Apparently, giving shots to dogs and spaying cats pays better than you'd think," Dirk added. "Doesn't she drive a beat-up old Jeep with three wheels in the junkyard and the other one on an oil slick?"

"Hey, her husband's rich," Brody declared most indignantly. "He's some kinda fancy-schmancy doctor that flies all around the world fixin' famous, rich people's brains or somethin', and I *like* her Jeep. I don't have to worry 'bout spillin' somethin' in it like I do you guys' cars. I can sit in hers with my shorts all wet and sandy after I been swimmin' and eat ice cream, and she don't get all miffed about it."

"Hey, I'll show ya miffed," Dirk replied over his shoulder. "I could be sittin' at home watching a heavyweight championship fight right now. But you wanted to come, so don't go puttin' down my ride, 'kay?"

Brody grinned. "Like don't pretend I just dropped my gum on the floor and stepped on it?"

"Don't even think about it!" Dirk glowered at Brody from his rearview mirror.

The boy giggled, obviously less than terrified. "Yeah, all right. That's what I figured."

"The cat food cereal was the one and only trick you get to pull today," Savannah told him over her shoulder. "I don't have the strength to pull Dirk off you twice in a twenty-four-hour period, so—"

"You have arrived at your destination on the left," the GPS announced.

"Holy sh—cow!" Dirk exclaimed. "You weren't kidding, dude. This *is* some place."

Savannah stared, awestruck, at the massive glass, cement, and steel residence. Half walls of stone and lush bower plants and bougainvillea climbing them softened the otherwise severe, straight lines, giving the sophisticated and contemporary home a warm, inviting charm.

A waterfall spilled from a stone wall in front of the house and flowed through a man-made creek bed and beneath a redwood bridge that led to the front door.

The water was lit with blue and green lights, as were the palmettos, hibiscus, and oleander that bordered the edges of the yard.

Through the floor-to-ceiling windows, Savannah saw more people than she had ever thought could fit into a private residence at one time. She felt her tummy do a somersault when she realized the other guests were dressed in elegant evening attire.

"So much for not having to fancy up because Dr. Carolyn doesn't care about such things," Savannah whispered to herself as she quickly glanced down at her simple cotton sundress, then Dirk's slacks and short-sleeve dress shirt, not to mention Brody's favorite jeans and bright red, superhero T-shirt.

"Clean and neat is all that matters, sugar," Savannah heard. It was Granny's voice whispering to her spirit. How many times had Gran told her that when they were underdressed for an occasion?

Too many times.

A wardrobe with a wide variety of choices was not a luxury that could be afforded in a family with nine children, subsisting on a grandmother's meager pension.

In spite of the intervening years and Granny's loving

advice, Savannah still felt a certain uneasiness deep inside when she found herself inappropriately attired. Especially in what appeared to be a potentially "stuffy" atmosphere.

But for the moment, another problem needed to be addressed. She noticed it at the same moment that Dirk said, "Where the heck am I supposed to park? This road ain't that long, and both sides are full."

Savannah and Brody looked up and down the short street, trying to help. But other than private driveways, Dirk was right. There wasn't one place to park any car—especially one the size of his old Skylark.

Then Savannah saw it. A narrow, but "large enough" space in the veterinarian's driveway itself, between a stone wall and a gorgeous Lamborghini that had been backed in and was facing the street.

"Hey! There ya go," she told Dirk. "Slide on in there. You'd fit just fine. I'm surprised nobody took it yet."

In an instant, Dirk bristled. "I ain't squeezing my baby into that little space! You'll bang the doors on those rocks and the guy with the Lambo might hit it with his door when he gets in."

Savannah gave him an eye roll and a *tsk-tsk,* as she frequently did when she believed he had just spoken some foolishness, several times any given hour.

"We *can* do this," she said with only the slightest touch of condescension in her tone. "Let Brody and me out first, then you pull close to the stone wall, I'll direct you, and you'll be far enough from the Lamborghini not to cause any trouble."

Dirk thought it over a few seconds, glanced up and down the packed street, and grumbled, "All right. I guess. But if that dude leaves a mark on my car, I'll . . ."

"Will you stop?" Savannah said, trying to sound far more patient than she felt in front of Brody.

Funny, she often thought, *how much more you have to watch what you say and do with a pipsqueak around.*

She reached over and patted Dirk's arm. "As upset as you would be to get a mark on your baby, the man . . . or woman . . . who owns that car isn't in the habit of throwing the door open with wild abandon without looking first to see what it might hit. That vehicle cost more than our cars, house, and everything in it, including the cats."

Dirk continued to grumble like a bulldog with a bumblebee in its mouth, as he waved a hand toward her door.

Savannah took the gesture as a sign of acquiescence. "Let's get out," she told Brody as she grabbed her purse from the floorboard, turned off her phone, and shoved it inside the bag. "Hand me that pecan pie up here and grab the drawing you made."

"Do you think he'll like it?" Brody asked as he and Savannah climbed out of the Buick, their birthday offerings in hand.

"I do believe he will," Savannah told the boy, as she looked at the construction paper and crayon work of art—the portrait of a woman with oversized blue eyes and short, orange hair. Of the ninety-six colors in Brody's giant crayon box, Mango Tango had been his choice to represent the veterinarian's strawberry blonde pixie cut.

"It bears a striking resemblance to Dr. Carolyn," she told him, "and her husband's sure to appreciate someone drawing him such a pretty picture of his pretty wife."

Something that Savannah couldn't quite identify crossed Brody's face. A bit of doubt, misgiving, maybe even anger? She couldn't be sure. Whatever the emotion behind it might be, it certainly wasn't positive.

But before she had time to analyze it, she had to direct Dirk into the spot next to the stone wall—a task that, undoubtedly, would have been more easily accomplished without her purse in one hand and an oversized pecan pie in the other.

Eventually, they got the job done without any of his prophesied tragedies coming to pass or her dropping the precious pie.

But just as he had put the car in park and turned off its engine, she saw someone approaching her from behind.

She turned and saw a tall, burly man with a shaved head walking a large, mixed-breed dog on a short leash of thick, sturdy leather. The animal's eyes met Savannah's for a moment, and she got the instant impression he was a no-nonsense fellow who would do whatever was necessary to defend his owner or the owner's property.

"I wouldn't do that if I were you," the man told her, his own expression as stern as his pet's.

"I beg your pardon," she said, glancing down again at the dog, noting Brody's proximity to it, and making sure she was between the animal and her charge. "You wouldn't do what?"

"Park anywhere near that Lamborghini."

Savannah had long since tired of the conversational topic involving how close one could or should not park next to an A-list sportscar.

With considerable effort, she managed to keep her tone casual and friendly when she said, "It's okay. My husband's picky about his vehicle, too. We made sure that we stayed well away from—"

"It won't matter. The bastard who owns it assaulted my son just for letting our dog here get too close to it. That led to an altercation and a trip to the hospital, and now there's a lawsuit pending, with my dog's life in danger. The court may tell me I have to put him down!"

"Oh, that's, um, just awful," Savannah replied, not sure as to what to say. "How unfortunate, to have such bad blood between neighbors."

"You're damned right it's unfortunate. It's worse. It's hell. That guy's crazy!"

The fellow's eyes blazed with rage, and the thought occurred to Savannah that he didn't appear to be all that far from "crazy" himself. A step or two in either direction and he could wind up in jail or committed to a place where he could "rest" and "rediscover" himself, whether he wanted to or not.

"He's nuts!" the guy was continuing to spew. "Especially when it comes to his new toys. I wouldn't put anything past him."

Savannah glanced around the lovely, exclusive street with its luxury homes and decided she was quite content, living in her quaint, Spanish-style, mini-hacienda. Yes, she was just fine with her nondescript street in the center of San Carmelita with no ocean view at all.

Joya del Mar didn't seem quite so joyful anymore.

Chapter 4

Savannah cut a quick look at Brody to see if he appeared to be upset by what he had just heard the highly agitated neighbor say.

The boy didn't seem to be the least bit fazed by it.

Very interested, yes. Taking in every word. But not one iota of dismay on his little face.

Then she reminded herself of the sorts of drama Brody had experienced while living with his biological mother—her many encounters with the police, not to mention her misadventures with her less-than-law-abiding friends and associates.

Mr. Brody Greyson had seen too much in his six years. Far, far too much. Savannah had hoped to provide a more peaceful environment for him.

"I'm sorry that happened to you, sir," she said, using the voice she had used back in the day when she had been a police officer, the one meant to defuse situations and calm upset feelings. "Hopefully, your situation will have a peaceful resolution."

For just a second, the man looked over at the front of the house with its massive glass windows and the celebratory crowd inside.

His expression darkened, and he said with a sinister tone, "Peaceful? No. Peaceful's not gonna happen. Not with a guy like that one. Some people you can reason with. Him, you can't."

He turned back to Savannah and something in his eyes made Savannah far more wary of him than his well-leashed, no-nonsense, guard dog. "Good luck," he said, "and don't even breathe on that car, if you know what's good for you."

As he led the animal down the street, Dirk walked around the Buick and stood between Savannah and Brody. "What was that all about?" he asked, nodding in the fellow's direction.

"That guy there don't like Dr. Carolyn's husband," Brody replied. "Not one bit!"

"Then it *was* our host that he was talking about?" Savannah felt something trickle through her bloodstream that she recognized as adrenaline.

She had a bad feeling about tonight, and experience had taught her to listen to those feelings.

"Yeah, it's Dr. Erling's car," Brody was saying. "He just got it for his birthday. He's real, real, real proud of it, too!"

Distracted while he stared, goo-goo-eyed, at the Lamborghini, Dirk said, "Any particular reason why the dude with the dog doesn't like him?"

Brody smirked. "Nobody likes Dr. Erling. He's nothin' but a great big ol' pain in the ass."

"Brody!" Savannah and Dirk exclaimed in unison.

"What? He *is.*" Brody looked genuinely confused. "Even that there guy who lives next to him said so. He called him something even worse than I did. So, what am I supposed to say about Dr. Erling? That he's be-e-e-u-tiful and his farts smell like roses?"

Savannah reached over and ran her fingers through his hair, trying to get it to lie down and behave. But other than the fact that his were golden and hers black, their locks were quite similar. Untamable. Every hair possessing a rebellious mind of its own.

Not unlike its owner.

"Usually, if you try hard enough, you can think of something good to say about almost anybody," she told the boy. "If you can't, then it's probably best to just say nothing at all and keep your opinion to yourself."

"That's what Granny says," Brody observed.

"I know. That's where I got it, and it's good advice. But once in a while, if you really think it's necessary to say something not nice about someone, you can find better words than the one you just used and much better than that man used. I'm sure you remember, darlin', there are certain words we've asked you not to say."

Dirk slapped him on the back, then pulled him to his side in a hug and whispered, "Until you're old enough to shave, drive a car, and vote. Then we'll revise the list a bit."

Having heard him, Savannah added, "Hopefully by then you'll have developed a vocabulary and be able to express yourself with words that are acceptable in polite company . . . like if you're having dinner with the president or whoever."

"Well, we sure wouldn't want all them superpolite people in the White House to get their panties in a twist," Brody grumbled as the three of them started up the walk to the front door. "Couldn't be havin' that. They might start a war or somethin'."

"What'd you just say?" Dirk asked, his big hand heavy on the kid's shoulder.

"I said, heaven knows we don't wanna see polite people havin' a kitten over hearin' the wrong words. There might be thunder and lightning shootin' down from heaven or a big ol' California earthquake or—"

"That's absolutely right," Dirk told him. "You catch on fast."

Brody glanced Savannah's way and lowered his voice, whispering to Dirk, "She's always sayin' I gotta learn to talk better, 'cause I might have dinner with the president or the pope or whoever someday. Like that's ever gonna happen."

"I know. She's always told me that, too, and I'm still waiting for my fancy engraved invitation for afternoon tea in the Rose Garden."

"I'll bet when the president spills his milk all over the White House kitchen floor, he says somethin' besides, 'Oh, dearie me!' "

Dirk chuckled. "Yes, in a situation like that, he probably says something downright salty."

"I'll betcha he don't leave the room just to fart neither, like she says we're supposed to do. Unless he's with the queen of some other country and she's got a thing about only fartin' in the bathroom, you know he just lets 'er rip wherever he's at, like any other guy."

"Yes, he probably does, son. But he's the president, so he gets to do a lot of stuff the rest of us don't. Especially when we're in the first grade." He glanced over at Savannah, who was grinning, but pretending she hadn't heard any of their exchange. "Unless he's got a persnickety first lady, like I do."

She stuck out her tongue at Dirk, he laughed, and Brody smiled, proud of himself, as though he had just pleaded his case before the Supreme Court and won.

They walked over the arched, redwood bridge with the rocky creek running beneath it. Brody cheered instantly at the sight of the glistening, orange, white, and red koi swimming beneath their feet.

"See there!" he told them, pointing. "That's just a little bit of what you're gonna see here. This is an awesome place. Dr. Carolyn brings a lot of the animals home from her clinic if the owners don't want them anymore, 'cause they're sick."

"How nice of her. She sounds like Alma," Savannah said, thinking of her sister who, as a child, had brought home every injured or neglected animal in the county and nursed it back to health.

Brody nodded and continued. "Dr. Carolyn's even got a llama with long eyelashes, like Bambi, and a five-foot-long, gnarly python! That's longer than me! He has ginormous, supersharp teeth!"

Savannah shuddered. "He sounds lovely. I think I'd like to see the Bambi-lashed llama."

"And the python!" Brody repeated, his excitement undimmed.

"Yeah. I heard you." She winked at him. "Like I said, I'm eager to lay eyes on the llama. The snake . . . not so much."

"Well, I like snakes. I like 'em a lot! Dr. Carolyn says they're good. 'They make good pets,' she says. You don't have to walk them, and they keep the mice away, and—"

"We have enough pets already," Savannah interjected. She saw where this was headed and was determined to cut it off with the sharp shears of logic before things got out of hand. "We don't have to walk Cleo or Diamante either, and mice are too terrified of them to even set one teeny foot on our property. So, with two cats and daily visits from the Colonel, I'd say we're covered."

Dirk nudged the boy and said, "You take her to see the sissy llama, and you can show me the snake. Deal?"

The boy brightened and scurried up the front steps ahead of them.

The sound of soft jazz and the aroma of exotic foods that Savannah didn't recognize wafted through the open door, graciously beckoning them inside the mansion.

For the first time since they had arrived, Savannah found she was actually looking forward to the evening.

Dirk took the pie from her. "Here, I'll carry that." He leaned his head down to hers, and whispered, "Looks like a bunch of stuck-up, high-society uppity-mucks in there."

"Then we'll fit right in," she told him with a wink.

"Yeah, right. We're gonna be about as welcome as half a worm in a half-eaten dill pickle."

Chapter 5

As Savannah, Dirk, and Brody entered the door, an elegant couple drifted by them. The lady's black silk gown shimmered as it flowed over what was clearly a fashionably perfect body. Her partner wore a suit that Savannah instantly recognized as the work of a high-end designer.

Dirk noticed, too. He nudged her with his elbow and whispered, "Ryan's got an outfit like that."

"I know." Savannah looked around the room and thought that their friends Ryan and John could have blended into this crowd seamlessly with their sophisticated manners and exquisite wardrobes.

"You should've borrowed Ryan's suit," she told him, "and I should've worn my prom dress."

"Or I should've stayed home to watch my fight, and you could've baked me and the squirt some chocolate-chip cookies."

Savannah looked around the room, trying to locate their hostess and see what Brody was up to. But she couldn't see either of them. Brody had dissolved into the crowd, and Dr. Carolyn was a diminutive woman, not easy to find among wall-to-wall tall men and women in high, high heels.

"What are we supposed to do?" Dirk asked. "I hate parties that don't have at least a horseshoe pit or dart-board or pool table."

"I'll take you downstairs and show you the snake!" Brody exclaimed, rushing back to them. "I put the picture I made of Dr. Carolyn on the piano, so I'm ready to have fun now."

Savannah could tell Dirk was eager to escape the crowded room, too, and she would have placed money on there being a less-dense population near the python's habitat.

"Go ahead," she told them. "You check out the slithery critter with the massive fangs, and I'll find Carolyn and let her know we're here."

Dirk looked so grateful, and Brody so pleased that she knew she'd made the right call by releasing them from their social drudgery.

"Gimme that pie back," she told Dirk. "I'm afraid to leave you two alone with it."

He quickly handed it to her and in three seconds they had disappeared, leaving her adrift in the sea of gloriously attired total strangers.

Savannah moved away from the door and ventured into the throng.

Considering the crowd of tightly packed people, it wasn't easy to see the room itself, let alone its décor. But she did notice the ultra-high teak ceiling, crossed with thick, dark beams. The wall to her left was stone, like the water feature in front of the home.

From the little she could see, she loved the Erlings' house. For all of its steel and concrete, it also had enough wood, stone, and greenery to impart the feel of nature and home.

But when she turned to her right, she saw something that ruined her cozy moment.

About fifteen feet away, stood a tall, handsome, blond man, elegantly dressed like the other guests crowded around them. He was drinking rather greedily from a glass containing what Savannah assumed was whiskey, judging from its rich, amber color.

He was staring at her over the rim of the lowball, and the look on his face was anything but warm and friendly.

In fact, the undisguised hostility in his eyes sent a chill through her and stirred other feelings that she seldom experienced, now that she was no longer a beat cop, patrolling rough and dangerous streets.

Back then, when someone had looked at her with that degree of intense anger, she switched into a high-alert mode and reminded herself that her Beretta was handy if absolutely necessary.

With her thoughts racing, she would also mentally rehearse the various ways to handle whatever circumstance developed.

Though no longer carrying a badge, she was as ready this evening as she had been on any other night in any dark alley.

As always when she left the house, her weapon was with her. Once a cop, always a cop. Tonight it was in her purse, as sundresses did nothing to conceal a shoulder holster.

A female servant in a black uniform glided by him, took his empty glass, and handed him one with at least two fingers of liquor inside. He took it from her and slugged back the contents, never taking his eyes off Savannah.

Their stare-down was intense and, to Savannah, seemed like hours, though it was probably less than twenty seconds long.

She gave him her best poker face, one that was neither hostile nor submissive.

Neutral. That was what she was going for as her eyes told him, "I see you. I don't know what the heck your problem is, but you should reconsider your position."

He didn't seem to reconsider anything. Or blink. Or show any sign at all of backing down and putting an end to his unspoken challenge. She had no doubt that his intention was to convey some sort of threat.

She was surprised and more than a bit confused by the experience. What on earth could she have done to cause a total stranger to show so much animosity toward her?

Certainly, she had always been gifted with a talent for ticking people off. But it usually took a bit longer than twenty seconds, and at least a word or two exchanged for her to find herself on their bad side.

She didn't need a conversation with this fellow to know he was quite upset with her. Angry enough for her to hug her purse tightly and get ready to swing it if he approached her.

While she would never discharge her weapon in a crowded room at a man who appeared unarmed, she would certainly not be averse to smacking him upside the head with it, should the situation warrant such.

The Beretta wasn't exactly a brick bat or the Reid women's cast-iron skillet, but it wasn't light either.

When he refused to break their little staring contest, she decided, for the sake of Dr. Carolyn and Brody, to do whatever was necessary to defuse this strange situation.

So, she blinked and looked away.

For several moments, she scanned the rest of the crowd with exaggerated interest, still looking for Carolyn Erling. The first thing she intended to do when she found her hostess was hand her the pecan pie, which seemed to be getting heavier by the moment, then ask her, gently, subtly, of course, "Who's that tall, blond, rude-as-all-get-out dude, and what in tarnation is his problem?"

When she decided it was time, she gave a quick glance back in the direction of the man with the attitude, only to find him gone. Completely gone. Not a sign of him where he had been standing, nowhere near there, or in the entire room.

He would have been fairly easy to spot, because of his height and hair color, so she assumed he had left.

She felt a sense of relief on one hand but couldn't help wondering where he had gone and what the whole thing had been about.

Ya never know, girl, she told herself. *It's best to just let it go. Maybe you bear an uncanny resemblance to an ex-wife or perhaps his fifth-grade English teacher who smacked him with a ruler when he couldn't rattle off his parts of speech.*

Dismissing him from her thoughts, she moved slowly through the crowd, continuing to look for Carolyn. She spotted several people she recognized. An up-and-coming actress whom she had recently seen interviewed on a television morning show concerning her soon-to-be-released movie. A fellow who was a Los Angeles news anchor for a major network station. The mayor of San Carmelita and his latest wife. A celebrity chef, whose book Savannah had bought only to try his recipes and find them nothing to write home about.

But there was no one there she knew or could hang out with and converse. Not one friendly, familiar face.

She found herself wishing Dirk and Brody would wrap up their snake visit and rejoin her.

Though Savannah could be sociable when the situation required, she didn't enjoy "breaking the ice" with total strangers. Especially ones who were dressed as if they were attending the Academy Awards, when she appeared to be dolled up for a Sunday afternoon picnic in the park.

Having convinced herself that Carolyn was not in the living room, dining area, or the poolside patio, Savannah decided to try the kitchen. Even during the most lavish, catered parties, hostesses often found themselves trapped there from time to time, supervising, lending a hand if necessary and putting out fires—hopefully, figuratively.

Carolyn would probably be no different.

Savannah wanted to unload the pie, but even more importantly, she desperately wanted to check out the kitchen. She never missed an opportunity to see a beautiful kitchen when she had the chance. She could only dream of such luxuries as having an island bigger than her own dining table with its extra leaf, a stove with six burners and a griddle, an undercounter wine cooler, and best of all . . . enough cabinets that she wouldn't have to store her Thanksgiving turkey roasting pan in her oven.

She followed her nose to find the source of the amazing, savory aromas that she couldn't quite identify. But it was her ears that led her to the kitchen, the voices, loud and businesslike, giving and taking directions, the clang of utensils and usual kitchen racket. It was all music to Savannah's soul.

She enjoyed good food—making it, eating it, savoring every luscious bite.

Sweetest of all, she enjoyed preparing and serving it to those she loved best in the world.

Gifts from her kitchen were gifts from her heart.

So, when she stepped from the patio through the open French doors into the enormous, gourmet kitchen, she took in every sight, every sound, and every scent.

Half a dozen workers were scurrying about, miraculously not colliding with one another, transporting platters laden with hors d'oeuvres that were miniature works of art.

As a couple of trays flew past her, Savannah caught sight of some tidbits that looked like nachos, only topped with caviar, sitting next to what had to be lobster sliders.

Just wait till I tell Ryan and John about those! she thought.

Her friends, who owned a wonderful restaurant of their own in the picturesque, downtown, historic quarter of San Carmelita, appreciated good food almost as much as she did.

She set the pie on a counter near the coffee station, then stayed close to the wall and out of everyone's way as she skirted the room, looking for Carolyn. She smelled something glorious and identified the dish as some beef tidbits that had been barbecued. Next to the bowl containing their sauce was a bottle of VSOP cognac.

Ah, she thought. *That's what I was smelling. I'll have to tell Ryan and John about that, too.*

Realizing she was in the way and should be moving on, she decided to leave the room and look for Carolyn elsewhere.

But, intending to make her way back to the living room, where she hoped to find Dirk and Brody, she chose the wrong door and instead entered a hallway that appeared to lead toward some bedrooms.

That was when she heard the argument. Just inside one of the open doors to her right.

A man and a woman were conversing in tense, angry tones. Especially the male.

"I can't believe you invited her here, to our home!" he was saying. "I fired her because I never wanted to see her stupid face again, and here she is at my birthday party! What the hell's wrong with you?"

"She just dropped by to pick up her check, Stephen. For heaven's sake, have a heart."

"She doesn't show her face around here! Ever again! And what's with that ragamuffin kid you dragged in off the streets? If you want him hanging around your clinic, that's up to you. But don't you ever again invite him here to our home. With our friends, our business associates, and him nothing but a—"

"I didn't invite him. He sorta invited himself, and I couldn't say no. He's a very sweet little boy, Stephen, as you'd discover if you'd take the time to get to know him."

"I don't want to know him, let alone his parents. Did you see them? What the hell, Carolyn? Where do you find these people? It's bad enough that you bring stray, dirty, diseased animals home with you, but—"

"Excuse me," Savannah heard herself saying. She

also heard her own pulse pounding in her ears and felt her face burning as she moved closer to the door. Three steps and she could see the couple inside the room.

They could see her, too.

Carolyn Erling gasped and put her hand over her mouth.

Stephen Erling, the tall, blond man who had been glaring at her earlier in the living room, did not gasp. Unlike his wife, who looked as if she wanted to simply disappear and be anywhere else on Earth than there, he seemed just peachy. Miffed, to be sure. But not at all ashamed or apologetic as he casually lifted a champagne glass and, in one hearty chug-a-lug, emptied its contents.

When he'd finished, Savannah was quite sure she saw him smirk.

She reminded herself of all that Dr. Carolyn meant to Brody. He treasured her and his visits to her clinic. He loved the chance to help animals—this child who had enjoyed so few good things in his short life.

Considering the possible outcome and the resulting ramifications, Savannah decided not to knock Dr. Stephen Erling, world-renowned brain surgeon to the rich and famous, into Kingdom Come with a blow to the side of his head with her Beretta-weighted purse, as was her initial inclination.

"Oh, Savannah," Carolyn said, rushing to her side and grabbing her arm. "I'm so, so sorry you overheard that. Please forgive us."

"*Us?*" Savannah asked. "I have no problem with you, Carolyn." She turned to Stephen Erling. "You, however . . ."

She paused to draw a deep breath. "My husband and I, we're a bit rough around the edges. I'll be the first to admit. But we *do* have the good manners to not remain where we aren't wanted. So, we'll be leaving. Now. But before we go, I want you to know that Brody—"

She choked and had to pause a moment to regain her control. "Brody is golden. Pure and precious. He's had a rough time, yes, a *very* hard life. Unimaginable. Far, far worse than yours, I suspect. Yet, he's a good boy. A truly wonderful little human being. He hasn't let his misfortune ruin him."

She looked Erling up and down. Such a handsome man with his inherent good looks, wearing exquisite clothing, standing in his immaculate house filled with the best of belongings the world had to offer.

Obviously, he was extraordinarily successful, abundantly blessed. But . . . ?

"I wonder, sir," she said, "what it was that ruined *you.*"

Before he could reply, she turned her back on Dr. Stephen Erling and walked away. Briskly. Without looking back.

The last thing she wanted was for a man like that to see her cry.

Chapter 6

Savannah hurried through the crowd, aware that several of the guests were staring at her as she passed by them. She wasn't sure if it was because of her inappropriate attire or the tears in her eyes.

She hoped it was the former. Playing the role of "Outcast" was bad enough. That of "Victim" was intolerable.

As she straightened her back, lifted her chin, and continued across the room toward the door with as much dignity as she could muster, she heard a voice deep in her soul—one that sounded a lot like Granny's—say, "It's not yourself you're crying for. Those tears are for your boy. Righteous indignation is a good thing. Especially when it's on behalf of the innocent. It's the evidence of a mother's love."

A mother's love? Am I really a mother? she asked herself,

for the first time in her life, as she exited the house and walked down the steps toward the wooden bridge.

A mother?

Me?

The question hit her so hard that the force of it caused her to stop in midstride, unable to move until it was settled in her mind and heart.

Since when is Savannah Reid someone's mother? came the next question. *Big sister? Yes. Wife? Yes. Cop? Not anymore. Good friend? I hope so. Temporarily a foster parent . . . But a mom?*

Last year, her doctor had spoken the word that had put an end to the dream of ever having a child of her own. "Menopause."

But at that moment, standing on the redwood bridge and looking at the beautiful, colorful koi swimming past, Savannah thought of little Brody.

In spite of the lack of affection and nurturing he had been shown in his young life, the child loved and wanted to protect and care for every animal he saw.

Even though he had been neglected and abused to the point that his tiny, vulnerable body would forever bear the scars of that mistreatment, Brody seemed to have decided that, if human beings treated him even halfway decently, he would choose to love them, too.

That's why Erling's words had hurt Savannah so deeply.

When she had heard Stephen Erling harshly denigrate Brody, dismissing him with such coldness, someone new had risen inside Savannah. Someone she had never met before and had never believed she would.

Momma Savannah.

Had she and that nasty man been alone when he had

uttered those words, she was pretty sure she would have been unable to resist slapping him stupid. Not a task that would have taken long. She might have even slugged him.

At the very least, she would have attacked him with far more words, uttered at the top of her voice. Words much more devastating than the ones he had used.

But she had walked away for Carolyn's sake, and even more for Brody's.

These days, she found that she chose so many of her words and actions based upon what was best for the little one in her care. The child she would happily defend under any and all circumstances.

Hers to defend.

Yes. *Hers.*

You're darned right I'm a mother! she assured herself. *If I didn't know it before, I sure as shootin' know it now.*

Liking the way that sounded in her head, the way it felt in her heart, she added, *In fact I'm a dadgum momma grizzly, so don't go messin' with me and mine!*

Her resolution in place, she walked over toward the Lamborghini.

For a few seconds, she stared at the beautiful sports car, knowing in her heart it was "his." An evil thought formed in her mind, the picture of her taking her keys from her purse and leaving an ugly scratch down the front, driver's side fender. But she quickly discarded the idea.

Even momma grizzly bears had to maintain some degree of decorum and pretense of civility, even when sorely offended.

So, she left her keys in her purse and took out her phone instead.

She needed to let the boys know that their snake-watching adventure was over, and it was time to go home.

Since she didn't want to tell them why, especially Brody, she decided to complain of a headache.

As she felt her pulse pounding in her temples and the associated pain, she assured herself it wouldn't be a lie.

Later, once she and Dirk were home and alone in their bedroom, she would fill him in on the dirty details.

She was a little concerned about telling him here and now. She knew that these days he was feeling as fatherly as she was motherly. But unlike her, Dirk wasn't as well-known for his patience and forbearance of his fellow man.

Something told her Dirk probably would have clobbered ol' Stephen, then and there, and possibly lost his badge in the process.

When she turned on her phone, it gave a little beep that told her she had received a message while it had been off. To her surprise, there were messages. Several. All from Dirk.

The first read, **"Where r u?"**

The second was, **"Done with snake. Can't find u."**

The third made her heart sink. **"Capt. called. Gotta go. Brody with llama. Pick u up later."**

"No, no, no!" she whispered, noticing for the first time that the Buick was gone.

We're stuck here? she thought. *After telling Carolyn and old Stephen Stink Face we're leaving, we can't? Oh, man. This bites the big one, big-time!*

Her mind raced, trying to find a solution. One simply could not flounce out of a place with great indignation and then come crawling back a few minutes later.

She could call her brother, Waycross, and his wife, Tammy. Ordinarily, they wouldn't mind at all. But their toddler had been teething and not sleeping well lately. So, neither had they. When Savannah had chatted with Tammy earlier on the phone, she'd mentioned they were planning on an early dinner and possibly a nap afterward.

Her sister, Alma, had said she'd be shopping for gifts for her bridesmaids. Savannah wouldn't dream of interrupting that important, festive activity by pleading to be rescued from a socially awkward situation.

Had they been closer to the center of town, Savannah would have asked her grandmother. But the drive was a bit longer than Granny was accustomed to. Savannah couldn't ask her grandmother to make it. Especially since sunset was imminent, and Granny didn't see as well in the dark as she once had.

So, other than take a cab or car service—which, even if they could get one that would be willing to make the trip, the cost would play havoc with her household budget—they were out of luck.

She decided that, as much as she loathed the idea, they'd just have to wait for Dirk's return.

"Wonder how large that llama's barn is and if he'd mind a couple of temporary roommates?" she muttered.

She texted Dirk a reply: **"Do whatcha gotta. Come bk soon as u can. We'll b with llama."**

No sooner had she sent it, than she saw someone coming out the front door. In that split second, she braced herself for another round with Erling. Was he going to deny her even the privilege of standing in his lah-dee-dah driveway, next to his whooptey-do car?

To her relief, it wasn't Erling, but a pretty, young woman with long, red hair and equally red eyes that told Savannah she had just been crying or was having a nasty allergy attack.

As the redhead hurried down the driveway, toward the street, she didn't appear to notice Savannah standing there. When she finally did, she jumped and said, "Oh. Hello." But she kept walking, as though reluctant to enter into a conversation.

Savannah wanted to respect her privacy, having just been in a crying mood herself, but she had to find out.

"Excuse me," she said, "but could you tell me where the llama is kept?"

The redhead just stared at Savannah, as though she had spoken to her in a foreign language. Then she seemed to snap out of it and become aware and present. "Oh. Yeah. The llama. His pen's around there."

She pointed to the right of the house, but all Savannah could see was a high stone wall with no gate or door of any kind.

"On the other side of the wall," the woman clarified. "You go through the house to the patio, turn right, and down the path. You'll see the bright red barn. Can't miss it."

"Thank you," Savannah said, feeling a choking sensation in her throat upon hearing the words *go through the house.*

That was just what she needed right now. To walk through that crowd and maybe even have the good luck of running into His Majesty King Stephen of the Peckerwood Forest once again.

"I can't get there any other way?" she asked the woman's back as she hurried on her way toward the street.

"Nope," she replied over her shoulder. "Not unless you can climb or pole vault over that wall."

"Okay. Thanks."

No reply.

"Maybe he insulted her kid, too," Savannah muttered as she saw the woman practically run to a small, blue SUV, dive inside, and drive away.

Savannah stood, staring at the house, wishing she had acquiesced and given Brody the cell phone he claimed he so desperately needed in order to ". . . be like all the other kids in my class."

After doing a bit of quick research at a PTA meeting, Savannah had discovered that "all the other kids" consisted of two prissy little girls, who had wanted phones so they could glue hot pink "diamonds" all over them, and one boy whose parents wanted to be able to GPS track him at all times, after he had set the neighborhood woods on fire.

But now she regretted her decision. If she'd given Brody what he wanted for his "Starting a New School Present," instead of a T-rex backpack and matching lunchbox, she could have just texted him now, rather than run the gauntlet of curious stares once again.

Oh, well, she thought with a toss of her head. *If gawking at me and my picnic dress is the highest form of entertainment they can find, it must be one dull party.*

As far as Stephen Erling was concerned, she decided that if he was still consuming alcohol at the rate she had witnessed before, he might be flat on his face on the floor somewhere, staring at his fine, hand-painted tiles.

One could always hope.

Chapter 7

Savannah took a deep breath to calm her nerves and strengthen her resolve; then she headed back toward the house and, once again, crossed the redwood bridge. The koi didn't seem quite so festive and classy now, and she was well "over" the house and its babbling brook and fancy-dandy stone walls and floor-to-ceiling windows.

At the moment, all she wanted in life was to get her kid out of there and return to a peaceful evening at her humble home with her kitties, her comfy chair, and maybe a game of Spider-Man Chutes and Ladders with Brody.

When she entered the living room, she was relieved to see that no one turned her way or even noticed her. Their backs to her, they were focusing their attention on the far side of the room, where Carolyn Erling was making a toast, her birthday "boy" standing next to her.

Carolyn looked anything but celebratory as she held a glass of champagne high and said, "I know we're all wishing him a very happy and exciting new year of life—"

"Hopefully, better than his last one," a male voice piped up from somewhere in the back of the crowd.

"Wouldn't take much," muttered a woman with long silver hair near Savannah.

Stephen Erling shot hateful glances toward the general regions where the speakers were standing, but it was clear he couldn't specifically identify his hecklers.

For the first time, it occurred to Savannah that maybe this crowd wasn't necessarily a gathering of the doctor's fans. After all, if his neighbor hated him and, having been in his company only a few minutes, Savannah loathed him, it might not be a stretch to think some individuals in that room might harbor resentments toward their host, even as they gobbled down his gourmet hors d'oeuvres and tossed back flute after flute of his champagne.

When Carolyn finished her speech, they all drank to his health. Or at least went through the motions of appearing to.

Savannah noticed that everyone else in the room, including Carolyn, was drinking from a standard, catererfare champagne flute. However, Stephen's was an intricately cut glass with a delicate tint of green.

Normally, Savannah would have liked the beautifully crafted piece of crystal. Antique, no doubt. But considering who was holding it, she decided to dislike it, along with its owner.

Both Carolyn and Stephen downed the contents of their glasses, like people who had just been rescued from the Sahara would guzzle cold spring water.

Carolyn gave her husband the slightest peck on the cheek and walked away without a word to him. She turned and hurried down a hallway, toward what Savannah now knew was the kitchen.

The woman looked exhausted, a mere shell of the vibrant, fun-loving, compassionate veterinarian, whom Savannah and Brody enjoyed chatting with in her clinic. This Carolyn moved like one who was deeply tired of life itself, trapped and resigned to her captivity.

Savannah's heart ached just to see her.

It occurred to Savannah that Carolyn Erling was exhibiting the same signs as many of the abused women Savannah had met while on the police force. The defeatist energy they radiated, the lost look in their eyes . . . it wasn't something Savannah could easily forget.

I'll have to take Diamante in for that ear cleaning soon, Savannah thought. *Maybe Dr. Carolyn and I can have a little girl-to-girl chat.*

But for right now, all she wanted was to get to the llama enclosure and Brody before he became concerned over her absence and before Dr. Stephen Erling looked her way. Or Brody's, heaven forbid.

She managed to slip out the door and hurry across the patio without incident. She turned right, as the red-haired woman had suggested, and followed a path that wound past a lush vegetable garden, some chicken coops, a rabbit hutch, and a pen with two adorable baby goats inside.

That was when she saw the red barn.

While the structure was cute in a fairy-tale sort of way, it wasn't much of a barn. Compared to the full-sized ones in rural Georgia where Savannah had been raised, this wasn't any larger than an oversized toolshed. But the pen was big enough for any animal to kick up its heels and run around.

An additional feature was the nearby apple tree, whose branches didn't reach quite near enough for a hungry critter inside the pen to nab a juicy bit of fruit.

Savannah wasn't at all surprised to see Brody standing next to the fence, picking apples from the tree and feeding them to a tall llama with a fluffy white fleece and long, floppy ears.

Both the child and the llama seemed perfectly at peace as Brody fed and chattered away to his woolly friend.

Savannah realized she hadn't needed to worry about him at all. As long as he had an animal buddy within reach, Mr. Brody Greyson was fine.

But when he spotted her, his face brightened, and he motioned for her to join them. "There you are! Come on over," he called to her.

As she approached, the llama noticed her and instantly laid its ears back and stared at her with a hostile look that was unsettlingly similar to Dr. Stephen Erling's.

"You better stay back," Brody warned her. "He looks at people like that right before he spits on 'em. You should see it! So-o-o nasty! It's kinda like poop mixed with slobbers flyin' atcha!"

"Lovely." Savannah took several quick paces back. "I think I'd like to avoid that if possible. It would be sorta like the cherry on the rotten day sundae."

"You're having a rotten day?" he asked, instantly quite concerned.

"Yes, sweetie. I'm afraid I am. Kinda."

"How come? I'm havin' fun."

"Then that's the best part of my day. But I do have a bit of a headache."

"Wanna apple? They don't taste all that bad. Just a little sour." Brody held out a small apple, pocked with worm holes, to her. It was balanced on his palm, as he had been feeding the llama seconds before. She could still see the animal's saliva glistening on his skin.

"No, thank you, darlin'. I reckon I'll pass."

"Oh. Okay." He turned and gave it to the llama. "I'll getcha another one if you change your mind."

"I'll let you know if I get a hankering for one."

She stood for a moment, allowing herself the momentary pleasure of looking out across the ocean, where the sun had dipped below the horizon, its rose-gold rays fading into night.

Strands of fairy lights, hanging from the house's various decks and balconies and strung across the yard had come on, turning the estate into a land of fantasy.

Too bad there's so much unhappiness here, she thought.

"You all right?" Brody asked.

She saw that he was watching her closely, a worried look on his handsome little face.

"I'm fine," she said. "Don't you worry about me. It's my job to worry about you, not the other way around."

He thought it over for a moment. "That doesn't seem fair."

"Sure it is. I'm the grown-up, and you're the kid. Kids should be allowed to just be kids, if at all possible, and not have to worry. There's plenty of time to fret about bills and jobs and the State of the Union and all that junk once you're an adult."

He gave her a big grin, made all the cuter for its missing front teeth. "I'm all for that!" he assured her. "But

I'm ready to worry about somethin' if you need me to. Just say so."

"If I get more than I can handle, you'll be the first to know."

She couldn't help grabbing him and giving him a big hug. As she clasped him close to her chest, she leaned down and kissed the top of his head, breathing in the smells captured in his hair. Fresh sea air, apples, the animal he had been feeding, hay, and little boy sweat. A precious combination.

He seemed to enjoy the embrace for a few seconds, then he abruptly pulled away, as he frequently did.

When he had first done it, Savannah had taken it personally. But she quickly decided that, after all he had been through at the hands of an abusive woman, he might need a bit more personal space than she was giving him.

After that, she had always allowed him to be the one to end any physical contact.

Though in the evenings, when the three of them were sharing family activities, she did notice that he appeared to feel more comfortable cuddling up to Dirk on the sofa and staying in that position for the length of a television show or even a movie.

Again, she figured it was because his abuser had been female, and Savannah was resolved to allow him the control he needed over who touched him and for how long. But it did make her a bit sad to feel him pull away before she was finished enjoying the embrace.

He looked up at her with loving concern. "Is your headache real bad?" he asked. "Do you need to go home now? If you do, it's okay."

"Thank you for that kind offer," she replied. "But with our ride gone, it's a long walk home."

"Oh, yeah. I forgot about that."

"Did Dirk say where the captain was sending him? What sort of case?"

"He said it was downtown. Somebody got their car broke into on Main Street."

"Doesn't sound all that critical. The captain could have put someone else on it. Did Dirk tell him he was at a birthday party?"

"Dirk told him. I heard him. Sounded like maybe the captain already knew that."

Savannah growled under her breath. "Yes, I'll just bet he did."

Dirk's and the captain's relationship was stormy, to say the least. Savannah recalled far too many times, even on their first anniversary, when Dirk's boss had used his position to make life unpleasant for his seniormost detective.

He seemed to enjoy assigning Dirk mundane tasks that were below his pay grade and expertise. Then Dirk made the mistake of grumbling about it, which was the captain's big payoff, assuring it would happen again. Soon.

"We looked all over for you," Brody chattered on. "Finally, Dirk said he had to go and asked me if I'd be okay just hanging out with Fantasia."

"Fantasia?"

Brody nodded toward the llama.

Savannah glanced over at the silly looking, lop-eared critter and noticed that it had lush, long eyelashes. But it was still giving her the stink eye, so she decided that, lashes and pretty name aside, they weren't likely to ever become best buddies.

"So, you've been here by yourself all that time, poor boy," Savannah told him.

"Except for the guy who was sneakin' around back here. The guy with the dog."

"Sneaking?" Savannah was instantly all ears. "What guy? What dog? What was he doing? Tell me exactly what you mean by 'sneaking.' "

Chapter 8

Savannah could tell by the slightly concerned and anxious look on Brody's face that she had over-reacted to his simple statement.

She chided herself and recalled it wasn't the first time.

Occupational hazard, she thought. *Once a detective* . . .

"It just sounds interesting," she told him with her most casual voice. "That somebody was 'sneakin' around the property. Usually, a sneaky Pete is up to something he shouldn't be."

"Yeah, but this guy's name ain't Pete. It's Dylan. He's the kid who lives next door. He was walkin' around, all quiet like, here by the barn when I came out. We talked for a minute."

"Would this be the kid who owns the really mean-looking dog?"

"Yeah. But Webster's not mean. He just looks it, 'cause

he's big and nature done stuck him with that ugly mug. He sure ain't winnin' no beauty contests anytime soon."

Brody paused to screw his face up into a frown with lots of wrinkles. It was a pretty fair impression of the dog Savanah had seen on the front side of the property.

"His name's Webster, huh?" she asked, trying to square the name with the face.

"Yeah. It's a fancy name for an ugly dog, but he can't help what his face looks like."

"True. We've all gotta work with what we've been given."

"He ain't overly smart neither."

"You could give him two nickels for a dime, and he'd think he was rich?"

Brody giggled and nodded. "Worse than that, he keeps comin' over here to see the llama and the other animals Dr. Carolyn's brought home with 'er. He even dug under the fence to get in here."

"A determined sort of fellow."

"He sure is, and Dr. Stephen don't want him on his property, 'cause he peed on his new Lamborghini's tires."

"Ah-h-h." Savannah thought back on the account the bald man had given her in the driveway. "There was more to that story than just the dog getting too close to the car."

"Lots more," Brody said, looking around before he continued to make sure they were alone.

"How do you know so much about this?"

"I was here! Helpin' Dr. Carolyn. We'd just finished raking the poop outta the llama pen, and she'd made me a big root beer float when it happened. I saw it for myself. The whole thing."

"A firsthand eyewitness. Do tell. . . ."

"Well, Dr. Stephen was looking out the front room window, and he saw Webster takin' a leak on his car wheel. So he came runnin' out, whippin' off his belt while he ran. He got outside and started whalin' on Webster with the belt with all his might, and Webster just hunkered down and took it."

"Oh, the poor dog," Savannah said, thinking other thoughts that she wouldn't share with a child, as they were of a far more violent nature.

She couldn't help wishing she'd been there, too. Somehow, she was sure she could have wrestled that belt away from Erling.

"Yeah, it *was* sad," Brody said. "I know what it feels like to get hit by a belt, so I hollered at Dr. Stephen to quit it. A bunch of times. But he didn't stop. I think he was too mad to hear me."

"Probably was. People don't hear much when they're angry."

"But Dylan heard his dog cryin', so he came tearin' over here and lit into Dr. Stephen, tryin' to get the belt away from him."

"I don't blame Dylan. Of course he did."

"But Dr. Stephen made the mistake of hitting Dylan, and that's when the trouble started."

"*That's* when it started?"

"Yeah. Nobody was bleedin' until that happened."

Savannah recalled that Dylan's father had said something about a trip to the hospital. She could only hope it was Dr. Stephen who had needed the ER's attention.

"Who was it that sprung a leak?" she asked.

"Dr. Stephen. At least twelve leaks, I'd say. A hole in his hide for every one of Webster's front teeth, top and bottom. Yep, ol' Webster had a real good hold on Dr. Stephen's arm, trying to save Dylan. Then Dylan's dad came over and the next thing you know, it was a knock-down, drag-out, right here in this rich folks' neighborhood."

Brody sighed and shook his head. "That sorta thing used to happen at my momma's house ever' Saturday night, but I bet the polite folks around here never seen the like o' that before."

"I reckon not."

"Now a judge is deciding if Dylan has to have Webster put down, 'cause of him being a violent, dangerous dog and all. Which ain't fair, 'cause he's a nice guy. Even when he got beat on, he didn't bite or fight back. It wasn't 'til he saw Dylan get hit that he got riled up. He's a dog! Protecting his owner, that's the most important part of his job!"

"It certainly was, and he was definitely provoked. Most dogs, good ones anyway, would have done the same. Hopefully, the judge will understand and give him a stay of execution."

She thought about it for a moment, then said, "Considering all that trouble, why would Dylan bring his dog back over here again today?"

"Dylan didn't bring 'im. Webster come over by hisself."

"It seems like Dylan and his parents would be really careful to keep him from getting off their property, considering what happened before."

"Oh, you can't keep Webster penned up to save your life. For such a dumb dog, he's real smart about getting out of anything you put 'im in."

"Is that what happened today?"

"I guess so. I didn't see when he first showed up. Just when Dylan was taking him back. Dylan said Webster especially likes to come over and say hi to the llama.

They're best friends. But Dylan was gettin' him outta here fast-like."

"That's why he appeared to be sneaking?"

"Yeah. He made me promise I wouldn't tell that I'd seen him here. But I don't reckon he'd mind me tellin' you. Just as long as Dr. Stephen don't find out."

Savannah made a motion of zipping her lips, locking them, and throwing the "key" over her shoulder.

She glanced down at her watch to see what time it was and how long Dirk had been gone. She could only estimate the time it might take him to investigate a car that had been burgled.

Depending on the circumstances, it could be a fairly simple case of someone reaching into an open car and taking a pack of cigarettes or some sunglasses off the dash, to a far more serious situation where a great deal of damage had been done to the vehicle. Possibly even the owner, if they came in contact with the perpetrator.

But whatever the case, she knew he would return as soon as possible. Especially since she had asked him to. He knew her well enough to know she hadn't made that request simply out of boredom or impatience.

"I'm sorry you got stuck here with a headache," Brody said, reaching for her hand and giving it a squeeze. "I shouldn't've asked you to come."

Savannah recalled what Carolyn had said to her husband about Brody pretty much inviting himself. But she couldn't find it in her heart to berate him for his little-boy bad manners.

Carolyn was a grown woman. If she'd truly been opposed to them coming or anticipated her husband might be, she could have refused the boy in a gentle way, and all would have been fine in the end.

Besides, it wasn't like the child or his parents had

made any sort of scene and ruined the party. If anyone had thrown a damper on it, that was the guest of honor himself.

She wondered if Brody was hungry. He was a kid with a hearty appetite, who needed to eat frequently and in shockingly generous amounts. The last thing she wanted was for him to suffer a hunger pang, a situation strictly forbidden in the Reid-Coulter household. But the thought of venturing inside the house for any reason, let alone to forage for food, made her feel like gagging.

"Don't you worry about anything at all," she told him. "If it's okay with you, we can just hang out here with Fantasia until Dirk gets back. My head doesn't hurt if I'm not inside with all the noise."

Okay, she thought. *It was only a little white lie.*

Surely lies didn't count if they were uttered to spare an innocent boy's feelings.

She never, never wanted Brody to know what had been said about him and his new family behind his back. Life had given the young child too much already that caused him shame. In whatever time Savannah had with him, she wanted to make sure his self-esteem was being built up, not torn down.

"That's okay," he said. "I don't mind waitin' 'til—"

A woman's scream came from the house. Then another.

Suddenly, men were shouting and the sound of the crowd, which only moments before had been laughing and casual conversation, now seemed agitated, even panicked.

Savannah heard a voice that sounded to her like Carolyn Erling's, shout, "Stephen! Stephen!"

For a moment, Savannah hesitated, weighing her next movement. The last thing she wanted to do was go anywhere she was unwelcome. But she had heard urgent cries like that before.

They usually meant something was not only wrong, but terribly wrong.

She didn't know if it was a situation where her presence would be helpful, but she knew she couldn't simply wait out here in the yard and act like all was normal.

She also had to protect the boy in her custody, while not exposing him to anything unsuitable for his age.

"What's goin' on?" he asked her, his eyes big as the shouting inside the house grew louder still.

"I don't know, but I think I'd better find out," Savannah said.

Brody nodded vigorously. "Yeah! Somebody might need arrestin' or CPR or somethin' like that, and you know how to do that stuff!"

"Okay. Here's what I want you to do. See that chair over there by the barn, the one kinda hidden behind the apple tree?"

He looked moderately disappointed. "You want me to sit there for the rest of my life, right?"

"Pretty much." She gave him a wink. "Don't fret. No matter how bad it is, I'll come back for you before you're, say, thirty. Deal?"

He sighed and started to meander, none too quickly, toward the chair. "At least I've got apples, so I won't starve. If I have to pee, I'll make sure nobody sees me watering the tree."

"What a fine lad! So well-mannered. You make me proud, son."

He just rolled his eyes and plopped down in the

chair. "At least come back in a little while and tell me what's going on. I might not die of starvation, but I might keel over dead from curiosity."

For a moment, Savannah thought how similar Brody was to the child she had been. Hungry for adventure of any kind. Eager to please but aching to be a part of everything around them.

"Just as soon as I see what's going on and the minute it's under control, I'll pop right out here and tell you all about it."

"Promise?"

"Double-dog promise with sugar frosting on it."

Without another word, Savannah turned and ran back toward the house, because the cries of distress and alarm coming from inside the mansion were getting louder.

Whatever the situation was, she had no doubt that it was getting worse by the moment.

Chapter 9

When Savannah stepped through the French doors and into the living room, what she saw was utter chaos. The formerly sedate crowd appeared to be rushing around in circles, helpless hands aflutter. The guests were, as Granny would say, "all in a dither."

It had been a long time since Savannah had encountered such a large gathering of people suffering so much collective distress.

Looking all around the room, she couldn't for the life of her discern the cause of the commotion.

As upset as they appeared to be and as much activity as there was in a crowded space, no one seemed to be punching, slapping, or even pinching anybody else.

None of the light fixtures were swinging, so no earthquake.

She'd heard no shots or explosions.

Maybe a medical situation? she wondered.

Savannah recalled seeing an extremely pregnant lady among the guests earlier and briefly fancied the mother-to-be's water might have broken.

But Savannah's instincts told her this was too much hubbub even for the imminent birth of a child.

One of the young servers she had seen offering drinks earlier pushed her way through the crowd and headed toward the doors that Savannah had just entered.

Savannah's curiosity got the best of her bad manners. She grabbed the woman by the arm and said, "What in tarnation's going on in here?"

Breathless and quite agitated, she could barely answer when she told Savannah, "Dr. Erling. Down."

Savannah's first thought was that something terrible had happened to Carolyn. "Where?" she asked.

The woman pointed toward the opposite end of the room, where only minutes before, Carolyn had given her husband's birthday toast with him standing next to her.

Before Savannah could ask again, the server twisted her arm out of Savannah's grasp, and a second later she disappeared through the double doors into the pool area.

Savannah looked over the crowd again and saw that whatever disturbing event had occurred, their attention appeared to be directed toward that fireplace area.

With little grace or courtesy, Savannah pushed her way through the guests until she made it to the opposite wall. Slicing one's way through a crowd was a skill she had honed during the years she had been a police officer. It was second nature to her, as was the well-practiced litany, "It's okay. Easy now. Easy. Everybody stay calm."

Sensing her alpha attitude, the highly agitated partygoers moved aside to let her through. They even seemed to settle down a bit, as though having someone take charge was a welcome development.

When Savannah finally reached the fireplace, she saw the source of everyone's distress. Though the sight was actually a relief to her, rather than a cause of great alarm.

It was Dr. Stephen Erling who was "down" on the floor and apparently unconscious. Not his wife, as Savannah had feared.

However, Carolyn Erling wasn't doing so well either. She was kneeling beside her husband, shaking him and shouting, "Stephen! Stephen! Open your eyes! Look at me! Oh, God! Honey, please!"

Savannah dropped to her knees next to Carolyn, then glanced around at the curious and alarmed visitors pressing in on all sides. She waved her arms at them and said, "Back! Move back and give him some air!"

The crowd parted and retreated a few feet.

"Is he dead?" someone shouted.

"No! He can't be! He's not dead, is he?" an equally insensitive guest replied at top volume.

Carolyn put her hands over her eyes and began to sob uncontrollably, rocking back and forth.

Savannah wrapped her arm around her shoulders and gave the woman a squeeze. Then she turned again to the crowd. "Has anybody called nine-one-one?" she asked.

They all looked at each other as though she had just uttered the most novel idea ever heard.

"Do it!" she shouted. "Now! Tell them we have a male in his forties—"

"Actually, he turned fifty today," said the woman with

the long silver hair who had commented earlier during the toast. As before, she had a sarcastic tone to her voice when she spoke.

Her inappropriate remark, nasty tone, and her ugly smirk caused Savannah to wonder if she was one of the most insensitive gals on the planet or if Stephen Erling had actually done something odious enough to warrant such a comment under terribly trying circumstances.

Certainly, Savannah was no fan of the man herself, but since he appeared to be dying or dead, this wasn't the time to be catty about the guy's age.

Savannah leaned down to press her fingers to his jugular, but Carolyn shook her head and said, "No pulse. I checked."

"Respiration?" Savannah asked, anticipating the answer.

Carolyn's reply was another head shake.

Savannah turned back to the crowd that seemed to be calming down quite quickly. She heard smatterings of comments circulating that contained the words, *"Stephen"* and *"Carolyn."*

But no one was doing anything.

Nothing at all.

"Why are you all just standing there with your teeth in your mouths?" Savannah yelled. "Call nine-one-one and say we have a male, fifty, down, unresponsive. Cardiac and respiratory arrest. Tell them to answer code three."

"I've got it," she heard a lady in a silk dress, dripping with diamonds, say with remarkable composure as she casually reached into her beaded purse and withdrew her phone.

Savannah could overhear her making the call and

speaking as calmly as if she was ordering a takeout dinner from her favorite restaurant.

Savannah was slightly confused at the change in the crowd, that had gone from hysterical to somewhat complacent in moments.

Could it be that they, too, had thought it was Carolyn who was in trouble? Savannah wondered.

"Is there a doctor in the house?" she shouted. "A doctor?"

When no one came forward, she said, "This's a doctor's birthday party, and there's not one lousy doctor here?"

Eventually, she heard a man from the back of the room say, "I don't know about any lousy doctors here, but I'm a pretty good psychiatrist."

"Then get over here and make yourself useful!" Savannah said as she rose and made room for him next to the frightfully still body on the floor.

Chapter 10

While the self-declared "pretty good" psychiatrist shuffled through the crowd to join Savannah, Carolyn said tearfully, "I can do it. The CPR."

She started to move over his chest, getting into position. But Savannah placed her hand on her shoulder and said, "I know you're a doctor, Carolyn, and probably know how, but this is your husband. You shouldn't—"

"Come sit over here with me," said a soft, sweet voice that Savannah knew very well.

She turned and saw Brody standing just behind Carolyn. He looked down at his friend, and after only the briefest glance at the body on the floor, took her hand in his.

"Come on, Dr. Carolyn," he told her, tugging at her. "That other doctor guy's gonna help him and so's Savannah. If anybody can bring him around, they can. You should wait over here with me."

Carolyn looked from the child to Savannah, who gave her a quick nod of approval.

When Carolyn didn't move quickly enough to suit her, Savannah gave her a nudge. "Please, darlin', let me get up there by his head, so I can start mouth-to-mouth."

Reluctantly, Carolyn stood and on unsteady legs, stumbled a few steps away and collapsed onto a love seat with Brody by her side, his comforting arms around her.

The psychiatrist knelt on the other side of the patient and checked again for a pulse, both at Erling's wrist and jugular.

"Nothing," he said.

"Then let's get 'er going," Savannah told him. "You first on the compressions."

The woman on the phone spoke up. "They said there's a wreck on the PCH. They can't get through for at least twenty minutes."

Savannah turned to her CPR partner. "Sounds like we're in it for the long haul. When you need a break, speak up, and I'll spell you."

As the doctor peeled off his tuxedo jacket and tore off his tie, he looked down at Erling and shook his head. "That's a 'No thanks,' on the mouth-to-mouth. You take care of that end, and I'll do the rest."

Within seconds, they had settled into a rhythm of his vigorous compressions and her rescue breathing.

As a stinking blast of sour whiskey breath blew back in Savannah's face, she understood why the psychiatrist had insisted on being in charge of the chest area, exhausting as that was.

It was going to be a long haul, indeed.

If she were honest, she would have to admit that she

wasn't thrilled to be in this position, engaged in such an intimate fight to save the life of a man she loathed.

But she saw his wife watching, her eyes so full of sadness, as though she already knew it was a losing battle.

Savannah decided that she could at least give Carolyn Erling the peace of knowing that everything that could be done for her husband was being done.

Better yet, Savannah saw Brody's big eyes, taking in every detail of the scene unfolding in front of him. Although she would have to talk to him later about not obeying and staying where she had left him, she had to admit, he was taking it very well. He had demonstrated far more maturity than most of the adults around him by the way he had taken charge of Carolyn and was offering her comfort.

Then there was the look of pride on his face. Profound satisfaction that his foster mom was trying with all her might to save a life. The life a man that neither she nor anyone else liked.

Savannah leaned down, positioned her mouth over Stephen Erling's and, again and again, blew her own breath into the man as hard as she could, willing it to reach the deepest parts of his body . . . parts that she was pretty sure were already dead or dying.

She fought down her own nausea as the air she had given him belched out of his body in foul-smelling clouds.

You get extra points for this, girl, she told herself. *Yes, when you get to heaven, Savannah girl, your crown should be a diamond tiara!*

About one hundred years later, or so it seemed to Savannah, the EMTs arrived at the Erling home and told the crowd what everyone had pretty much figured out by then.

Dr. Stephen Erling was dead.

Savannah sat on a leather ottoman next to the chair that someone had vacated for Carolyn, holding the young widow's left hand as she heard the pronouncement. Kneeling next to Carolyn, Brody was squeezing her other hand. He wore a terribly serious look on his face for one so young.

Savannah deeply regretted her decision to attend this party. She knew the child would remember this for the rest of his life and feel the pain of it.

She or Dirk would need to have a long talk with him about it later. Maybe more than one conversation. As sad and troubling as it was, an event like this was an excellent opportunity to plant early, healthy ideas in a young, developing mind about death, one of the most upsetting but inevitable events life had to offer.

But for the moment, the person who needed her most seemed to be Carolyn Erling.

Savannah patted the trembling, cold hand that lay limp in hers and said, "I'm sorry, Carolyn. So sorry."

"You have nothing to apologize for," she replied. "You tried your best, and for so long. I'll never forget that. I'll never forget how hard you tried to save him."

With the amount of adrenaline in Savannah's bloodstream beginning to finally decline a bit, she realized for the first time since the ordeal had begun how exhausted she was. Her clothing and hair were wet with perspiration, and she was shaking from the exertion and stress of the ordeal.

The psychiatrist, who had been doing the chest compressions, was far worse. He had refused to let her switch positions to give him a much-needed break from his exhausting task. Now he was lying on the floor near Stephen Erling, gasping for breath. His face was darkly flushed and far more sweat-soaked than Savannah's.

She wasn't surprised that one of the EMTs was checking his vitals, as well. The last thing anyone needed was a second man coding. One death per party was far more than enough.

Looking down at Stephen, lying ashen and still on his silk, hand-knotted rug, she couldn't help noticing how young, virile, and handsome he was. Fifty years old was far too young to die . . . and so unexpectedly.

Or was it?

Knowing that she shouldn't, but unable to help herself, Savannah turned to Carolyn and quietly asked, "Had he been sick?"

Carolyn shook her head vigorously, "Not at all. Stephen is the healthiest . . . *was* the healthiest person I ever knew. I swear, he never even caught a cold."

"Took good care of himself then?" Savannah pressed.

"He was vain about his appearance, so he worked out quite a bit. He ran on the beach and lifted weights every morning." Carolyn glanced quickly at Brody, leaned closer to Savannah, and whispered, "He had a few bad habits. In the past."

"Bad enough to cause"—she nodded toward the body—"that?"

Carolyn hesitated then shrugged. "I don't think so. I'm not sure."

Quietly, they watched as the EMTs placed a cover over Erling and began to collect their equipment.

They had rushed into the house, ready to save a life if possible, but now they were taking their time, displaying no sense of urgency at all.

Nothing more could be done for the man on the silk rug.

Savannah's mind was spinning with possibilities. Healthy fifty-year-olds didn't tend to just fall to the floor and die in the middle of their birthday parties.

Considering the quantity of alcohol Savannah had seen him consume, she thought it might have been alcohol poisoning. But something about the expert manner he had knocked back his whiskey and champagne told her that he was no novice drinker and would probably have a high tolerance level.

She thought of the trays of hors d'oeuvres being passed around the room at the time and asked Carolyn, "Could he have choked on some food?"

"No. I don't think he'd eaten anything. He never did at parties."

"Then what happened? Did you see him go down?"

"I don't know what happened. I was standing right beside him, and he was talking, acting normal. Then, all of a sudden, he told me he was feeling really sleepy, that he had to sit down. He took one step toward the sofa and a second later, he hit the floor."

Savannah looked around the area where Erling was lying. She hadn't noticed anything out of the ordinary before. But she had been concentrating on him, on saving his life, not looking for clues to his death.

Lying at the edge of the hearth, broken into several pieces, was the pale green, cut-crystal, champagne glass that she had seen him drinking from earlier. It looked to her as though it might have been dropped, rolled toward the fireplace, and broken on the marble hearth.

That needs to be bagged for evidence, the detective's voice in her head stated. Quite firmly.

It was a voice that Savannah had heard countless times over the years. One she had come to respect and obey whenever possible. So far, it had never led her astray. In fact, more than once, it had literally saved her life.

Unfortunately, it hadn't saved her career as a detective sergeant with the San Carmelita Police Department, working alongside Dirk.

Years back, her badge had been taken from her. Not because she was a bad cop, but because she had investigated people in high places and, when threatened, had refused to stop.

But, thankfully, her husband still had his badge, and she needed to speak to him, as quickly as possible.

Something wrong had just occurred in this house, among the folks who were standing around, their drinks still in their hands, wearing expressions that ranged from horrified to mildly curious.

She could feel it.

People were going to start to leave soon, if they weren't already. Critical evidence could be destroyed in the process—accidentally or intentionally.

She debated whether to remain with Carolyn, holding her hand and trying to comfort her, versus walking away and phoning Dirk.

She searched Brody's worried little face and felt two people warring inside her. The detective who sensed something terribly amiss in the Erling household and wanted to investigate it, and the mother, who felt the need to "be there" for the child in her care.

To her enormous relief, at that moment she saw Dirk walk through the front door. He glanced around, obviously looking for her. When he spotted her, he immediately began to push through the crowd, making his way toward his wife.

He gave only a quick glance at the body on the floor before rushing to her and kneeling next to the ottoman where she sat.

"You okay?" he asked, searching her face.

She nodded as he reached up and pushed her sweat-damp curls out of her eyes. "Yes," she said. "I'm glad you came back though. Perfect timing, in fact."

He looked over at Brody. "You all right, too, partner?" he asked with equal concern.

Brody looked as happy to see him as Savannah was. "Sure." The boy gave Carolyn a quick, sideways look and added, "I mean, we're mighty sad, but nobody's hurt, 'cept him."

Dirk turned his attention to the body on the floor and stared at it a few moments.

Savannah watched as her husband, with his detective's keen eyes, studied the corpse, then its immediate surroundings. She knew when he spotted the broken glass.

He turned back to her and gave her a questioning look. She nodded ever so slightly.

"So, that's Dr. Stephen Erling," he said, his voice much softer than his usual gruff, cop tone.

Carolyn nodded and sniffed. Savannah dropped the woman's hand long enough to dig into her handbag for a tissue.

"I'm really sorry, ma'am," Dirk told Carolyn as she dabbed at her eyes and wiped her nose.

"Thank you, Detective," she whispered, her soft words getting lost in the low rumble of the crowd's conversations.

"He hadn't been sick or nothin'!" Brody piped up, his eyes wide. "Healthy as a horse. But he just up and keeled over dead!"

Savannah gulped and thought, *Ah, the painfully awkward, blunt, honesty of youth.*

She started to chastise Brody, but before she could think of how to frame it in a way that was kind, Carolyn spoke. "Yes, Brody," she said. "You're right. He was fine. Until the moment when he . . . wasn't."

Dirk looked Savannah over, her wet hair and face, her crumpled dress. Then he glanced down at the psychiatrist, who was now sitting up, but was wearing an oxygen mask, provided by the EMTs.

"Let me guess," Dirk said to Savannah. "You gave mouth-to-mouth while he did the compressions."

She nodded.

"How long?"

"Twenty minutes. At least."

"Wow."

"Yeah."

Dirk looked around at the crowd, then once more scanned the room itself: the furniture, the floor, the broken glass lying next to the marble hearth.

Rising, he said, "I think I'd better get to work here. Dr. Carolyn, I need to speak to a few of your guests, just get their names and contact numbers. Stuff like that."

"Okay," she said. "Whatever you feel you need to do."

"Would it be okay if you and Brody went to another part of the house for a while?" he asked. "Maybe to your bedroom or wherever you'd be the most comfortable?"

"There's a study down the hall," Carolyn told him, pointing toward a door on the opposite side of the room. "It's my favorite place. My 'safe' place."

"Then go there. Rest. Try to relax if you can." Dirk turned to Brody. "Is that all right with you, son?"

Brody nodded vigorously. "Sure it is. I'll take good care of her for you. I promise."

Dirk offered Carolyn his hand and helped her to her feet. "If you need anything at all, just have Brody come get one of us, okay?"

"Yes. Thank you."

Brody grabbed Carolyn's arm and holding it tightly, led her through the door she had indicated.

Savannah watched and noted that not one guest attempted to reach out to Carolyn as she passed close to them, not even to offer her the smallest comfort or condolence. Something told Savannah that those present at this gathering were Stephen Erling's people, not his wife's.

Although none of them seemed particularly grief-stricken at his departure. Other than the initial screams she had heard from the backyard, they were behaving as though it was just your standard cocktail birthday party.

With a bit of unorthodox entertainment to go with the cognac-seasoned barbecue wings.

Chapter 11

Eventually, when Savannah, Dirk, and Brody returned to their own house, they were all exhausted.

They also had an overnight guest with them.

As Dirk pulled the Buick into their driveway, Savannah turned around in the front passenger's seat. She said to Carolyn, who was sitting in the back next to Brody, "I'm so glad you decided to come home with us."

"I should have just stayed," Carolyn replied. "Or gone to a hotel. I hate putting you out like this."

"You couldn't have stayed," Dirk told her.

Carolyn was silent a moment, then said, "Why not? I don't understand. No matter what happened, it's still my home."

"I'm sorry to say, your place is a potential crime scene now," he replied. "You can go back once it's been processed."

"Crime scene?" Carolyn looked shocked. "Why? What crime?"

Savannah thought fast. She wanted to be gentle to this newly widowed lady. At least, more gentle than Dirk, which Savannah figured shouldn't be too hard.

She wanted to spare Brody, too. Precocious as he might be, he was very young to have witnessed what he had that day.

Stephen Erling dying was bad enough for the two of them to process without adding "possible homicide" to the mix.

Savannah took a deep breath and plunged in, using her softest, most sensitive and sympathetic Southern drawl. "You see, anytime a young, healthy person dies, suddenly like that, there has to be an investigation. Everyone wants to know what happened. To understand how and why he passed."

When Carolyn didn't answer, Savannah continued. "Especially you, Carolyn. You deserve to know why your husband was taken from you like that. No one can bring him back, but it may give you some peace of mind to know exactly what happened."

"I understand the need for autopsies and coroners' reports, but why can't I stay in my home?"

"'Cause if it turns out that his death was foul play, the CSU has to go over it with a fine-tooth comb, find out who done it, so's we can nail 'em," Dirk interjected, without a trace of sensitive Southern drawl and precious little sympathy.

Savannah cringed and thought, not for the first time, that Dirk would be far happier living on a desert island. As long as he had a handful of his favorite people, the cats, cold beer, and a TV to watch his favorite sports, he would have been perfectly happy.

She doubted society would miss him all that much either.

"It's just a routine part of the investigation, Carolyn," she said. "Nothing to worry about."

"How long will it be until I can go home?"

"Not too long," Savannah told her. "Meanwhile, you're welcome to stay with us."

"You ain't puttin' nobody out," Brody added. "At least, if that means causin' problems or makin' a nuisance of yourself, you won't be. We're happy to have you. Di and Cleo will be glad to see you, too."

Carolyn smiled down at him and shook her head. "I doubt that. Most of my patients run when they see me. I'm the one who examines their owwies and sticks needles and thermometers in them. I'm usually their least favorite person on Earth."

"That's not true," Brody said. "Everybody loves you. Especially critters. We're lucky you're stayin' with us. I wanna show you my room. You get to sleep in it tonight. It used to be Dirk's man cave, but he gave it to me! It's pretty cool. It's got a big, round baseball rug and Dodgers stuff everywhere 'cause me and Dirk, we're big-time Dodgers fans."

"I can't take your bed, Brody." Carolyn leaned forward and said to Savannah, "Seriously. I didn't realize I'd be kicking him out of his bedroom, or I would have—"

"I sleep on the couch a lot," Brody insisted. "Ever' time Granny comes over, I give her my bed, and I don't care a lick."

"He doesn't," Savannah assured her. "He really doesn't."

"I don't." Brody grinned broadly, his smile charming, if a bit gap-toothed, as he had been keeping the Tooth Fairy quite busy recently. "It's fun when we have company that I like, and I like you. With all you been through, you oughta be with people who like you, what with your husband fallin' down dead all of a sudden thata way."

Again, Savannah cringed at his childish candor.

But Carolyn seemed to take it in stride. Softly, graciously, she replied, "Thank you, Brody. I'll never forget your kindness and your family's efforts to help me in my time of trouble."

Savannah quickly added, "No one should be alone after a night like this. You're always taking care of others, human and animal alike. Let us take care of you for a change, Carolyn. It's our honor to do so."

Casting a quick look at Dirk, Savannah saw that he seemed less enthused than Brody about having company for the night. Maybe even less pleased and willing than Savannah.

However, Dirk had been the one to suggest it, initially, there at the seaside mansion. No sooner had Carolyn retired to her study with Brody than Dirk had whispered to Savannah, "She stays someplace else tonight. With family or friends or at a hotel."

"I don't know if she has friends or family in the area, and being alone in a hotel when your husband just died . . . that seems a bit cold and lonely," Savannah had replied.

"Okay. If necessary, she comes home with us. As soon as I've got all these people's names and numbers, they're outta here, and I'm sealing it up. As far as I'm concerned, this place is off-limits to civilians until Dr. Liu and CSU tells me otherwise."

But now, whether it had been his idea or not, Dirk seemed to be having misgivings about their overnight guest. Savannah made a mental note that, as soon as she could get him alone, she'd be sure to ask why.

The four of them got out of the car and made their way along Savannah's newly laid stone walkway to the front door. The rockwork had been one of numerous gifts from her sister's rich and famous fiancé.

Savannah was finding out there were many perks to having one of the world's most popular movie stars in the family. Little Alma was the envy of millions of Ethan Malloy's fans, marrying a guy who had been chosen "The Handsomest Man in the World."

A flood of guilt swept over Savannah when she recalled all the sisterly, maid-of-honor, wedding duties she had been neglecting lately. It wasn't easy, maintaining her old life while taking on this whole new one as a mom.

Now, just to make things more complicated, she was front and center in what might be a murder case.

One day at a time, old girl, she told herself as they reached the front door. *One hour or even minute, if it comes to that.*

As Dirk turned his key in the door lock, Carolyn looked up at the matching bougainvillea vines that graced both sides of the door. They began in their oversized terra-cotta pots, hugged the frame, left and right, and intertwined at the top.

"How beautiful," Carolyn said. "What a colorful and inviting sight to welcome you home."

"They're named Bogey and Ilsa," Savannah told her. "I planted them the first day I moved in. They've been growing ever since."

Carolyn thought it over for a moment. "That's sweet.

Some couples are just meant to be together." In a voice that sounded rather sad and wistful to Savannah, she added, "While others aren't."

Dirk opened the door, then stood back for the women and Brody to enter. Savannah ushered Carolyn inside and flipped on the foyer light. At their feet was the household's usual welcoming party, the two, ebony mini-panthers, Diamante and Cleopatra.

They mewed their joy at their humans' return, until they saw Dr. Carolyn. Black tails twitched, and in less than two seconds, the foyer was completely kitty-free.

"See. I told you," Carolyn said as she slipped out of her sweater and handed it to Savannah, who folded it neatly and placed it on the top shelf of their coat closet.

Savannah took Dirk's leather bomber jacket and Brody's sweatshirt. As she put them away, as well, she asked Dirk, "Could you and Brody fetch us each a glass of iced tea from the fridge? I'll make us something to eat in a minute, but I could use a refresher first."

Dirk gave her a grateful smile but said, "Don't worry about dinner. I'll order some pizzas." He looked at Carolyn, then down at the boy. "If that's okay with Dr. Carolyn and Mr. Brody here."

Everyone withheld their verdict as they waited for Carolyn's, which she delivered without hesitation. "Whatever everyone else wants is fine with me. I doubt I can eat anyway. But refreshing tea sounds good."

"I've gotta warn you, it's sweet tea," Savannah said.

"I wouldn't have expected anything else from a Georgia-born lady," Carolyn replied.

"Okay. Tea comin' up," Dirk said as he and Brody took off for the kitchen.

As soon as the guys were gone, Savannah reached into her purse and pulled out her Beretta.

She saw Carolyn give it a double take, but she didn't appear to be upset at the sight of a firearm, as some folks were.

"Sorry," Savannah said. "I want to put it away while the boy's in the other room. He's the inquisitive sort, so I keep it up here."

She reached to the top of the closet and punched in the numbered code of the small safe she and Dirk had installed once they began to entertain children in the household.

"Good idea," Carolyn said as Savannah stowed the weapon inside, closed the door, and tried the handle to make certain it was locked. "You can't be too careful with any child, let alone one as spirited and curious as Mr. Brody Greyson . . . as he likes to call himself."

"Isn't it a hoot how he always introduces himself that way?" Savannah said. "I take it as a good sign. A strong sense of himself."

"Oh, he has that, all right, and with you two taking care of him, he'll only grow more of it."

Savannah flushed with pleasure at the praise. She hadn't been at this mothering business long enough to garner many reviews.

Carolyn's words were more reassuring than Savannah might have expected them to be. Carolyn Erling was, after all, an intelligent woman and a close friend of Brody's, having known him even longer than Savannah and Dirk had.

"Thank you," Savannah told her, as she led her from the foyer into the living room. "I'm glad to hear it. I know he thinks the world of you. Letting him hang out there at the clinic like you do means so much to him. He'd rather hose the poop out of your outdoor enclosures than go to Disneyland."

Carolyn chuckled, but it was a hollow sound, as though she was forcing it. "That's high praise, indeed," she said. "Thank you. I love having him there. He's a fun little guy to be around, and he's a hard worker, too. Does a good job for me."

"I heard that!" Brody said as he came bounding out of the kitchen, holding a frosty glass of iced tea in each hand. "You're talkin' about me in here."

"We are, indeedy," Savannah told him as she nodded toward Carolyn, indicating he should serve their guest first, before her. "Dr. Carolyn here is telling me that, there at the clinic, you thump the dogs' ears and tweak the cats' tails."

"I most certainly do *not!*"

Savannah had assumed he would know she was teasing, but on second thought, she realized Mr. Brody Greyson wasn't the sort to joke about thumping or tweaking animals.

Considering that he, himself, had been on the receiving end of physical mistreatment, Savannah couldn't blame him.

"As a matter of fact," he said, "if I caught wind of somebody doin' such a thing, I'd thump their ears and tweak their tail-ends for *them!* We'd see how *they* liked it!"

Savannah reached down, put her hand under his chin, and lifted his face so he was looking into her eyes. "Brody, I apologize. That was a dumb joke, and if I'd thought about it twice before saying it, I'd never let it fly out of my mouth like that. Do you forgive me?"

He gave her an affectionate grin. "Sure. I know you didn't mean it on purpose. But you owe me an extra cookie or piece of pie or somethin' for it. Deal?"

She nodded and pushed a strand of hair out of his eyes. "Deal."

Dirk handed Brody a glass of tea, then sat on the far end of the sofa with his own.

Savannah noticed he didn't kick his sneakers off and shove them under the coffee table, as he usually did as soon as he arrived home. He had also left his usual seat, the end of the sofa nearest Savannah's comfy chair, available for Carolyn.

But although he was using his "company manners," Savannah couldn't help noticing that the disgruntled look on his face was a bit more intense than his trademark Dirk scowl.

Although Savannah and Brody were treating Dr. Carolyn Erling with all the gracious attention offered to any other guest in their home—even more, since she had, only hours ago, lost her husband—Dirk was being civil to her, but not exactly warm and inviting.

Yes, Savannah decided, *I definitely want to have a word with him alone, as soon as possible, and find out what's up with him.*

She drank down her tea as quickly as she could without giving herself a brain freeze, then said to Dirk, "I'm going to go look for that pizza coupon I clipped yesterday. Okay? Then we can phone our order in before it gets much later," she said with what she hoped was just the right amount of nonchalance.

"Yay!" Brody plopped down on the sofa next to Carolyn and slipped his arm through hers. "I want one with everything! All right?"

"Of course," Savannah said as she rose from her chair and walked toward the kitchen."

"But *no anchovies!*" he added. "I'd rather eat a mouthful of salty beach sand with dead, rotten fish in it than one of them things!"

"You sound a little undecided about that," she told him. "If you change your mind, just let me know, and I'll tell them to put extra on for you."

Savannah grinned at the boy, but as she walked past Dirk, she shot him a knowing look, which he intercepted and acknowledged with a slight nod.

She passed through the dining area and into the kitchen. There she fiddled with the miscellaneous items of her official junk drawer, making what she supposed was a convincing amount of "searching" racket.

Finally, after a reasonable amount of time, she called, "Dirk, could you come help me find that pizza coupon?"

"Sure," he replied, far more enthusiastically than he would have normally. Once Dirk was settled on the sofa for the evening, he seldom rose again except to shower and go to bed.

"Excuse me," she heard him tell the others. "Brody, find out what Dr. Carolyn likes on her pizza and if she wants a salad or whatever."

A moment later, he appeared in the kitchen and joined Savannah beside the drawer.

"I thought I saw it in here yesterday," he said, loudly jiggling some items inside. A hammer, a wrench, a flashlight, and some miscellaneous screws.

Leaning his head down to hers, he whispered, "What's up?"

"What's up *with you?*" she replied softly. "Are you sorry you asked her to come home with us?"

He thought it over, shrugged. "I guess so, a bit. I'm pretty sure her ol' man didn't croak from natural causes."

"Me, too."

"But until I hear for sure it was murder, I can't really take her to the station and grill her. Wouldn't be right to put the squeeze on an innocent gal who just became a widow."

"You were hoping to interrogate, I mean, talk to her tonight? Here?"

"Sure I was. Now I'm thinkin' it's gonna be awkward . . . because of the boy. Her bein' his good buddy and all."

"You don't want him to see you being a cop with somebody he loves."

Dirk winced and frowned. "I haven't forgotten how it went down the last time I tried to arrest someone in front of him. Somebody he cared about. Even if it *was* his worthless mother."

"The child does have a protective streak a mile wide," she said. "Not to mention a mean right hook."

"Please, don't remind me. Clocked by a six-year-old. I'm still livin' that down at the station house."

She stood on tiptoes, kissed his cheek, and said, "Took that black eye weeks to fade away, as I recall."

"I'd just as soon *not* recall the gory details, if that's all right with you."

Savannah thought for a moment, then said, "Would you be just as satisfied if I was the one who did it?"

"If it was you who got to squeeze her, you mean?" he asked. "Where'd be the fun in letting *you* do it?"

Shaking her head, Savannah said, "No. I have no intention of 'squeezing' a woman who just watched her husband die in front of her."

"Then what good are you?"

She resisted the urge to take some utensil from the

junk drawer and give him a brisk lesson about "Being Respectful to One's Wife at All Times . . . Especially If She Happens to be a Reid Female."

But a lecture she had recently given Brody about using one's words, rather than impromptu weaponry, came to mind.

"I prefer to think of it," she said, "as gaining her trust while plying her with alcohol. Then, when she thinks of me as a dear sister-of-the-heart, ask some leading questions that'll get her to spill her guts. If she's innocent, no big deal. We've had a nice bonding experience. But on the other hand, if she's guilty as sin, she might actually say something that can later be used against her in a court of law."

He thought it over for only a second, then said, "That's supposed to be better? Sounds underhanded and sneaky to me. Worse than just plain ol', honest, run-of-the-mill squeezin'."

She did a quick replay of the words that had just tumbled out of her mouth.

He was right.

She hated it when he was right.

But fortunately, it wasn't something that happened often.

"How about this?" she whispered. "While you do the bedtime chess routine with Brody, I take her out back in the garden, give her a good, strong, hot toddy and see if she wants to share whatever's on her mind? Of course, all the while I'll be offering genuine concern and support, not to mention a soft place to fall in her time of grief and loss. Is that better?"

"Yeah, well, I guess." His shoulders sagged. He released a deep, weary sigh of resignation. "I suppose it doesn't matter who does it, as long as the mission is accomplished."

She kissed him again, then reached into the drawer and pulled out the coupon that had been there, front and center, all the time.

"Let's have our pizza. Without anchovies, heaven forbid," she said. "Then leave the rest to me."

Chapter 12

"Do they play a game of chess every night?" Carolyn asked as Savannah led her from the kitchen and out the rear door.

Savannah glanced back at her "boys," who were sitting at the kitchen table, their heads bent in intense concentration over the black-and-white checkered board and its classic figures.

As always, Brody was wearing a cocky grin, while Dirk glowered.

The stakes were high. At least for Dirk, who was a novice player himself and hated to lose to a "six-year-old pipsqueak, who likes to rub it in when he wins," as Dirk put it one night after a particularly dismal defeat.

"Yes. They play a game every evening at bedtime," Savannah told Carolyn. "For someone who calls rooks, 'castles,' and knights, 'horsies,' he's surprisingly good."

"Well, he *is* only six," Carolyn replied.

"I was talking about Dirk. Brody knows the proper nomenclature."

Savannah handed Carolyn one of the mugs she was carrying. They were filled with steaming hot toddies.

The aroma of the lemon and orange slices, cloves, and a cinnamon stick mingled with the strong whiskey scent, a promise that a great deal of tasty comfort would soon be forthcoming.

Savannah led her guest down the back stairs and across the lawn toward the wisteria-draped arbor. Beneath it were several comfortable chaise lounges, Savannah's second favorite seating in the world.

A million years ago, before she had become a mother, as well as a working woman, she had spent many blissful hours in those chairs, reading romance novels, nibbling chocolates, or just communing with her own thoughts.

Now, nibbling, communing, and sometimes even thinking, were luxuries she could scarcely afford. But she wouldn't have it any other way.

She motioned for Carolyn to make herself comfortable in one chair, and she settled onto the one beside it.

Carolyn looked around, taking in the delicate wisteria blossoms overhead, lit by a few twinkling, accent lights and the silver moonlight. She breathed in the fragrance of the nearby flower garden, its evening perfumes enhanced by the dewfall.

"This is lovely," she said.

Savannah smiled, recalling her visit to Carolyn's seaside mansion only hours before. Though it felt like years.

"You have a pretty nice yard yourself," she told her guest. "Especially the view. Nothing tops the Pacific Ocean for beauty and grandeur."

Carolyn looked down at the mug in her hands and said, "It will never be the same after today. Nothing will ever be the same."

Savannah tried to think of something encouraging, uplifting, something hopeful. But she knew all too well that during life's worst moments, the power of mere words wasn't enough to take away a mourner's pain. Sometimes, well-meaning platitudes made it even worse.

"No," Savannah said softly. "You're right. Nothing will be the same as before. I'm so sorry."

Carolyn wiped her eyes, then lifted her chin and sat up straighter. ""How did Brody learn to play chess?" she asked, apparently wanting to change the subject.

"He enjoys hanging out with some friends of ours, Ryan and John," Savannah told her. "They're interesting fellows. Former FBI agents who now own a fancy-schmancy restaurant downtown called ReJuvene."

"Oh, I've eaten there before. With Stephen," Carolyn added, her voice breaking as she spoke his name. It took a moment for her to recover her composure. When she did, she said, "The place is beautiful, most elegant, and the food is divine."

"I agree. Ryan and John are so kind to our family. Brody loves going in there, and they enjoy having him. They make him gourmet hot dogs with truffle French fries, hamburgers, and pizza. Once in a while, he even gets a cooking lesson from the chef, Francia. Between the lunch and dinner crowds, John or Ryan play chess with him, teach him new moves to use on Dirk."

"Poor Dirk."

"Exactly. I told Dirk to ask Ryan and John for some lessons when he drops by to get a free beer from time to time. But the male ego being what it is, it ain't happenin'."

Carolyn chuckled, but there was little merriment in the sound.

Savannah took a sip from her mug and savored the heat of the drink that warmed her mouth, delivered the whiskey burn to her throat, then carried the sensation down into her stomach. From there, she could feel something akin to warm, liquid relaxation trickle through her belly and into her limbs.

It had been a hard day, and it wasn't over yet.

She watched from the corner of her eye as Carolyn did the same and waited for the beverage to take effect.

After a few sips, she appeared to relax a bit, sinking a little lower in the chair, closing her eyes for a moment, then sighing.

"I'm so sorry, Carolyn," Savannah said. "I can't imagine how you must be feeling."

Carolyn was quiet for a while, as though considering her response carefully. Finally, she said, "Honestly, I'm not even sure myself how I'm feeling. Terribly sad, of course, but . . ."

When she didn't continue, Savannah said softly, "But . . . ?"

"Would it sound terrible to say, also a bit relieved?"

Savannah carefully wiped any trace of surprise off her face to have heard such an admission. She thought how excited Dirk would have been if he were within earshot.

When Savannah didn't reply right away, Carolyn repeated her question. "Does it sound terrible? Am I a horrible wife to even think such a thing, let alone speak it out loud?"

Savannah searched her mind for a response that would be both kind and honest. Finally, she said, "If it's the truth, then it doesn't matter how it sounds. Truth is truth."

"I can tell you and Dirk have a happy marriage," Carolyn continued, her hands wrapped tightly around the mug, as though welcoming its comforting warmth. "That must be really nice."

Savannah gave a slight nod. "It is . . . most of the time. Everybody has a bad day once in a while."

"Our marriage wasn't a happy one." Carolyn turned to face Savannah and there were tears in her eyes when she said, "I used to think we were happy. But eventually, I figured out that I wasn't a wife to him. I was nothing more than a means to an end."

"How so?"

"When we first met, it seemed like love at first sight. He told me he adored me and, stupid me, I believed him."

"Did you love him?"

"Of course I did. How could I not? He was gorgeous, ambitious, brilliant. Everyone told me how lucky I was to have caught him. 'A rising star.' That's what everybody called him."

"You're quite successful yourself, Dr. Carolyn."

"I consider myself successful. I fulfilled my lifelong dream. Being a neighborhood vet was all I ever wanted to be. It's what I love doing."

Savannah nodded solemnly. "I must say, I agree with your definition of success. Following your passion, doing what you believe is your life's work, it doesn't get better than that."

"Stephen would have disagreed with you. He saw things very differently. He didn't believe in such silliness as callings or passions or fulfilling one's destiny."

"What did he believe in?"

"Stuff. The biggest, best, fanciest, fastest, whatever would impress others and set you above them."

Savannah thought of the sportscar and the mansion on the water. They were impressive, indeed. But they hadn't caused her to think any higher of Stephen Erling. Not one notch.

"Stuff is just . . . stuff," Savannah said. "Toys, expensive or otherwise, they're just objects that have to be dusted, maintained, fixed, stored, repaired, and eventually discarded. You get too much of it, and you can start feeling like *it* owns *you,* rather than the other way around."

"I tried to tell Stephen that, to convince him that sometimes less truly is more, but you can't change people's minds. Especially those who are quite sure they're right 99.99 percent of the time."

"And that .01 percent was the time when they thought they were wrong, but they were mistaken?"

"Exactly."

Savannah took a sip of her toddy. "You were telling me about when you and he first got together."

"Ah, yes. When Stephen and I met, I had a good practice that was well established. I lived simply, so I was in very good shape financially. I realize now that he was more interested in my finances than my feminine charms. He owed a lot for those Ivy League medical degrees he'd accumulated. I had a sizable savings and had made some good investments."

Savannah heard the bitterness and pain behind her words and thought, once again, how interested Dirk would be if he were eavesdropping.

Having an unhappy marriage wasn't necessarily a motive for murder. Thankfully, or much of the population would have to sleep with one eye open. But she had a feeling that, if she could keep Carolyn Erling talking, she might uncover even more elements that, combined, could form a solid motive.

"When did you start doubting your husband's sincerity?" Savannah asked.

"Even before the wedding. We had a row. He showed his true, controlling, nasty side, and I knew it was a mistake," she replied. "But I married him anyway. After all, I had the ring, the gown, the invitations had been sent out. Stupid, huh?"

"There's nothing stupid about wanting to trust the ones we love, to give them the benefit of the doubt."

"I'd say that depends on how often and how long you keep doing that, in spite of evidence that they don't deserve your trust."

"True."

"I found out on our honeymoon that he'd been having an affair with my maid of honor, my best friend. There's no getting around it. When it came to that guy, I was an absolute fool."

"I'm so sorry. But you're not alone in your foolishness. When it comes to love and marriage, we tend to follow our hearts rather than our brains. We're only human."

Carolyn's face softened, and she said softly, "He was so beautiful. I'd look at him and just melt into a big puddle of love and lust. I guess if a person really wants to believe something badly enough, they'll find a way."

"Yes, I do believe we human beings are particularly skilled at that."

Carolyn took a long drink from the mug and closed her eyes. When she opened them, she looked angry.

Savannah had never seen that particular expression

on her friend's face before, and she was surprised at how it changed the woman's appearance.

The gentle, loving vet was gone. This woman . . . she was someone Savannah wouldn't want to tangle with on one of her worst days.

"I put up with a lot of that man," Carolyn said, her tone as bitter as her countenance. "Let's just say I shoveled a lot of dog crap for those highly specialized medical degrees of his. While I was in my clinic, expressing dogs' impacted anal glands, checking for ear mites on rabbits, and lancing abscesses on quarrelsome tomcats, he was living a life of fame and fortune, jetting around the world, performing surgeries on celebrities of all sorts. I was so proud of him. But he was ashamed of me. His wife, who wasn't even a doctor to human beings."

"Really? He looked down on you for that?"

Carolyn nodded.

Savannah found it hard to believe. "I've always been in awe of veterinarians," she told her. "Regular doctors only have to know about the human body. You guys treat everything from a pet python, to a parrot, to a hamster."

"That was his point. My patients are dogs and cats, horses and pigs. His were movie stars and ambassadors and even presidents. But that wasn't the worst of it."

Here it comes, Savannah thought. *The rest of the motive. . . .*

"My maid of honor wasn't his only conquest. There were other women, too. Many, many women. He flaunted them right in my face, daring me to leave him. Knowing that I wouldn't."

"Why not?"

"Because I would lose the life I'd worked so hard to create. Gradually, he'd gone from being financially dependent on me to me depending on him. His practice, mine, our home, and more importantly, my clinic—they were all tied up together. I couldn't get rid of him without losing everything else that mattered to me."

Savannah nodded. "A lot of people remain married because of financial entanglements. Sad, but true."

"But still . . . even that wasn't the worst."

"Tell me the worst, Carolyn," Savannah said, wondering if it was the alcohol that had loosened her tongue so effectively.

It had been a long time since Savannah had interviewed someone who had opened up and shared so freely.

Had it not been highly illegal, she would have suggested to Dirk that, in the future, he give his suspects a hot toddy before grilling them at the station house.

"I could have stood it all," Carolyn continued, "the infidelities, the adolescent squandering of our money, his arrogance, and the put-downs. But he waited until after we were married to mention to me that he would never want children. He said there was no room for such annoying distractions in a neurosurgeon's world. 'Annoying distractions.' That's what he called any children we might make together."

She looked at Savannah with so much sadness in her eyes that Savannah had to fight back her own tears of empathy. "I'm sorry, Carolyn. So sorry."

"Can you imagine anyone referring to little Brody that way?"

Savannah recalled some of the horrible names Brody's mother had called him. Casually. With no consideration for his innocence or what such vile language and harsh labels could do to a tender soul.

"Not being able to have a child of your own is awful enough," Savannah said, speaking from experience, because of her own premature menopause. "But to have someone deny you that joy, and not even talk to you about it before marriage, that's rough. I can understand you'd be heartbroken and furious about that."

"I guess that's why I enjoy having children, like Brody, come into the clinic. It's not like having a little one of my own, I'm sure, but I figure it's the next best thing."

Savannah smiled. "Especially when the kid is Mr. Brody Greyson."

"Yes! Especially when it's him, little live wire that he is."

The two women sat in companionable silence for a while, finishing their drinks, soaking in the healing power of the moonlit garden.

Finally, Savannah decided to gently ask the difficult questions.

"What do you think happened to Stephen this evening? You may not be a physician, for people anyway, but you have extensive medical training. What do you think caused him to pass so quickly like that?"

Carolyn thought long and hard before replying, then said, "I have no idea. Stephen took very good care of himself, physically anyway. He worked out, ate right, drank too much, but not enough to kill him. If he got the sniffles, he'd run to a specialist."

"So, you don't think it was disease?"

"No. Of course, it could have been. But I don't think so."

"He hadn't suffered any sort of injury lately?"

"Not even a small spill."

"Back at your house, you said he had some bad habits in the past. Did he do any sort of recreational drugs?" Savannah asked, hoping Carolyn wouldn't take offense.

The question didn't seem to upset her. She answered quite matter-of-factly, "He used to."

"What was his drug of choice?"

"Cocaine. But he got treatment for it and was able to stay off it. He'd been clean for years."

"Maybe he relapsed."

Carolyn shook her head. "No. I would have seen the telltale signs a mile off. Believe me, I knew what to look for."

"Then what do you think caused him to . . . pass?"

Carolyn set her mug on the side table between them and put her hands over her eyes, as though wanting to blot out some terrible sight that only she could see.

After a few moments, she dropped her hands and turned to Savannah, who could see tears rolling down her cheeks. "I have a bad feeling, Savannah," she said. "I don't think it was disease, and he hadn't suffered any sort of accident or injury. He wasn't depressed or the sort to harm himself. So that only leaves one thing, doesn't it?"

Savannah nodded. "Yes." She decided to broach the topic, since Carolyn appeared understandably reluctant to do so. "If he wasn't sick and hadn't been in any sort of accident, then I'm thinking he might have been the victim of foul play."

"But how? He was in a crowded room, being watched every second."

"He might have ingested something."

"Something . . . toxic?"

"Yes. I mean, maybe not. Perhaps there's still a perfectly logical answer that isn't immediately obvious to you or me. But perhaps something he ate or drank was, well, not good for him."

Savannah chided herself for her awkward choice of words. But since Carolyn had chosen not to say the word that was on both of their minds, neither would she.

Apparently, the newly widowed veterinarian preferred not to use the word *poison.*

Savannah could hardly blame her. She pulled a tissue from the box on the side table and handed it to her friend.

As Carolyn wiped her eyes, Savannah said, "Can you think of anyone who might have wanted to harm Stephen?"

"You mean like an enemy?"

"Precisely like an enemy. Did he have one?"

"One? One single enemy? *My* Stephen?" She gave a wry chuckle. "Stephen made enemies everywhere he went, and he traveled all around the world. He wasn't happy unless he was seriously on the outs with someone at all times. He thrived on conflict."

"Does anyone in particular come to mind?"

Carolyn shrugged. "Any of the women he was messing around with. Some of them got very upset that he wouldn't leave me and marry them, which he never would have done because that would have meant dividing up the toys."

"Okay. A bevy of disgruntled girlfriends and who else?"

"Their husbands and boyfriends. He got death threats from more than one of those."

"You may have to produce a list of them. Names. Addresses if you know them. Who else?"

"His co-workers. My co-workers. Our neighbors. Estranged family members. Patients who had bad outcomes. Their relatives."

"Wow."

"Yes. I'm telling you. For a guy who was so sure of his own superiority, there are a lot of people who won't be sorry—quite the contrary, in fact—when they hear he's gone."

"Were any of them at the party?"

Carolyn thought it over for a few seconds, then nodded. "At least six, maybe eight of them."

Oh, goody, Savannah thought. If it did turn out to be a homicide, Dirk was going to have his hands full. As senior officer of little San Carmelita's two-man Major Crimes Unit, he was bound to catch the case.

There was nothing quite like trying to find justice for a guy that half of the world hated, and other half didn't know.

Later, after Savannah had shown Carolyn the guest room and upstairs bathroom and, once again, expressed her condolences, Savannah walked on down the hall and entered her own bedroom.

To her surprise, instead of finding Dirk in bed, he was pulling off his jeans and getting into a pair of blue and gray plaid, L.A. Dodgers pajama bottoms.

"You're wearing jammies to bed?" she asked him. "Since when? You haven't worn clothes to bed since the last earthquake."

Like a lot of Southern California folk, Dirk harbored a fear of running out of his house in the middle of a major quake and encountering his neighbors, au naturel.

For several months after a shaker, he had worn pajamas to bed. But eventually, once the aftershocks had died down, he'd return to his old habits. They hadn't experienced any tremors over 5.5 on the Richter scale in quite a while.

"I'm not going to bed yet," he said, pulling a T-shirt over his head.

"Really? But you hardly got any sleep at all last night. I thought you'd be dog-tired."

"I am."

"What do you intend to accomplish this late, sporting those Dodgers britches?"

"I'm gonna go downstairs and keep an eye on Brody."

Savannah flashed back to the image of the little boy, sound asleep on the sofa with a purring, black kitty tucked beneath his chin. She had given him a kiss on the forehead as she and Carolyn passed through the living room on their way from the backyard to the upstairs bedrooms.

"I just checked on him. He's finer than frog hair," she told him.

"Good. I intend to make sure he stays that way."

He walked over to her, enfolded her in a tight hug, then kissed the top of her head. "You go on to bed. No point in both of us staying up. Besides, I'm the one who was stupid enough to invite her to spend the night with us. Don't know what I was thinking."

As Savannah tried to process what he'd just said, he added, "I guess I'm just not used to having a kid in the house. If it was just you and me, it'd be okay, but a little guy like that, downstairs, by himself and out of earshot . . ."

"Dirk, are you suggesting you need to protect him from Carolyn?"

He shrugged. "Why not? I'm pretty sure that Dr. Erling guy was murdered, and she's my number one suspect, and she's sleeping under the same roof as my kid."

"Whatever you think of Carolyn Erling, I guarantee you, she would never, ever hurt a hair on that little towhead."

"Okay. I appreciate you sharing your opinion on the matter, but I gotta do what I gotta do."

"What are you gonna do, that you just gotta do, Mr. Manly Man? Sit on the end of the sofa all night with a shotgun across your lap?"

"No, Miss Smartie Pants. Since you won't be parked on it yourself, I'm gonna sprawl out in your comfy chair. I don't need a shotgun to deal with Dr. Carolyn, if she starts trouble."

He headed toward the door, and she rushed to intercept him.

"Honey, really." She grabbed his arm. "You're so tired. You nearly fell asleep with your face in your pizza at dinner. If you really think someone has to keep watch over him, I'll do it. I can nap tomorrow while you're at work, probably investigating this case."

He took her hand off his arm, kissed her knuckles then ruffled her hair with his big bear hand. "Van, I don't have to tell you, of all people, how many nights I've sat in a cold car outside of some bum's house, waiting for him to show up or do a drug deal, or whatever. Go to bed, darlin'. I got this."

A moment later, he was gone.

Savannah looked over at the bed that looked all the bigger now for being empty, and she felt a pang of loneliness.

But she also felt enormously proud of Dirk.

For a guy who had driven her nuts for the first fifteen years of their working-turned-personal relationship, he'd turned out to be a pretty awesome husband. Now, it appeared he was an equally incredible dad.

Yes. Dirk Coulter.

Go figure.

Chapter 13

When Savannah set the platter of fried eggs and sausages on the table, it occurred to her that there was a lot less laughter in her home than there had been twenty-four hours before. No pranks. No giggling. No banter between her and Dirk or little boy snickering.

Brody and Dirk sat, quietly buttering their toast, no doubt out of respect for Carolyn, who was having a simple bowl of cereal—minus the cat food tidbits.

As Savannah lowered herself onto the chair next to Dirk's, she stifled a groan. She had awoken to savage pains in her back, the disgruntled muscles complaining bitterly about yesterday's unaccustomed workout.

She wouldn't have minded at all if her CPR activities had actually saved a life. But more than once during her career as a police officer, she had performed the arduous task, pushing her body far beyond its limits, to no avail.

It made the subsequent back pain harder to bear.

"You okay?" Dirk asked, keeping his voice low.

She nodded but thought, *If by "okay" you mean am I gonna live? Yes. Barely. But I'll never be the same.*

One quick, sideways glance at Carolyn told Savannah that her guest had heard Dirk's question and felt bad about it.

Carolyn's expression was one of abject misery, mixed with something that looked like guilt. "I think I owe you a day at one of our better downtown spas," she said. "At least a nice massage to work out some of that soreness."

"Oh, I'm all right," Savannah lied. "At least, I will be, once I get going. I just slept funny. Got a little crick in my neck."

"That's sweet of you to say, Savannah. But what you did yesterday, I've done myself," Carolyn told her. "I know it's terribly hard work. I'm not surprised you're stiff and sore today."

Brody perked up and shoved a spoonful of cornflakes into his mouth. "You've done that mouth-to-mouth stuff, too, Dr. Carolyn?"

The vet gave him a smile. "More like mouth-to-snout. A Labrador retriever, a poodle, a hamster, and a Siamese cat."

"At least it wasn't that python," Savannah muttered under her breath.

Brody grinned and snickered. "Cool! I'm gonna be a vet, you know, when I grow up. I wanna do that mouth-to-snout stuff, too!"

Carolyn turned back to Savannah. "I hope he has better luck with his patients than you had with yours."

"That's for sure," Savannah said, offering her the platter with the eggs and sausages.

She shook her head and said, "No, thank you, Savannah. I'm sorry that you went to so much work to make this full breakfast. But I just don't have an appetite this morning."

"That's 'cause you're sad about your husband," Brody said with the authority of a psychiatrist delivering a complicated, expert diagnosis.

Savannah cringed at his bluntness, but Carolyn reached across the table and patted his hand. "You're absolutely right, Brody. I *am* sad, which is to be expected under the circumstances. When we lose someone close to us, we can't help it."

"Like when people need you to put their pets to sleep. Only not really to 'sleep,' you know . . . and then the people cry there in the clinic, 'cause they're super sad."

"Yes. Exactly like that."

Savannah slid the platter to its usual place on the table. Next to Dirk's plate.

He wasted no time before wading into it. But just as he was transferring an obscene amount of sausage links to his plate, his phone chimed.

Savannah had a feeling about who would be calling. Dirk didn't possess a particularly active social life. Almost always, when someone called his cell phone, it was concerning business, not pleasure.

"Yeah, Captain. Whuzzup?" he asked, still chewing.

After listening for a moment, he glanced quickly over at Carolyn and said, "Yeah. Okay. Gotcha. I'll be coming in soon."

He ended the call and shot Savannah a loaded look.

She knew what it meant. The captain had assigned him a case, and she had a sneaking feeling it was Stephen Erling's.

So, the not-so-popular, former brain surgeon to the rich and famous was now officially a "case"?

She wondered what new developments there might be.

The fact that Dirk resumed his breakfast without saying, told her that she shouldn't ask. At least, not in front of the widow.

"I'm going in a little earlier than usual," Dirk told Brody. "If you can get ready quick, I'll drop you off at school on my way."

"Okay!" Brody shot up from his chair, grabbed his bowl and plate, raced to the sink, placed them inside it, then disappeared. Seconds later, they heard him pounding up the stairs and running down the hall to his bedroom.

"Wow!" Carolyn said. "Is he that eager to go to school every morning?"

"He is. But he particularly likes it when Dirk takes him," Savannah admitted.

"He likes you, too," Dirk told Carolyn. "He's crazy about you."

"But I'm a girl," she replied, "and every boy that age knows that us girls are icky and have cooties."

"Yeah, well, give him a few years, and he won't mind cooties. Especially icky girl ones." Dirk gave her a wink as he stood and carried his own plate to the sink.

Who says a wife's nagging doesn't pay off in the end? Savannah thought as she watched him rinse off the plate before sticking it inside the dishwasher. *You've just got to stick with it and not give him a moment's peace until he adopts the rules of society, one by one.*

"Then you're saying we girlies *do* have cooties?" she asked him playfully.

He walked back to the table, stood beside Savannah, and toyed with one of the curls that was forever hanging down into her eyes. "Present company aside, of course," he said, tucking it behind her ear. "But once the adolescent hormones get to flowin', we guys start noticin' that you ladies have other charms that make up for any cootie infestations."

He left Savannah and walked behind Carolyn's chair. Laying his hand on her shoulder, he said, "I'm sorry, Doctor, for what's happened to your family. If there's anything we . . . I . . . can do for you, don't be shy. Speak up, okay?"

"You've done quite enough already, Sergeant Coulter," she replied. "I really appreciate you taking me in like you did last night. I don't know what I would have done if you hadn't."

"Think nothin' of it," he said as he picked up his phone from the table and shoved it into his jeans pocket. "Glad to have ya."

Savannah looked up at him, noticing the dark circles under his eyes. She could hear the fatigue in his voice.

In the middle of the night she had gone downstairs, intending to relieve him of his Brody guard duty, whether he wanted her to or not. But she had found him fast asleep, sitting in her chair, with a very contented Cleopatra curled on his chest. Savannah had decided it was best not to disturb him.

But he couldn't have gotten any true, quality sleep, comfortable chair or not. Nothing was as good as the coziness of one's own bed.

She had already predicted that, true to habit, tonight

he would be ready for bed right after dinner. She was determined to make sure that he hit the sheets far earlier than usual. No matter what was going on.

No one could be on duty twenty-four hours a day. At least, not for long.

"Be safe," she told him as he scooped his keys up from the kitchen counter.

She realized, of course, that those two simple words, uttered at the beginning of each and every one of his shifts couldn't actually ward off bullets or knife blades, or flying fists or broken bottles, let alone wrong-way speeding vehicles on the freeways.

There was no foolproof talisman that could protect a police officer from all the various harms that could befall him "out there." There were no magic words that would ensure he would return to his family at the end of his shift as healthy and whole as he had been when leaving his home.

But she had to say them anyway, because in her heart Savannah was absolutely sure those two simple, routine words of benediction helped.

Though she wasn't sure how.

Perhaps it was the love behind the words that provided the badly needed protection. *There might not be a lot of strength in simple words,* she told herself, *but there's a heap of power in love.*

He smiled at her and headed out of the kitchen and into the living room, where he called for Brody to "Shake some tail feathers up there, buddy. Get a move on!"

As always, when Dirk left Savannah's presence, she missed him. Even before he'd stepped out of their house and into that unpredictable, anything-but-safe world out there.

When she heard Brody tearing down the stairs like a herd of wildebeests, shouting, "Okay, my tail feathers are all shook! Let's go-o-o!" and the door slamming behind them, Savannah realized . . . now she had *two* beloved boys to worry about and miss.

Every woman should be so fortunate.

Chapter 14

Less than five minutes after Dirk and Brody left, Savannah was in the upstairs hallway, beside the linen closet, handing Carolyn her best guest towels for her shower, when she heard the front door open and close.

"Dadgum. Brody must have forgotten his lunch pail again," Savannah said.

"I'm pretty sure he had it with him," Carolyn told her. "Red with a dinosaur on it?"

"That's the one."

Then Savannah heard a cheery voice, virtually dripping with honey and liquid, golden sunshine, and she groaned.

That particular voice was a bit too sunny most mornings for Savannah's taste. On an especially bad day, before she had reached an optimal percentage of caffeine in her bloodstream, Savannah found such unbridled gaiety unbearable and had to restrain herself from getting physical with her assistant/best friend.

She thought she should at least be allowed to apply a bit of duct tape to her mouth and by doing, buy herself half an hour of blissful peace and quiet.

"Savannah! Yoo-hoo! It's just little ol' us! Are you home?! Sa-vaaa-nah?" warbled the familiar, female voice. Since its owner was one of Savannah's favorite people in the world, she chose to forgive her for her habitual, overt, and ill-timed displays of joie de vivre.

After all, nobody was perfect.

"That's Tammy, my assistant, sister-in-law, and best friend," Savannah told Carolyn. "Not necessarily in that order."

"Hmm. She sounds . . . chirpy."

"Oh, you don't know the half of it. She can make a robin who just ate a fat, juicy worm sound positively suicidal. The happiest person I know. From the moment she jumps out of bed at the crack of dawn. But I love her anyway."

Savannah handed Carolyn the soft, white, terrycloth bathrobe that was reserved for very special guests, like Gran when she stayed overnight. Then she called out, "I'm up here, Tamitha. I'll be down in a minute. Make yourself at home."

She turned back to Carolyn and took a quick inventory of all she had just placed in the woman's arms: towels, robe, jasmine-scented bubble bath, and her best shampoo and conditioner.

"There are pink votive candles on the windowsill," she told Carolyn, waving a hand toward the open bathroom door. "Feel free to pull the shade down and light them."

"What a luxury! Candles and a bubble bath in the morning? How deliciously decadent."

"If everyone would treat themselves to a candlelit bath when they first rolled out of bed in the morning, in my humble opinion, the world would be a more peaceful, loving place."

Carolyn looked at the label on the yellow, jasmine bottle. "Not to mention a more fragrant one. Thank you for this treat."

"My pleasure. Enjoy it for as long as you want."

While you have the chance, Savannah added to herself, knowing all too well that, if Dirk's and her suspicions proved true, life would be getting terribly complicated for Carolyn Erling very soon.

As Carolyn disappeared into the bathroom, Savannah turned to walk down the hall toward the staircase and saw that Tammy was on her way up. She was carrying little Vanna Rose, Savannah's adorable toddler niece and namesake, on her hip.

The moment the tiny girl, with bouncing red curls and an angelic face, saw Savannah, her smile turned into peals of baby laughter. Savannah's very favorite sound in the world.

The toddler started jumping up and down so wildly that Tammy nearly dropped her. Her tiny arms were outstretched, reaching for Savannah, as she squealed with delight.

"Settle down, sweetcheeks," Tammy told her. "You'd think you hadn't seen Auntie for ages, instead of two days."

When Tammy reached the top of the stairs, she set the little girl on her teeny feet, which were adorned with penguin booties with bells on them.

The baby and the accompanying, jingling penguins practically flew to Savannah, who scooped her up in her arms and placed a flurry of kisses on her chubby, pink cheeks.

"Wow! You're getting that walking business down pat, puddin'," Savannah told her. "At this rate, you'll be ready for the San Carmelita Marathon next month."

"Oh, we've already registered!" Tammy told her. "She'll be participating, too. In the stroller, of course."

"Of course."

Savannah smiled, thinking how different Tammy's life was now, compared to only a few years ago. Back then, Tammy was known in the town as the beautiful, athletic woman with the long blond hair, who could be seen running along the foothill road every morning without fail.

In the middle of a torrential rain with the sides of the road transformed into rivers, Tammy ran. Earthquakes, brushfires, nothing stopped her. Year after year.

Then, the townsfolk noticed that the slender young woman was gaining a bit of weight—especially in her tummy area. After a few months, it became obvious that the extra poundage was a baby bump.

"That's it," they said. "She's a mother now. Her running days are coming to an end." They added that they would miss seeing her, receiving her friendly waves and her radiant smiles.

As winter faded into spring, the bump grew larger and larger, then for a few days, no one saw her on the roads.

Less than a week later, she reappeared. Still running but pushing a stroller.

Now Savannah couldn't tell who enjoyed the mother/

daughter runs the most—Tammy, Vanna Rose, or the townspeople, who felt they had somehow shared in the pretty, blond lady's journey.

Savannah looked Tammy up and down, taking in her sweat-damp running gear. "Don't tell me you cut your run short just to come visit me," she said. "That day will never dawn."

Tammy shook her head and looked annoyed. At least, as annoyed as Miss Tammy Sunshine and Lightness ever got. "No. A wheel popped off the stroller, and I need a screwdriver to put it back on. We were just a few blocks away, so I thought we'd come borrow one from you rather than ask Waycross to pick us up. He's putting a very special paint job on that old Studebaker he's been restoring. Heaven forbid that I should interrupt that!"

"He'd be glad to come rescue his girlies no matter what he was doing," Savannah said, kissing Vanna's baby hand. "But you know where the toolbox is. Just help yourself. I'll keep our fairy princess here occupied. Let me know if you need a hand."

"Thanks." Tammy turned to leave, then reconsidered, stopped, and turned back to Savannah. "Oh! I forgot to tell you. I've got some news, if you haven't heard it already."

"What's that?" Savannah asked, thinking Tammy's face was even more flushed than from her routine run. It had to be something juicy.

"It's awful. That veterinarian friend of Brody's, Carolyn What's-Her-Name, her husband died last night."

Savannah raised one hand in traffic cop fashion, "Um, actually—"

"I heard they suspect foul play."

"Well, you shouldn't—"

"Apparently, he wasn't a very popular guy. A real jerk they say, especially with women, if you know what I mean."

"Sh-h-h. Tammy, seriously . . ." Savannah said, glancing behind her at the bathroom door.

To her horror, Carolyn was standing there, wearing the robe and a stricken expression on her face.

Savannah turned back to Tammy, who moved a step closer, so she could see what Savannah was looking at. When Tammy spotted the open bathroom door and Carolyn standing there, a look of horror spread across her face.

Savannah's heart sank, feeling for both women. Carolyn, of course, didn't need to hear something like that at such a time. And poor Tammy was the politest person Savannah had ever known, the least likely to commit such a dreadful faux pas.

The three women stood for what seemed like ten years in awkward, embarrassed silence.

Only little Vanna seemed to be enjoying the moment as she pulled one of Savannah's curls and squealed with delight to see it bounce back when she released it.

Finally, Savannah found her voice and said, "Um, Dr. Carolyn, meet my dearest friend in the world, Tammy Hart-Reid. A truly lovely person who, instead of swatting flies like the rest of us, traps them under drinking glasses. Then she releases them outside, after thinking long and hard about which pleasant spot in the garden she would want to be released in if she was a fly. So, I can assure you that, at this moment, she feels lower than slug slime at the bottom of a roadside ditch."

Savannah turned to Tammy. "Tammy, as you may have guessed by the scarlet glow of my cheeks, this is Brody's good friend, Dr. Carolyn Erling. She spent the night with us because . . . well, you already know. Brody says she's about the nicest person he's ever known, so she probably won't hold what you just said against you." She sighed. "At least, we hope not."

Tammy gulped. Then choked. But remained speechless.

Carolyn stared at Savannah, a helpless, lost look in her eyes.

Another ten years passed. Savannah could feel herself aging by the moment. Her skin wrinkling, her hair turning white, her chin, butt, and boobs sagging.

Finally, at long last, Carolyn spoke. "I just wanted to ask if I can have a washcloth."

A few minutes later, Savannah walked out the back door of her house and onto the patio. She was still holding the squirmy Vanna Rose with her left arm. In her right hand was a bunch of tissues.

She walked over to Tammy, who was bent over the stroller, screwdriver in hand, fastening the wheel onto its axle and sobbing.

Shoving the tissues at her, Savannah said, "Buck up, buttercup. Could've been worse."

Tammy looked up at her with red, tear-filled eyes. "How?" she asked. "How could that have been any awfuller than it was?"

"Well, yeah. You've got a point there. Positive spin: Nowhere to go but up."

Tammy glanced over Savannah's shoulder, then all around the yard and up at the house's windows, making sure they were alone before she added, "Thank goodness I didn't mention that people are also saying it may have been his wife who did him in. Talk is she and he were about to get divorced."

"Glad you left that little tidbit out," Savannah said. She bent down, closer to Tammy, and whispered, "Is that really what they're saying?"

Tammy nodded. "Yes. That's the consensus."

"Who is 'they'?"

"Social media comments. The town's page posted a short little obit-thingy for him, 'Famous San Carmelita Brain Surgeon Dies at His Birthday Party.' Then under the post, a ton of people chimed in about how much they didn't like him. Some even hated him. You know how people are. Especially when they're anonymous."

"Yes. I do. They're like a pack of hyenas on a zebra corpse. Can you get me a copy of that? I want to see what they said, and if I can, figure out who those anonymous ones are."

"Then it's true?" Tammy stood and dusted off her hands and knees. "He was murdered?"

"We won't know until we hear from Dr. Liu, but it might be homicide. We were there last night, you know."

"Get outta here! No way!"

"Brody got us invited to the birthday party."

"Did you meet him, the victim, before . . . you know. . . ."

"Yes, and after spending maybe a minute conversing with him, I can tell you now, you can add me to the list of potential suspects who would have enjoyed doing him in."

"That bad?"

"Worse. Way worse." Savannah glanced up at the bathroom window to make sure it was still closed, and the shade drawn. "Are you busy this afternoon, after you get home?"

"Not really. Why? You want me to do some sleuthing?"

Tammy's whole demeanor changed so dramatically that Savannah was glad she'd asked her. No more sobbing. Her eyes were twinkling like a kid's the night before their birthday.

Tammy was quite sure that she had been born to "sleuth." It was the only pastime she loved even more than running.

"That would be helpful. Just in case it turns out it wasn't natural causes. That way we'd get a head start."

"We?"

"Dirk caught the case."

Tammy nodded and snickered. "Yeah, ol' Dirko can use all the help he can get."

"That's my husband you're speaking of there, girlie," Savannah said, lifting her chin and her right eyebrow. "He has his flaws, like spitting toothpaste specks on the bathroom mirror three times a day, but he's a darned good detective."

"Oh, right. I keep forgetting. You're a loyal wife and don't want to hear anything bad about your hubby."

"No, I don't." Savannah thought it over, reconsidered, and added, "Unless, of course, it's me saying it."

"Where do you want me to start?" Tammy asked. "Like who's on your suspect list, if it turns out to be homicide?"

"I hear he fools around. A lot. See if you can find out who his latest squeeze was. Also, the neighbor who lives next to him, the north side. The guy's got a son, Dylan. There was some sort of kerfuffle involving a dog named

Webster who peed on Erling's Lamborghini's tire and then bit him and Erling wound up in the hospital."

"Doesn't sound like something that would turn into murder, but—"

"You never know, human nature being what it is. Brothers have killed each other over who got the bigger steak at the family barbecue."

"Anything else?"

"Check out Dr. Erling himself, of course."

Tammy glanced back at the house again and whispered, "Her, too?"

"Sure. You know what they say. . . ."

"It's usually the spouse."

"Makes sense when you think about it. Especially in this case."

"What do you mean?"

"Apparently, Erling was a donkey's hindquarters. I hate to think it, let alone speak it out loud, but she was his next of kin, the one who spent the most time with him."

"It stands to reason she was on the receiving end of most of his orneriness."

"Exactly. The more he hurt her, the stronger her motive would be." Savannah thought back on the brief contact she'd had with the surgeon the day before and added, "I've gotta tell you. I wouldn't put it past her. Or blame her. If I was married to a guy like that, chances are good he'd wind up being a suspicious smell in the attic."

Chapter 15

Once Savannah had sent Vanna Rose and Tammy on their way with kisses, hugs, and a restored stroller wheel, she walked back into the house, hoping to enjoy one more cup of coffee, sipping and savoring it quietly in her comfy chair, while she decided how to best spend her day.

Her calendar had been full already with grocery shopping, picking up the shoes that had been dyed to match her maid-of-honor gown for Alma's upcoming wedding, and collecting Dirk's suit from the cleaners so he would have something to wear to the "tasting" tonight at Ryan and John's restaurant.

That, she was anticipating with great eagerness. Their friends were gourmet cooks in their own right and the restaurant's chef was superb. They were going to cater Alma and Ethan's wedding reception.

No doubt tonight's preview meal would be a culinary delight.

If she made it that far.

As she refilled her coffee cup and trudged toward the living room, she was wondering how she and her sore neck, legs, and everything in between were going to get through the day.

But before she entered the room, she heard Carolyn's voice. Her guest was having a one-way conversation with someone, and she was speaking softly in a low voice, as though she might not want anyone to overhear.

Savannah assumed she was on the phone.

At first, she intended to return to the kitchen and give the woman her privacy. Considering all that had happened, it might be a sensitive call.

But then she heard some words that stopped her.

"Please don't say that. I love you. I want you in my life. Everything is, you know, different now."

Savannah warred with her conscience. She didn't like to eavesdrop. Granny had always taught her, "Don't do anything to others that you wouldn't want done to you."

She figured that probably included snooping.

But the investigator in her head spoke louder than the memory of Gran's words when it said, "To heck with that! This could be good stuff here. You don't wanna miss a word of it!"

So, she listened and heard, "We're going to put all that behind us. Please. I need you."

Whatever the person on the line said in reply, Savannah assumed it was encouraging because Carolyn's voice sounded far lighter and happier when she said, "Oh, good! Thank you! I'm so relieved. We're going to work hard at forgetting all that unpleasantness. Things are going to be much better from now on. You'll see."

There was another pause as Carolyn listened. Then she ended the conversation with "Okay, great. Thanks again. I'll see you there. Bye."

Quickly, Savannah took a few steps back into the kitchen, where she took a spoon from the drawer and began to stir her coffee, doing her best to appear busy.

She could hear Carolyn's steps as she made her way across the living room. A moment later, she entered the kitchen.

"Hi," Savannah said. "You're all done with your bath?"

"Yes, and I'm smelling like a bouquet of roses. Or, jasmine as the case might be."

An awkward, silent moment passed between them, both women recalling what had transpired before. Finally, Carolyn said, "Did you get your friend with the broken stroller on her way?"

"Yes. I did, and she's mortified beyond belief. She's really a sweetheart, and if you knew her, you—"

"I'm sure that if she's one of your closest friends and a member of your family, she's a wonderful person. I'm sorry she feels so bad about it. She doesn't have to. No harm was done."

"Really?"

"Really. I'm going to have to get used to things like that being said behind my back. Probably even to my face. Hopefully, not by anyone who truly matters to me, whose opinion I value."

Savannah studied her friend's expression, trying to read her. But either Dr. Carolyn Erling was particularly skilled at donning a neutral, poker face under difficult circumstances. Or she was one of the most stoic souls Savannah had ever met.

"Just one day at a time, Carolyn," she told her. "One hour or one minute if necessary. But now it's time for a bit more coffee. Would you like another cup? It's my own proprietary chicory blend."

Carolyn hesitated, then said, "All right. It is delicious. Reminds me of some coffee I had in New Orleans. But just one more cup, and then I've got to get going."

"I understand, and I'd be happy to drop you wherever you need to be."

"I've decided to go to work today. But you don't need to take me to the clinic. I'll call a car service."

Savannah handed her a steaming mug of coffee, then pushed the small tray with the creamer and sugar toward her. "You're my guest, and you won't be calling any car service. If you really want to go to work, I'll take you. But I'm sure that nobody would expect it of you, considering."

Carolyn poured a dollop of creamer into the mug and said, "Maybe not. But I expect it of myself. My patients need me. I can't turn my back on them just because I had a crummy day yesterday."

"Okay." Savannah motioned her toward the living room. "Let's go sit a spell and have our coffee. Then you can get to the clinic and those ailing critters of yours."

As both women left the kitchen, Savannah couldn't stop replaying Carolyn's words, ". . . just because I had a crummy day."

She kept thinking, *What woman refers to the day her husband died, a day most people would consider one of the worst of their lives, as simply "crummy"?*

Maybe Carolyn Erling had a gift for understatement.

Or perhaps, the day before hadn't been the worst day of her life. Maybe for Dr. Carolyn, it was Independence Day.

As Savannah drove Carolyn to her veterinary clinic in Savannah's classic, 1965, red Mustang, the two women had little to say at first. They hardly spoke until they passed the waterfront promenade and looked across the beach to the pier. The normally gentle waves were crashing against the outermost pilings, creating impressive saltwater sprays.

A storm was coming.

Storms weren't all that common in San Carmelita. Not even gentle showers. Frequent, gentle rain was one of the things that Savannah missed most about Georgia—other than the peach and pecan pies.

But a few times a year, especially in the spring, when the ocean decided it was time to shake up the peaceful little town, it would line up one massive storm after another in the Pacific. One by one they would come onshore, bringing torrential rain with them.

People living on the hills, enjoying their panoramic views of the ocean and coastline, suddenly started to worry about mudslides. Horribly destructive at times, they could tear a mansion off its foundation and carry it down the hill, leaving a crumbled mess on their neighbor's property.

With equal drama, Momma Nature bombarded the beach dwellers with high tides and massive waves that turned their meticulously decorated living rooms into giant aquariums.

When it was storm season in sunny, sleepy San Carmelita, boredom was the least of anybody's problems. They were having too much "fun" sandbagging, plugging up roof leaks, shoring up retaining walls to keep their up-the-hill neighbor's new swimming pool from sliding down into their outdoor firepit area.

"It's going to be a doozy," Carolyn said when they saw a particularly giant wave crash into the pier and spray the hearty souls who were strolling along, soaking in the ocean's intoxicating power, its roar, its fury.

"I like a good storm once in a while," Savannah said. "At least here, we don't have to crawl out of bed in the middle of a downpour and go huddle in a dark, flooded ditch while the tornado warning sirens scream."

Carolyn shuddered. "That sounds dreadful."

"Not as bad as having to share your shelter with an equally terrified water moccasin or two." Savannah could feel her skin literally crawl as she spoke the words. "I hate snakes," she added. "Mostly, because of the memory of those nights."

Carolyn smiled. "I love snakes."

"Oh, that's right. I forgot. You have a pet one. Brody loves it, too. Couldn't wait to show it to Dirk." She glanced over at Carolyn, whose expression was completely neutral and told her nothing. "I'm sorry if I offended you," she said. "It's just a personal preference, or aversion, rather. I'm sure snakes are very nice."

"You didn't offend me. A lot of people feel the way you do. If I'd had your experiences, I would probably feel the same way."

"Oh, good, because I'm lying my butt off here. I don't really think any of them are nice at all."

"Maybe one of these days, I could introduce you to

my Burmese python. He's very friendly, cuddlesome even, and an excellent conversationalist. He might change your mind."

"Someday I might change my mind about Limburger cheese, the screech of nails on a blackboard, or my husband's snoring, but I'm afraid the snake thing is deeply embedded in my DNA code."

Abruptly, Carolyn changed the subject. "When do you think I'll get to go home? I have to at least drop by there today to feed and tend my animals or make arrangements for someone else to."

Savannah debated whether to give her the shortest answer possible—usually the safest response, if a bit cowardly—or tell her the truth.

It depended on the results of the autopsy that was probably going on at that very moment or might already be finished.

If Dr. Liu found Stephen had expired from something like a congenital heart problem, then Carolyn's return home would be green lit almost instantly. If it was a homicide, heaven only knew when Carolyn would be able to sleep in her own bed again.

Also, Savannah couldn't help wondering if she, Dirk, and Brody were going to have their overnight guest indefinitely. Under most circumstances, Savannah was most hospitable. She was never happier than when she could house, feed, and entertain one of her fellow human beings.

But she didn't want to find her husband sleeping in her comfy chair every night for the next week or more, and she didn't want to have to do so herself.

The chair was soft and invited one to dive into it, stretch out, and let the troubles of the day sink into its overstuffed cushions and armrests. The chintz upholstering was a lovely rose print with vibrant, warm shades of crimson, cinnamon, maroon, and gold. But come bedtime, no chair—comfy, rose-spangled or not—could compare to her bed's memory foam mattress and bamboo pillows.

"I'm not sure when you'll get to go home, Carolyn," she finally admitted. "I'd say that, by tonight, you'll have a much better idea about what's going on and what you can expect down the road."

"Depending upon whether it was natural causes . . . or something else," Carolyn added in an emotionless monotone that Savannah could only describe as a "flat affect."

A symptom of depression, she reminded herself. Commonly seen in victims of domestic abuse.

"That's exactly right," Savannah replied. "Time will tell."

"Will you let me know as soon as possible? So that I can make arrangements."

"Of course you'll be told. But it will probably be Dirk who gives you that information. It's his case, after all."

"Oh, right." Carolyn smiled. "I keep forgetting that you aren't on the force with him. You two seem like partners."

"We were for so long. It's hard to step out of that role. Gets me in trouble sometimes."

"I can imagine."

"But for the most part, he appreciates the help my agency and I give him from time to time. Just as we appreciate it when he assists us. We all work together."

"That must be nice."

Savannah heard the pain in Carolyn's voice, and this time, when she turned to see her facial reaction, she saw tears in her friend's eyes.

"Sharing your life with a good man can be wonderful, Carolyn," Savannah said softly. "You'll see. Once this is all behind you, eventually, you'll get back out there in the world again. You'll find there are plenty of fine fellows, any one of whom would bring you a lot of joy, if you'd let him. They aren't all like your former husband. Thankfully."

Carolyn shook her head. "The last thing I want right now is another man in my life. I want to be alone. Heal. Try to get back the bits and pieces of myself I've lost over the years."

"You will. I have faith in you."

"Good," Carolyn replied. But this time her tone was anything but flat and empty. Her voice was full of sadness, bitterness even, when she added, "Someone needs to have faith in me. Faith in myself is one of the most precious things I've given away."

Chapter 16

When Savannah and Carolyn arrived at the veterinary clinic, Savannah parked the Mustang near the door. But as she turned off the key and started to get out, Carolyn said, "Oh, no. No, you don't have to walk me in."

She seemed agitated all of a sudden, and the anxious energy she was giving off made Savannah suspicious. She reminded Savannah of a kid who had eaten half of the snacks in the cookie jar and their mom was about to lift the lid.

Savannah continued to climb out of the car.

If for some reason Carolyn didn't want her to go inside, she was all the more determined to do so.

"Don't you worry none, darlin'. It's no trouble at all," Savannah said, her tone as sweet as Georgia acacia honey.

"But you already drove me here and—"

Carolyn's objection fell flat as Savannah beckoned her out of the car and led the way to the clinic's front door.

"I need to pick up some more of those ear drops for Diamante anyway. I'm about out," Savannah said, trying to sound casual. Trying to sound like she wasn't lying enough to set her bloomers ablaze at any given moment.

She wasn't even remotely close to being "about out." But with any luck, maybe Carolyn wouldn't recall how recent her last visit had been.

"If you've gone through all of that medication already," Carolyn replied, giving her a suspicious look as they passed through the door, "then you're using way too much. That bottle should have lasted you two months at least, not two and a half weeks."

Okay, Savannah thought. *Dr. Carolyn keeps track of such things. A very close watch. Good to know.*

She abided by a personal code: Unless absolutely necessary, like in the line of duty, don't lie. But if you do, try not to lie to smart people, who will catch you.

She had been taught a better, stricter code by Granny. But somewhere along the line, she had decided it was a tough old world out there and one had to be practical about such matters.

Especially cops, private detectives, and the mothers of small boys.

When they walked into the clinic's main waiting room, Savannah was surprised to see how many patients and their masters were present. All different species of pets were enclosed in carriers, wrapped in towels and held on laps, while others sat patiently and obediently at their owners' feet, or ran around, sniffing the other critters' backsides and making a general nuisance of themselves.

But it was the owners who captured Savannah's attention. Because of the way they looked at Carolyn.

The quick, darting glances were unmistakable, filled with some compassion, empathy, and respect. But most were pure curiosity.

During her years as a police officer, Savannah had seen thousands of such expressions on the faces of lookie-loos, the morbidly curious who drove oh-so-slowly past traffic accidents, fender benders and head-on catastrophes alike, hoping to catch a glimpse of the evidence of someone else's misery.

The gorier, the better.

Back in those days she would have waved them on, assuring them there was "nothing to see."

Even if there was.

Especially if there was.

Most citizens didn't know what a police officer knew: Once you see it, you can't unsee it. It's part of you forever. A terrible part with the power to wake you at night from dreams that gave you soul-deep shivers and cold, drenching sweats.

Yes, she thought, *they're looking at their vet like she's a vehicle accident with fatalities.*

For all practical purposes, she is, was her next thought. *People will be people. They just can't help themselves.*

She wondered how many of them had set their appointments days ago, versus how many had decided that very morning that Fido or Fluffy simply couldn't wait another day to have their toenails trimmed.

One sideways glance at Carolyn told Savannah that she, too, had noticed the crowd and the intense scrutiny they were giving their favorite vet. Savannah wondered if Carolyn might be regretting her decision to return to work so quickly after her tragedy.

But a moment later, the waiting room assembly was the last thing on Savannah's mind as she saw a young woman hurry from behind the desk in the office area, and rush toward Carolyn, her arms outstretched.

Savannah recognized her instantly. She was the young, distraught redhead whom Savannah had seen leaving the party in tears the day before. The one who had reluctantly given Savannah directions to the llama barn and then had practically laid down rubber as she peeled off, making her hasty escape.

Right in the middle of the room, in full view of those waiting, the red-haired beauty grabbed Carolyn around the waist and hugged her tightly for what seemed like an extraordinarily long time.

As they embraced, the redhead looked over Carolyn's shoulder and saw Savannah.

It was obvious to Savannah that she recognized her, too. The woman's initial reaction to seeing Savannah was a combination of displeasure and uneasiness that bordered on fear.

Why would she be afraid and unhappy to cross paths with me? Savannah asked herself. It's not like I'm going to arrest her.

Savannah quickly reminded herself that she had a husband who could, and might, if Savannah uncovered some felonious reason why this gal couldn't look her straight in the eye.

"I'm so glad you came in," Savannah heard Carolyn whisper to her. "I was surprised when you said you would. So pleased. I didn't think you would, under the circumstances. Thank you."

Okay, so she's probably the one Carolyn was talking to on the phone, Savannah surmised.

"I'd do anything for you, Carolyn," the young woman replied, also whispering. "You know that."

Carolyn ended the embrace and looked around the room. Everyone waiting there, even their various pets, seemed fascinated by this public and somewhat intimate exchange between the two women.

For a moment, Savannah wondered if maybe the two had a history, a romantic one. She also entertained the thought that such a relationship might have presented a problem, considering that until yesterday, Carolyn had been married.

On the other hand, they might just be close friends, Savannah reminded herself. She and Tammy made spectacles of themselves on more than one occasion when either extremely happy, upset, or sad. What were a few hugs, kisses, and tears among best buddies?

Something told Savannah that this woman was the reason Carolyn hadn't wanted her to come inside the clinic with her.

Savannah had every intention of keeping the question "Why?" front and center in her mind until she had a satisfactory answer.

Savannah stood, waiting for Carolyn to make the next move. Perhaps introduce her? Tell her to pick up the ear meds they both knew she didn't need or . . . ?

"Savannah," Carolyn said, "I'd like to introduce you to my dear friend and former assistant, Patrice Conway."

So, the redhead has a name, Savannah thought. She also wondered, if Patrice had been Carolyn's assistant, why this was the first time Savannah had seen her, other than the day before when she had been fleeing the party.

Savannah extended her hand as Carolyn told Patrice, "This is Savannah. She's been bringing her gorgeous black cats here since they were kittens. She's Brody's mom."

"Hello, Ms. Greyson," Patrice said, shaking Savannah's hand. "Brody's such a cute kid. Bright, too."

"My last name is Reid, and Brody is my foster son. But thank you. We think he's a pretty smart cookie, too."

With the simple introduction made, an awkward silence settled over the three of them, and Savannah got the distinct impression that her lukewarm welcome inside the clinic was over.

"I should go—" she began.

"I understand!" Carolyn replied far too eagerly. She hid her enthusiasm behind what she, no doubt, hoped was a nonchalant semi-smile and added, "I mean, if you need to leave, I don't want to keep you."

Savannah thought of the old Southern phrase, "Here's your hat; what's your hurry?"

Savannah turned toward the door, then said, "If you'd like to stay with us again tonight, you're more than welcome. Just give me a call or drop me a text."

"She'll be staying with me," Patrice inserted with such authority and certainty, that Savannah was a bit taken aback.

Carolyn looked surprised. "I am?" she asked Patrice. When the redhead nodded, Carolyn smiled and ducked her head. "Oh. I didn't expect, I mean, thank you."

Patrice slipped her arm around Carolyn's waist and gave her a sideways squeeze. "No problem. You're with me . . . for as long as you want."

Savannah mumbled a good-bye, and when a response wasn't immediately forthcoming from either woman, she turned and walked back to the door.

As she left the building and returned to the Mustang, Savannah thought about how eager she was to tell Dirk about this strange development.

But her enthusiasm faltered when she ran the story through her own head, considering how she would describe the past five minutes.

"I took Carolyn to the clinic, went inside even though I got the idea she didn't want me to, and met a friend of hers who hugged her a bit too hard and long in front of a waiting room full of clients."

She could just hear him now saying, "So what?"

She had to agree. For all the uneasiness she felt deep in her gut, she couldn't explain why.

Flutters of intuition aside, her little trip to the clinic hadn't exactly been a lead story news event.

No sooner had Savannah climbed back into the Mustang and started the engine than she heard her car's phone ding. It was a frenetic, fast, and frenzied tone that reminded her of her husband when he was being impatient.

Dirk handled the biggies in life with unexpected grace and calm. If you'd just had an accident in your vehicle or were waiting for the results of a biopsy, he was your man.

On the other hand, if he was stuck in a grocery line with two items in his hand and someone buying lottery tickets in front of him, life for him was hardly worth living.

"Yes, Detective Sergeant Coulter," she said in her most officious voice. "Whatcha got for me?"

Normally, that would have garnered her a suggestive

response. One that, uttered with his deepest, "bedroom" voice, would have given her a major case of the quivers.

But instead she heard only a one-word response. "Murder."

"For sure?" she asked.

"Yeah. Liu just called me. I'm on my way to the morgue now. Wanna meet me over there?"

Again, it was no time for phone flirtations. Funny how the word *murder* brought thoughts of romance to a screeching halt. Homicide was a definite mood killer.

"Sure! I'm only a couple of blocks away. I'll meet you in the parking lot."

She heard him hang up. No good-bye.

Dirk was in "detective" mode, and Savannah knew he would live there until he arrested the killer. As would she.

Everything took a back seat to murder. Not just romance.

Chapter 17

When Savannah pulled into the county morgue's parking lot, she looked for a shady spot. Since she wasn't expecting Dirk to arrive for several minutes, she had a fantasy that involved her sitting in a quiet place, under a leafy tree, communing with nature, and eating the candy bar in her purse.

She hadn't received "fortification" for a couple of hours. As a result, she was in desperate need of the life-sustaining nutrients that existed in chocolate and nowhere else on Earth.

She had no doubt whatsoever that a fairly regular intake of chocolate, administered several times daily, had kept her alive for years. Heaven only knew how many deadly diseases she had avoided with that miracle food.

It had to be true.

Nothing that tasted as heavenly as chocolate could possibly be bad for you.

Even if it was, she figured the stress of giving it up would do her more physical harm than the substance itself. So, why risk it?

She had just reached inside her purse and was about to draw out the beautiful bar in all of its foil-wrapped glory, when a voice—the nasal tone of which curled her toenails—exploded in her left ear.

"Savannah! Sweetheart! Wow! Fancy meeting you here!"

She jumped. Shoved the bar back into her purse and began to roll up her window as fast as she could. Then she locked the doors, reminding herself that her Beretta was next to that candy bar, should the need arise.

With Officer Kenny Bates in close proximity, a gal couldn't be too careful.

"Hey, whatcha doin'?" He rapped hard on her window with his knuckles. "Don't act like that, gal, shuttin' me out thadda way," he complained. "You'll hurt my feelings."

"I'll hurt more than your feelings if you don't get away from my car!" she shouted back.

From where she sat, all she could see was his belly, thankfully, mostly covered by his uniform, pressed against her window.

She knew it was him, not only from his twangy, outrageously loud voice, but from the gaps in his too-small shirt, where the two sides didn't quite meet tightly enough to keep his thick belly hair from poking out between the buttons.

To her horror, instead of backing away as instructed, he shoved his girth against the Mustang, causing it to rock from side to side.

The thought of him even being near her precious,

red pony was enough to enrage her, let alone for him to be rubbing his disgusting self against the car's waxed-to-perfection door and meticulously polished window.

Usually, at any given time, even someone who wasn't a detective could read the "clues" on the front of Kenny's shirt and divine what he'd eaten for the past few days.

Shc had known hardworking chefs who had less food on the front of their aprons at the end of a five-course dinner service than Kenny wore almost every day on his uniform.

"If you get that nacho junk that you called last night's 'dinner' on my car, boy, I *will* murder you. Badly. Painfully. You won't see it coming, and you'll never get over it, I swear."

She heard him laugh loudly, like it was the funniest thing he'd ever heard.

Not exactly the reaction she'd been hoping for while trying to instill terror in the teeth-suckin' yayhoo.

Unwilling to be held hostage in her own vehicle, but quite sure she could never push the door open hard enough to dislodge him, she decided to get out on the passenger side.

This involved lifting herself over the console and very nearly bringing her girlie parts to grief on the shift. Yet another reason to despise Kenneth Bates with every atom of her being.

"Come on, Savannah. Just a hug. One nice, lo-o-ng hug! It's been ages since I seen you. You hardly ever come around anymore, and when you finally do, you're usually with *him* and *he* makes a big squawk about it if I try anything."

He belly-bumped the car a few more times, enraging her even further, as she frantically searched her mind for what sort of disinfectant she would have to use to kill the Kenny Cooties he was depositing on her driver's door.

She opened her purse and the first thing she saw was her Beretta. Time slowed for her as she heard Kenny yell, "Come on, baby! They've got cameras all over inside the building now. Out here like this—this is our big chance!"

For half a second, her fingertip stroked the barrel, and she entertained a short, evil fantasy that involved inserting a bullet into Kenny's right buttock.

But she quickly banished the thought.

Not because Kenny didn't deserve a sore backside. But because she chose to live in a civilized society where one didn't shoot one's fellow man simply because he "had it comin'."

Instead, she reached for her "other" weapon, her pepper spray, and jumped out of the Mustang.

Leaning across the roof of the car, she pointed it straight at Kenny's somewhat startled face and said, "Step away from the vehicle, Bates. Do it! Now!"

"What's that? Bug spray?"

For a fleeting moment, she pictured him as a six-foot-tall, 350-pound cockroach in an ill-fitted, soiled uniform, wearing a slightly askew toupee and a leer on his ugly mug.

Yes, he was every woman's dream. At least, inside Kenny Bates's demented imagination, where every woman was swooning with desire for him.

Especially Savannah. Lucky her.

"You aren't gonna spray me, girl," he said with a wink. "You and me, we got chemistry. I know you can feel it . . . felt it the moment we laid eyes on each other."

"The only chemistry you're going to feel, Bates, is

the capsaicin in this spray if you don't turn around and walk back into that building."

"You don't mean that. You're just tryin' to be a good wife, faithful and all that. I understand. But what he don't know won't hurt him."

"Won't hurt *you,* you mean."

"You wouldn't tell him if I just got me one little kiss. He's already beat me up once. You wouldn't wanna see that mess again."

She shrugged and smiled. "Actually, I rather enjoyed it. As I recall, he only hit you once. A single upper cut and you hit the floor. Hard. Out like a light bulb run over by an eighteen-wheeler's tires. It was a first-round K.O."

When her words didn't have the desired effect of causing him to crumple into a quivering wad of fear and remorse, she added, "Just for the record, I don't need my husband to protect me from the likes of you. As I recall, I beat the puddin' out of you one time with your own porn magazine. The one you were shoving under my nose and telling me to look at, 'cause the gal in the centerfold looked like me. Remember that?"

He instantly sobered. "Of course I do. I'd just gotten that magazine. Hadn't even read it yet, and you beat me with it until it was in pieces."

"Aww, don't grieve its passing. It died for a good cause. Who would've thought that stabbing somebody with the end of a rolled-up magazine could cause that much pain, that many bruises, eh?"

He grumbled some obscenities under his breath and looked less happy than he had a minute ago. Thankfully, the memory of that humiliating experience seemed to have dampened his ardor a bit, as she had intended it to. After all, he had suffered months of teasing from his fellow officers as the security video of Savannah's retaliatory attack had circulated among the SCPD personnel and eventually even gone viral on various social media sites.

"I forgave you for that," he said, half whimpering. "I decided not to let that one little fit you threw come between us and—"

"There is no 'us,' Kenny. There's never been an 'us' and there won't be."

"Why not?"

"So many reasons. So many, they plumb boggle the mind."

"Name one."

"I loathe you."

"Why? I've only been nice to you."

"You've invited me over to your apartment one hundred times, while describing in detail the kind of sex you're expecting us to have."

"Yeah. Okay. I'm an optimist."

"You're a pervert, who's humping my car like a demented ferret and about to get sprayed."

He moved away from the door, and she dared to think he might be complying. But then he started to make his way around the hood, and she realized he was coming toward her, not retreating as she'd hoped.

Just as Savannah was thinking she might have to follow through with her threat, she saw, in her peripheral vision, Dirk's Buick pulling into the parking lot.

She knew what was coming next.

From the instant look of fear in his eyes, she knew Kenny did, too.

"I wasn't doin' nothin'!" he told her. "Nothin' but talkin' to you, so he better not—"

"Maybe you should hightail it into the building, pronto. If there's anything worse than getting sprayed, it's having that spray get into brand-new, open wounds. That stings worse than tomato juice on a paper cut."

But her warning was too late.

Dirk had spotted his wife aiming a pepper spray canister at the morgue's receptionist/resident sleaze. He gunned the Buick, shot across the lot, and brought it to a smoking stop only a few feet away.

He jumped out of the car, and in seconds had grabbed a handful of the back of Kenny's collar. "You better tell me right now, Bates," he said, "why my wife's about to spray your ass?"

"I have no idea," Kenny croaked. "She's got a temper. But I don't have to tell *you* that."

Dirk turned to Savannah, and as he reached behind his back for his cuffs, he asked her. "Well, what'd he do? What's the charge?"

She watched as her husband cuffed her tormentor, and she struggled, not sure how to phrase her complaint. To her knowledge there was no cop 10-code for "belly bumping a car in a lascivious manner with an indignant woman inside."

"No charge," she finally said. "He was just being his rude, obnoxious self. But I had it under control."

"You sure?" Dirk asked. "If you were mad enough to spray him, he must've been doing somethin'."

Savannah thought of how both she and Dirk had been warned to never lay hands on Officer Kenny Bates again. The only reason they hadn't been charged before was because she had threatened the city with a sexual harassment case against both Bates and the town.

"Let 'im go," she told Dirk. "He ain't worth it."

Dirk uncuffed him, stared at him, nose-to-nose for several long moments, then gave him an unceremonious push toward the building.

Bates wasted no time making use of his avenue of escape.

As he scurried away, Dirk walked over to Savannah and put his arm around her shoulders. Pulling her close to his side, he said, "What exactly did he do?"

"He asked for a hug and a kiss. His usual."

"Dirty rotten rat fink."

"But the worst thing was . . . he banged his stomach against my door and window."

"Like in a sexual way?"

"Sorta. It did seem, I don't know, dirty, I guess." She sighed. "But then, Kenny Bates could read a pancake house menu and make it sound like the script for a porn flick."

"Yeah. Some guys are just 'gifted' that way." He reached for her hand and squeezed it. "One of these days I'm going to catch that guy actually breaking the law and then . . ."

"You'll put him away for life?"

"Yeah. For jaywalkin'."

Chapter 18

When Savannah and Dirk entered the dull, square, gray building that housed the county's morgue, no one was manning the front, reception counter. Normally, Bates would be sitting there behind his desk, eating, playing video games, or looking at pornography. But blissfully, he was absent, and Savannah was grateful. One Kenny Bates encounter per year was about all she could stand.

They knew the drill and walked up to the counter to sign the visitors' list. Dirk scribbled his customary, illegible scrawl. But Savannah followed her usual habit of using a pseudonym. She had never written her real name on Kenny's stupid list, and in all the years she had entered this dreary place, she had never been questioned for her noncompliance.

Today's nom de plume was: K.B. Ura Maggot.

As they walked down the gray hall with its worn and torn linoleum and flickering fluorescent lights overhead, heading toward Dr. Jennifer Liu's autopsy suite, Savannah's curiosity got the best of her.

"Did she actually call you and tell you it was murder even before she'd finished the autopsy?" she asked him.

He looked moderately uncomfortable and shrugged. "Naw. I called and asked her if she was done yet."

"She was still in the middle of it?"

"Yeah, and so she told me in no uncertain terms."

Savannah laughed. Dr. Jennifer Liu, the county's first female medical examiner, wasn't known for being patient, overly polite, or tolerant.

"She just loves it when you interrupt her work by nudging her to go faster."

"She mighta mentioned that, too, in passing. Eh, who cares? She hates me anyway, and I wanted to know now, not next month, when she's good and ready to tell me."

"Dr. Liu is fast and efficient, and no matter how much you aggravate her, she'd never hold back information that you needed."

"Yeah, I guess. She did tell me she's sure it's a homicide and to come on over if I wanted. As long as I brought you."

"Does she know I don't have any freshly baked, macadamia-chocolate-chip cookies with me?"

"No way. I may be dumb, but I ain't stupid. You think she's so efficient and all that because she wants to help solve crimes, support the cause of Truth, and the American Way. But I'm tellin' you, her motivation is the cookies and chocolate stuff you bring her."

Savannah thought of the candy bar in her purse that she hadn't yet eaten. She was hungry, but if push came to shove and Dr. Jen demanded a treat quid pro quo, Savannah would reluctantly sacrifice the sweet treat on the altar of Justice.

They reached the large, swinging double doors that led into the clinical, austere rooms where Dr. Liu spent much of her workday, exploring human bodies for clues to their untimely deaths.

Savannah couldn't imagine doing such a grim, gory thing for a living. But she was infinitely grateful that stronger souls than hers existed in the world. Thankfully, they were willing to fulfill gruesome duties which most folks could hardly bear to witness, let alone perform.

She and Dirk paused at the doors and drew deep breaths. They both admired Dr. Liu. On a good day, they even liked her. But she was hard work, not easy to deal with, especially in a professional capacity.

She expected perfection from herself and wouldn't tolerate anything less from her fellow workers.

"Okay, let's get 'er done," Dirk said. He pushed the door on the right wide enough for Savannah to enter, then followed her inside.

As always, when Savannah walked into the suite, the first thing that struck her was how bright it was. The white walls, the stainless-steel cupboards, counters, sinks, and examination tables, and the high-powered lights over those tables made the room so bright that she felt the need to wear her sunglasses indoors.

But then, those who looked for minute clues hidden in human biology needed all the light they could get.

Off to her right, on a table with one of those searing lights above it, Savannah saw a body which she instantly recognized as the tall, blond, and handsome Dr. Stephen Erling's.

Though he was considerably less handsome in his present state.

Next to him stood Jennifer Liu in all her exotic loveliness.

Savannah had decided long ago, the instant she had met the medical examiner, that she was one of the most beautiful women she had ever seen. Tall, slender in an athletic sort of way, Dr. Liu had the bearing of royalty, the face of a cover girl model, and the body and wardrobe of a courtesan.

Although she wore the traditional white doctor's smock, beneath its bottom hem, only an inch or so of black leather skirt showed, followed by an impressive length of shapely legs with black stockings and silver studded, black stilettoes. Her waist-long, silky black hair was tied back with a colorful silk scarf.

She glanced up when she saw them enter and gave them a curt nod.

"You done yet?" Dirk asked, his brusque tone causing Savannah to cringe.

When would he learn that pecan pie, homemade fudge, and chocolate-dipped cheesecake were far more effective when dealing with human beings than an acerbic tone?

Rather than answer him, Dr. Liu turned to Savannah and said, "Good morning, Savannah. So nice to see you." She glanced down at Savannah's hands that, other than holding her purse, were empty. "Even though you didn't come bearing edibles."

"I'm sorry." Savannah gave her a bright smile, hoping to compensate. "It was a spur-of-the-moment visit. I'll make it up to you next time."

"I'll hold you to that."

Dr. Liu covered the body on the table with a white

sheet up to the waist. Then she peeled off her gloves, removed her mask, and tossed the items into a nearby bin.

"Yes," she said to Dirk, "I'm done."

Dirk stepped closer to the table and looked down at the body with its distinctive *Y*-shaped incision running up the center of the chest, then branching out to each shoulder. "What'd you find?" he asked.

"Not a great deal," the doctor replied. "He has a slight bruising on the back of his right hand."

"Any idea what hit him?"

"No. It's an unremarkable, even bruising from the base of his fingers almost to the wrist."

Savannah moved nearer so that she, too, could see what Dr. Liu was pointing to. She saw the slight discoloration, but she wasn't sure she would have noticed it if the doctor hadn't pointed it out to them.

"How old is it?" Savannah asked.

"Not perimortem. I'd say it happened a couple of days ago. Maybe three."

"Anything else?" Dirk said.

"Yes." Dr. Liu lifted the left arm to show its underside. "This. A bite, and a pretty bad one at that."

"Somebody bit him?" Dirk looked surprised.

Dr. Liu chuckled. "Don't get overly excited. It isn't a human bite. It's the wrong shape."

"Then what?" Dirk wanted to know.

"A dog," Savannah told him. "The one we saw the guy walking when you were parking the Buick next to the Lamborghini." She turned back to Dr. Liu. "He's a big fellow, a mixed breed named Webster. He made the mistake of taking a potty break on the tire of this guy's new fancy car. Dr. Erling here commenced to whacking both Webster and then his owner with a belt. Really hard, too, from what I hear. So, the dog called a halt to it."

"Good for Webster," Dr. Liu said. "I would have bit him, too."

Dirk was growing impatient with the women's casual conversation. "This dude here didn't die from a bruise on the back of his hand. Was the dog's bite infected or—?"

"No infection," she told him, "and otherwise, he was completely healthy. No disease at all."

"No other signs of violence on the body?" Savannah asked.

"Nothing."

"Then why did you tell me on the phone that it's definitely homicide?" Dirk wanted to know.

"Because, since I couldn't find anything else significant, I had the CSU run some quick, preliminary tests on the blood and tissues samples. Just to see if anything showed up."

"Well? Did it?" Dirk asked.

"Big-time. He was inebriated, to be sure. But not enough to cause alcohol poisoning."

"Then what—?" Savannah said.

"Pentobarbital."

The word bounced around a few seconds in Savannah's brain, until finally she made an association with it.

Capital punishment.

Dirk was the first to say it. "That's the stuff they use when they carry out a death sentence in prisons."

Dr. Liu nodded. "Sometimes, it's part of a cocktail of drugs that's administered during an execution."

"What else is it used for?" Savannah asked, trying to think of who might have access to such a substance.

"It has numerous uses besides its notorious one. It

can be administered in an emergency situation to a patient experiencing seizures. Some anesthesiologists use it as a pre-op sedative. It's even used, once in a while, to treat insomnia."

Dirk nodded toward the body. "Sure worked on this guy's insomnia. He'll never have another sleepless night again."

Normally, Savannah would have been put off by any disrespectful comment directed toward the dead, but in this case, considering it had been directed at good ol' Dr. Erling, she decided to let it slide by without even a disapproving wife glance in Dirk's direction.

"Sounds like something that, as a surgeon, he'd have access to himself," Savannah commented.

"Yes, and those around him in a hospital or clinical setting." Dr. Liu looked down at the man on her table and shook her head. "Stephen Erling here was an obnoxious human being. You're going to have a hard time finding anyone who *didn't* have a motive to kill him."

"Wait! You knew him?" Dirk asked.

"Unfortunately, I've spent a few evenings here and there in his company. Let's just say I didn't enjoy a moment of it."

"But how did you . . . ?" Savannah's mind raced, trying to find a connection, then added, "Oh, you're both doctors. Medical-type gatherings, huh?"

"Social gatherings."

The way the doctor said, "social," and the suggestive lift to her left eyebrow caused Savannah to picture gatherings that were non-professional in nature.

Years ago, Savannah had resigned herself to the belief that Dr. Jennifer Liu led a colorful life outside the drab, gray confines of that building. She had never claimed to have a steady romantic entanglement. But the way she simply exuded overt sensuality suggested to Savannah that Dr. Jen might have numerous outlets for any intimate desires she might want to fulfill.

Savannah also knew that, on any given night in quiet, conservative little San Carmelita, there were gatherings where those desires might be pursued in all sorts of novel forms.

"Did our guy have his wife with him at these 'social' gatherings?" Dirk asked, obviously thinking along the same lines as Savannah.

"He did not," Dr. Liu replied, "though he always brought a partner."

"The same one?" Dirk asked.

"Yes. The same lady, every time. A petite platinum blonde with large eyes and a Betty Boop mouth."

"Would you happen to know her name?"

"He called her 'Lissa.' "

"No last name?"

Dr. Liu shook her head. "No. But I heard them joking about how glad they were that someone named 'Jerry' had been called out of town or they wouldn't have been able to attend."

"Maybe Jerry was Lissa's husband or boyfriend," Savannah wondered aloud.

Dr. Liu nodded. "That's what it sounded like. As if they were happy to be getting one over on Jerry as much or more than they were enjoying the party. Or each other, for that matter."

"This pentobarbital . . ." Savannah said. "Was the amount the lab found in his blood enough to kill him?"

"Absolutely. A couple of times over."

"How did it get inside him?" Dirk asked. "A shot, something he ate or drank?"

"I found no punctures on the body other than those bites. No needling at all. There was no food at all in his stomach. I would say he drank it."

"He was downing alcohol like crazy," Savannah said, "but the drink he took only a few minutes before he went down was a special toast. A birthday speech given by his wife, followed by everybody chugging champagne. He drank his from that green cut-crystal glass that was broken, lying next to the fireplace hearth where he fell."

"The lab is aware of that fancy green glass," Dirk said. "When I dropped the stuff off there, I told Eileen to give it a thorough goin'-over."

"I talked to her half an hour ago. She's checking that glass right now for pentobarbital," Dr. Liu said, "and all the bottles that had been opened, too."

"If that glass or any of those bottles have pentobarbital in them, check them for fingerprints, too," Dirk added.

The doctor rolled her eyes and sighed. "No, Detective Coulter. What crime scene unit would ever think of checking for latent prints?"

Dirk gave her a grunt and turned to leave.

He had only taken two steps when Dr. Liu said, "Before you walk out in a huff, there's something else that might interest you."

Savannah knew Dirk didn't want to stop, turn around, and ask. But of course he would. Offended or not, huffiness aside, nothing mattered to him half as much as solving a case.

"What?" he asked, none too graciously.

"Surgeons and hospital staff aren't the only ones who have access to pentobarbital," she told him.

"There's another common use for that particular drug."

"What's that?" Savannah asked.

"It's often used for a humane, but sad purpose."

Savannah had a feeling that she already knew the answer, even as she asked the question, "What purpose is that?"

"Veterinarians use it, too. On those heartbreaking occasions, when they need to put one of our pets to sleep."

Chapter 19

"I told you it was your veterinarian friend," Dirk said as he and Savannah walked across the morgue parking lot, returning to their cars.

She grabbed his arm and pulled him close enough that they would have been nose to nose, if she had been six inches taller. "Are you telling me, that you really believe that sweet lady who spent the night with us, Brody's good buddy, who has devoted her life to caring for innocent animals, decided to put her husband down like he was some old, blind beagle with a bad ticker?"

"He messed around on her. Apparently a lot."

"Then she could have just castrated him in his sleep. I'm sure she's got the equipment and the know-how to get 'er done in a jiffy. He probably wouldn't even have noticed . . . until the next time he tried to fool around."

"That is not funny, Van. Maybe to a woman, but not to a guy."

They continued on to the cars and paused beside hers. She glanced around and, seeing no one else in the vicinity, she moved close to him and slipped her arms around his waist.

"Sorry," she said. "Low blow. But seriously, we've got other suspects now besides Carolyn."

"I guess you mean that Lissa and Jerry that Dr. Liu mentioned?"

"For starters. Want me to call Tammy and have her check them out?"

"You haven't already got her going on this case?"

She chuckled. "Of course. But she doesn't know about the pentobarbital, Lissa, or Jerry."

"Sure. If you and your Magnolia gang have nothin' else to do but work my case for me, knock yourselves out."

Savannah walked to the Mustang's driver's door, unlocked and opened it. "I'll call her on my way home," she told him.

"Call her with your cell from my car."

"Your car? But I—"

"You'll want to go with me to pick up Carolyn, right? Knowing you, you'll wanna be there, front and center, when I squeeze her."

"You're gonna squeeze her?"

"I most certainly am."

"Dang." Savannah glanced down at her watch. "I've got stuff to do this afternoon."

"Well, if you don't wanna—"

"I'll go."

He grinned. "I knew you would. If for no other reason, to make sure I do it right. Not too hard."

"Or in the wrong places."

"Whatever would I do without a wife to tell me how to behave? To tell me whether I'm hungry or not, when it's time to go to bed or take a shower? What not to eat. How much to drink—"

"Not to spit toothpaste on the bathroom mirror or wad the towel in a ball and shove it between the rod and the wall."

"Heaven forbid!"

"Without my constantly running, background commentary, you'd be lost, darlin'. An uncouth heathen who hurls his underdrawers willy-nilly on the floor and—"

"I'll admit I've tossed my boxers on the floor from time to time, yes. But I'll have you know I've never hurled my willy on the floor or anywhere else it wasn't welcome."

"And"—she continued—"he doesn't know how to talk to his fellow human beings without risking getting hit."

"Like that guy who was your partner for all those years, back when you were a cop and a happily single lady?"

"Yeah. Now that you mention it, you're a whole lot like him."

"Then why did you marry such a barbaric brute?"

Savannah closed the Mustang's door and locked it. Then she put her hands inside his old leather bomber jacket and slid them around his waist to the small of his back. Giving him a tight squeeze that brought their bodies close enough that she could feel his warmth through their clothes, she whispered, "I married that brute because . . . when he kissed me, it made my knees weak, my toes curl, and my girlie parts wake up and say, 'Whoa, howdy!' "

He chuckled and the deep sound of it had quite the same effect on her as their first kiss had. " 'Whoa, howdy'? That's what they say when I kiss you?"

"Among other things."

He growled and pulled her closer still. "Then I'd like to spend some serious time chatting with you and the girlies in the future. The very near future, that is."

"I'm sure that can be arranged."

"Maybe if that gal doesn't spend the night with us again, and I get to sleep in my own bed instead of—"

"Don't fret. She's found other accommodations."

"Oh, darn. I'm bitterly disappointed."

His hands slid from her waist down to her ample rear and pulled her even more tightly against him.

She giggled. "Whoa, howdy! I can tell."

By the time they had gotten into the Buick, snuggled for a minute, and then pulled out of the parking lot, Savannah was in a much better mood.

She wasn't sure why. It could have been her husband's caresses, but she knew herself well and figured it was more likely that her mood uptick was due to having a case to work on.

Even if she didn't have a paying client, work was work, and Savannah thrived on hers.

She grabbed her cell phone and called her home landline. Tammy answered immediately.

"Hi!" was the too-bright greeting from the other end. Savannah was astounded, as always, when in her friend's presence how anyone could be so happy so much of the time and not be a cocker spaniel puppy.

"Hi yourself," Savanna replied. "We just left the morgue."

"Was it murder?"

"Yes. An overdose of something called pentobarbital."

"Okay, I'll check it out—see who might have it, who can buy it, and where."

"One thing you should probably know before you get too far down the road is that vets use it to put animals to sleep."

"Oh, that doesn't sound good for Carolyn."

"I know, but it'll take a lot more than that to convince me she had anything to do with it."

The silence on the other end told Savannah that maybe Tammy wasn't as sure as she was, but she decided not to hold it against her. Or mention it to Dirk. He didn't need reinforcements.

"How's it going on your end?" Savannah asked. "Got anything for me?"

"Tons of stuff."

"Tons?"

"Well, I know that Dylan, the kid who lives next door to Carolyn and Stephen and who owns Webster, has been in trouble. I'm trying to find out what, and it isn't easy. With him being a juvenile, they've expunged the record. On the other hand, his dad, Shane Keller—his record is there for anyone to see. Pretty lengthy. Bad stuff, too."

Savannah wasn't all that surprised. Even if he did live in a seaside mansion, the guy had given off a dark, angry vibe that Savannah had felt from others. Some of whom had been felons. "What were the charges?" she asked. "How bad?"

"Assault and battery."

"On whom?"

"Interestingly enough, a former neighbor. Other than Erling."

Savannah mulled that over and gave Dirk a thumbs-up. "A guy who's battered a neighbor moves next to a dude like Erling, a narcissistic conflict junkie. Gee, what could go wrong with that?"

Savannah and Dirk were only half a mile from Carolyn Erling's veterinary clinic when Savannah's phone chimed.

She looked at the screen and grimaced. "I don't like this," she said.

"Who is it?" he asked, glancing down at her screen as he turned the Buick off Main Street and onto Sundown Avenue. They were heading into a less picturesque part of town where San Carmelita's signature, quaint, hand-carved, wooden signs with gilded lettering gave way to graffiti scrawled on long-ago painted stucco walls.

"It's Ms. Pomeroy."

"Brody's teacher?"

"Yeah."

"Shit."

"Sh-h-h. Hello, Ms. Pomeroy," she said, as cheerfully as she could manage with her heart pounding in her throat.

"Hello, Mrs. Coulter."

Savannah didn't have the patience to explain to the woman, for a third time, that she had kept her maiden name when she'd married, so she let it slide.

"What's wrong?" she asked, knowing it wasn't the most sophisticated response, but not caring.

Somehow she didn't think a schoolteacher would

call in the middle of the day if a child had just won the National Spelling Bee or had been nominated for a Junior Nobel Peace Prize.

"Is Brody okay?" she heard herself saying, her voice quivering with fear. "Has he been hurt or—"

"No, Mrs. Coulter. Nothing like that," the teacher replied, as calm as Savannah was rattled. "There's nothing to worry about. I'm sorry if I alarmed you by calling you like this."

Savannah turned to Dirk and whispered, "He's okay." Then she told the teacher, "No. Don't apologize. You can call me anytime for anything. You'll have to forgive me. I'm new to this parenting stuff, and I'm still trying to figure out when to panic and when not to."

"Well, you don't need to panic, but I would like very much to see you, if you could drop by the school."

"Yes, of course. When?"

"Today, after school. Around two forty-five, if that's convenient."

Today? Right after school? she thought, as her anxiety meter instantly soared to new heights.

She might be a novice at all this parent stuff, but she knew that a same-day request for a parent-teacher meeting had to be something important. Something had to be badly amiss.

"It might be better," the teacher was saying, "if you come without Brody. Assuming you can arrange for someone else to care for him, of course."

Savannah thought of Tammy, Waycross, Granny, Ryan and John, Alma and Ethan, and she instantly felt grateful that she had such a great backup team for all things Brody. Few of the parents she knew were fortunate to have such a long list of supporters.

"Yes, I can come alone," she said. "Where?"

"In my classroom, if you like."

"Sure. That's fine."

"Good. Thank you, Mrs. Coulter."

Savannah weighed her next words, thinking that if she hung up before getting at least a hint about what the problem might be, she would go completely crazy. Possibly within minutes.

She hated to do that to Dirk. She was all too aware that a "crazy as a sprayed-roach" Savannah wasn't a pretty sight.

"Ms. Pomeroy," she said, "please don't think I'm being overly dramatic when I tell you—if you don't let me know at least a little bit more about why you're calling me in today, chances are I won't be able to make that appointment, because I will most likely suffer an anxiety-induced heart attack long before I can get there."

She heard a lengthy silence on the other end. It lasted long enough for her to figure out that she should have chosen her words more carefully or taken another tack.

"Ms. Pomeroy?" she asked, thinking they might have lost their connection. "Are you there?"

"I am, Mrs. Coulter. I'm sorry if I've upset you. Brody is a bright and wonderful child. He hasn't been physically harmed or hurt anyone else. But we've had a bit of a problem here today, and he drew a picture that, well, I think you should just come here and see it for yourself."

"Oh. Okay." Savannah felt her entire body go weak as she settled into the knowledge that she was simply going to have to wait a few hours before finding out the particulars. This tidbit had made her feel worse, rather than better. "I'll be there at two forty-five, and either his great-grandmother or Aunt Tammy or Uncle Waycross will pick him up at two-thirty, as usual."

"Thank you, Mrs. Coulter. I'll see you then."

As soon as she ended the call, Dirk wanted to know every word that had passed. He looked as worried as she felt when she related the conversation back to him.

"He drew a picture, and we need to go talk to the teacher about it?" he said.

"I don't think you have to go," Savannah began. "She just asked if I—"

"Of course I'm going. He's my son!" Dirk hesitated a moment then added, "You know what I mean. Foster, but close enough."

"I know exactly what you mean. But you have a homicide on your hands."

"Stephen Erling can wait long enough for me to go with my wife to see what's wrong with our kid."

She smiled at him, reached over, and placed her hand on his knee. "Thank you."

"You don't need to thank me. It comes with the territory."

He drove the Buick into the clinic's lot and pulled into a parking space. Then he added, "I'm not gonna take Carolyn to the station house. I don't have time. I'll just ask her some questions here and, depending on what she says, I might take her in later."

"Gotcha." She squeezed his knee. "I'm glad you're coming along."

"It's not like I'd get anything done if you were there without me and me someplace else, wondering what was goin' on."

"I need to call Tammy back and ask her if she can pick up Brody herself or get Granny or Waycross to do it. Go on inside, if you want."

"I'll wait. Make your call. We're a team."

As Savannah phoned Tammy, she thought about what he'd said. They had been a team for many years, back in their "coppering" days. But their connection had deepened, as she expected, when they'd married.

What she hadn't anticipated and was happy to discover, was the exceptionally strong bonding effect that parenting together had created. Brody was a new and wonderful kind of glue that strengthened their marriage.

She didn't want any of that to change.

She wondered about the "bit of a problem" that Ms. Pomeroy had mentioned, and the picture Brody had drawn.

Whatever the issue might be, she was glad not to be alone in dealing with it.

Sometimes, it's a comfort to be part of a "team," she thought. *Even if the team consisted of only "he" and "me."*

Chapter 20

Savannah's first impression, when she and Dirk entered the clinic and saw Carolyn behind the counter, talking to someone on the phone, was that the vet wasn't the least bit happy to see them.

The convivial smile slipped off her face the moment she turned and saw them standing there, waiting for her to finish her call.

"Yes, that's right, Mr. McKee," she was saying. "Four drops, three times a day until it clears up. If you don't see an improvement in a couple of days, give us a ring. You're most welcome."

Having ended her call, she set the phone on the desk behind the reception counter and walked over to them. "Hello, Savannah, Detective Coulter. What a nice surprise."

It occurred to Savannah that their visit was neither a surprise nor nice, but she painted an equally false smile on her face to match the vet's and replied, "Good to see you again, too."

Dirk merely grunted.

Carolyn glanced around, looking embarrassed and uneasy.

Savannah noticed that the clients in the waiting room and the office workers behind the counter were watching, listening, while pretending to do neither.

"Can we talk? Privately?" Savannah said it in a near-whisper, but she had no doubt that everyone heard every word.

Carolyn gave them a curt nod and beckoned them to follow her down the hallway and to the room at the end.

Savannah knew it was the doctor's office, as she had sat in there many times before to discuss her pets' health care over the years. Lately, since Brody had drawn them closer, and Carolyn had become as much a friend as the family vet, they had even traded recipes in that office. Chocolate-based, of course.

Savannah sincerely doubted this visit would be as pleasant.

The three of them entered the small, cozy room, and Carolyn closed the door behind them. She sat behind her desk and gave a wave of her hand, indicating they could sit on the two side chairs.

As Savannah had every time she'd entered this office, she glanced over the doctor's shoulder to the beautiful black-and-white photos that lined the wall behind the desk. While most of the pictures were of dogs and cats, other species were represented in the lineup as well. Parrots and budgies, ducks and chickens, turtles and fish, hamsters and guinea pigs, rabbits and geckos. There was even a raccoon and a skunk.

Most of the pictures were signed with paw-print "signatures" and bore messages thanking Dr. Carolyn for her loving care.

Many times before, Savannah had considered that wall a testimony to the happiness Carolyn had provided for others in her practice. Not only had she saved the lives and health of those animals, but she had given a beloved animal back to a worried family and prolonged those all-too-short years for them to enjoy together.

She had thought that Dr. Carolyn Erling must be a happy woman, knowing how valuable her care was to so many. Anyone that important must feel a strong sense of self-satisfaction.

But today, as Carolyn nervously rearranged pens, papers, clips, and files around on her desktop, avoiding Savannah's and Dirk's eyes while doing so, Savannah wondered how happy, how self-satisfied, Dr. Carolyn was today.

Not very, Savannah told herself. *She looks plumb miserable and not in a grief-stricken, my-precious-husband-just-died sorta way either.*

Savannah waited for one of them to speak, but Carolyn was pressing her lips together so tightly that they were white, and Dirk seemed content to watch her, intently studying every movement she made, every expression that crossed her face.

Most of the cops Savannah had known in her life, herself included, had a way of scrutinizing a suspect that was quite predatory. But Dirk had perfected the "all-penetrating stare."

For a guy who had no idea where his sunglasses might be and who wasn't sure where ice cubes were kept in his own house, he was a master at being observant when on the job.

Finally, he spoke, and Savannah was glad to hear him using his "soft" voice when he told Carolyn, "I'm very sorry to have to say this, Dr. Erling, but the medical examiner has ruled your husband's death a homicide."

Carolyn didn't look surprised, Savannah decided, watching her with her own investigator raptor eyes. Upset. Uneasy. Yes. But not shocked.

"I was afraid you'd say that," she replied. "I had a feeling. . . ."

"Why?" Dirk asked. "Why did you think it might be murder?"

She shrugged. "I don't know. Everything, I guess. Because Stephen was so healthy and young. Fifty is young, right?"

"Very young," Savannah was quick to admit. "Getting younger all the time."

"Why else?" Dirk asked. "What other reasons did you have for thinking he might have been murdered?"

Carolyn hesitated for what seemed like a long time, then seemed to come to a decision and said, as though confessing to something terrible and shameful, "Stephen wasn't liked."

"Why didn't people like him?" Dirk asked.

"People hated my husband because, to be honest, Stephen wasn't a good man. Far from it, in fact."

"Did *you* hate him, Doctor?" Dirk asked, staring into her eyes, her soul.

"Sometimes" was the honest reply.

Dirk held the direct gaze for several long seconds then said, "Did you kill him?"

"No."

Savannah waited, holding her breath, to see if Carolyn was going to add something to her curt, one-word denial. But she didn't elaborate.

"Do you know who did?" Dirk asked. From the suspicious gleam in his eyes, Savannah was quite sure that he didn't fully believe her.

Carolyn looked down at her desk and began to fiddle with the pens and straighten the paper stacks again. "No."

Lie.

Savannah had a built-in polygraph, and its bells and whistles had just gone off, shrieking loudly in her head.

One glance at Dirk told her that his personal lie detector was sounding alarms, too.

"Would you tell me if you knew?" Dirk asked.

Carolyn seemed to be considering her answer carefully, then she said, "I'm not sure, Detective. I guess it would depend."

"On what?"

"Who they were. Why they did it."

Dirk sat up straighter in his chair, then leaned toward her. Savannah noticed that Carolyn crossed her arms over her chest and pulled back as far as she could.

"Are you telling me," Dirk began, "that if you knew, for sure, that somebody had murdered your husband in cold blood, you wouldn't tell me?"

Tears filled Carolyn's eyes as she said, "I'm just trying to be honest with you, Detective. Your wife and I are friends. I adore the little boy in your care. You were kind enough to take me into your home and shelter me on a terrible night. I realize that you're doing your duty, and I want to cooperate with you—or at the very least, be honest with you."

"I appreciate that, Doctor, but don't you want justice for your husband?"

The tears streamed down Carolyn's cheeks as she

said, "For all I know, Detective Coulter, what happened to Stephen *was* justice."

Savannah reached into her purse and pulled out a clean tissue. As she placed it in Carolyn's hand, she gave her friend's fingers what she hoped was a comforting squeeze.

Savannah glanced over at Dirk and slightly raised her right eyebrow. It was their customary sign, suggesting that she would like to step in. He responded with an almost imperceptible nod.

Turning back to Carolyn, she said, "Here in your clinic, do you use a drug called pentobarbital?"

Carolyn answered immediately. "Of course. It's commonly used in veterinary medicine."

"What is it used for?" Savannah asked, knowing, but curious to know what Carolyn would say.

"Some use it as a surgical anesthetic. I don't. I have other drugs I'm more comfortable with."

"But you *do* use it?" Dirk interjected.

"Yes. I do, when I'm required to euthanize an animal. It's reliably effective, and I believe quite humane. It provides a gentle passing."

Savannah couldn't help wondering if Carolyn had somehow engineered a "gentle passing" for the husband who was tormenting her.

"Where is your pentobarbital stored?" Dirk asked.

"Right over there." Carolyn pointed to a sturdy, metal cabinet on the wall to the left. Its door was secured with a large, shiny, combination padlock.

"Who has the combination to that lock?" he asked.

"No one but myself."

"No one? Not even your most trusted workers?"

"No. That's a new lock, and I'm the only one who can open it."

A new lock? Savannah thought. *What happened to the old one?*

"Why did you have to get a new lock?" she asked.

Yes. There it was. A certain look on Carolyn's face that told Savannah the questioning was about to pay off.

"We had to buy a replacement," Carolyn said, "because the old one was broken."

"Did it break by itself?" Dirk asked. "Or did it have help?"

"Quite a bit of help," Carolyn replied. "Judging from those marks on the front of the cabinet."

Savannah jumped up from her seat and hurried to the other side of the room, where she bent down and studied the stainless-steel surface near the lock. She saw several fresh, deep gouges. "A crowbar, I'd say," she told them as she returned to her seat.

"That's what we thought," Carolyn said. "They used it on the back door to get in. Damaged it so badly, we had to replace the doorknob and both locks."

"When?" Dirk wanted to know as he pulled a small notebook and pen from the inside pocket of his bomber jacket.

Carolyn hesitated. "Um, sometime, maybe a week and a half or—"

"No, not 'sometime,'" Dirk said. "No 'maybe' either. I need to know exactly when."

Reaching for her phone, Carolyn said, "Okay. We found everything broken on the morning of the day that we lost a favorite patient here. Loki, a Great Dane that we've treated since he was a puppy. He had a lot of health problems, and it finally just got to be too much. His owner was devastated. It was awful."

As she scrolled down the screen, Savannah could see she was looking at her calendar.

"Here it is. Thursday, the sixth, was when we discovered it."

Dirk scribbled away on his notebook. "Then Wednesday night was when you think they broke in?"

"Yes. We closed late that night. About eight-thirty. We'd had an emergency surgery on an injured cat."

"What time did you open on Thursday morning?" Dirk asked.

"About eight-thirty."

"Who opens in the morning?"

Carolyn glanced away, reached down, and picked up a paper clip. Staring at it, she said, "Usually Patrice opens. She was, she's my assistant."

"Did Patrice open that morning?" Savannah asked.

"No. She wasn't working here then. I opened myself."

"What did you think when you found the back door pried open?" Dirk wanted to know.

"I figured it was a break-in, and I assumed they were after our drug supply. There's not much else in a veterinary clinic that a criminal would want."

"You came in here and found the cabinet there open?" Dirk asked.

"Yes. Just as I feared."

"What did they take?"

Carolyn looked confused. "Do you mean, which drugs?"

"Yes, and how much of each one. You must've had some Schedule I drugs in there."

"I do have some Schedule I drugs on the premises."

"You're supposed to keep tabs on those. So, you do

know how much you had before the break-in and how much you had afterward. Don't you?"

"Yes. Of course I do, Detective. Forgive me. I'm just not thinking really straight right now."

Dirk softened instantly and said, "No, of course you aren't. But if you could let me know what was stolen, it might be important."

She turned to a laptop computer she had open on the desk. "I can print out a list for you. I have it here, because we had to reorder."

It took her a moment to find the information she was looking for and print it. Then she handed the sheet to Dirk.

He held it so that Savannah could see it, too. She read aloud, "Diazepam, morphine, oxycodone, fentanyl. Lots of those. But one bottle of pentobarbital."

"Wow!" Dirk said. "Those are some pretty potent potions there. Your burglars must have been pretty happy."

"I'm sure they were once they got home and sampled the wares," Carolyn replied dryly. "Hope they enjoyed them. That stuff had to all be replaced, and it doesn't come cheap."

"Can I see a copy of the police report?" Dirk asked.

"The, um, police . . . ?" Carolyn dropped the pen and clenched her first.

"Yes, the police report," Dirk repeated. "Expensive drugs like those, having to replace the door lock and the one on this cabinet. That would add up to a tidy sum. You must've reported it to us and to your insurance company for reimbursement. Right?"

"I . . . I—"

"Yes?"

"I intended to. But I haven't had a chance. With the

burglary and planning Stephen's birthday and some difficult cases lately, I just haven't gotten to it. I will."

"If you'd called us, we might have been able to lift some prints off the door or the lock or that cabinet there before everybody touched them," Dirk told her. "I'd think you'd want to know who broke into your clinic, Doctor. If they were caught, they wouldn't steal from you again or anybody else."

"I'll do it! I swear. I've just had so much going on."

Carolyn started to cry again, and Savannah reached into her purse for another tissue.

Savannah couldn't help feeling sorry for the woman. Although Savannah harbored some suspicions that Carolyn might have caused her husband's untimely departure, she also chose to trust that her friend was innocent until proven guilty.

She wished Dirk would bring the interview to a close. But she could tell, as he scanned the words on the printed list one more time, that he had something more on his mind.

"Did they take all of your pentobarbital? Was this one bottle all you had?" he asked.

"We had four. One was taken, leaving us three. I guess they were more interested in the other stuff. They took all we had of those."

"How big a bottle was it?" he asked.

Carolyn walked over to the medical cabinet, opened the combination lock, and reached inside.

A moment later, she walked over to Dirk and placed in his hand a small, clear glass bottle, containing a pink liquid. On it was a bright yellow label with the words *For Euthanasia* in bold, black lettering.

"That's one of the bottles they left behind." As she

settled back into her desk chair, she added, "It's a lucky thing they didn't take it all. As I told you, we had to put down that Great Dane friend of ours that morning, and he was enormous. In spite of his bad condition, he didn't go down easily. I needed to use a lot more on him than I'd expected."

She paused a moment, drew a deep breath, and said, "That was a pretty crummy day, all the way around, now that I think of it. But obviously, nothing like yesterday."

"I'm sorry, Carolyn," Savannah said. "You *will* get through this and out the other side, you know. You really will. Somehow. Someday."

"Of course I will," Carolyn replied with a tired smile. She shrugged. "After all, it's not like I have a choice."

Chapter 21

"I told you she did it," Dirk insisted as he drove them from the clinic's parking lot and headed down Calida Avenue toward the 101 Freeway entrance ramp.

"Yes, you did tell me that," she replied, feeling her cheeks blush and her ears begin to ring, as they often did when she was feeling highly provoked. Usually at Dirk. "You've told me several times, in fact. But since you're a human being and therefore not infallible, you might have been wrong the umpteen times you told me before, and you might be wrong right now."

"Nope. I'm sure."

"Or you might just be full of hooey. That's the other possibility."

"Nope. I feel it in my bones."

"That's probably arthritis. Is it in your tailbone? Arthritis is sometimes caused by overuse, and you use that bone a lot. Sitting at your desk in the office, in the car all day on stakeouts, watching baseball, football, basketball, not to mention boxing all weekend and—"

"Whoa!" He cut her a sharp sideways look as he pulled onto the entrance ramp and headed south, back to the central part of town. "You're hittin' some low blows there, lady. I'll be singin' soprano for a month."

Savannah opened her mouth to release yet another zinger, when she realized he was right and shut it.

He wasn't correct, in her less-than-humble opinion, about Dr. Carolyn's guilt. But he had a point about her being snippier lately than her usual feisty self.

She had no reason to complain about his couch time. She wasn't exactly famous for logging hours of intentional exercise herself. In fact, she was about the polar opposite of Tammy, whose dedication to fitness was legendary.

Savannah's claim to fame was her maraschino cherry and pecan Christmas fudge.

Dirk mowed the lawn ninety percent of the time and hauled the garbage to the curb twice a week. In a pinch, he would even clean the gutters and help her weed her garden and prune the roses. So, she figured she really shouldn't complain about him being glued to the sofa, watching his favorite teams, a few hours every weekend.

However, she knew she shouldn't have chocolate-dipped, peanut butter cheesecake for breakfast either, but just knowing something wasn't a good idea had never kept her from doing it if she wanted to badly enough.

Dirk reached for her hand and squeezed it. "I'm a little worried about you, Van," he said.

"Well, don't be. I'm all right." She didn't squeeze back.

"I don't think you are. You don't seem as peaceful and relaxed as you used to be."

"I am so! I'm so peaceful I feel like going to bed right after dinner, and I'm so relaxed I can hardly put one foot in front of the other when I come downstairs in the morning to get my coffee."

"Both of those sound more to me like exhaustion and burnout than they do peaceful and relaxed."

"I can be mellow and worn to a frazzle at the same time. They aren't mutually exclusive, you know. Are they? No! They aren't. I can be all of those things."

"Yes, you can, my dear. Far be it from me to say you can't." Then he added under his breath, "Mellow, frazzled, peaceful, and argumentative as hell. That's my girl."

"Smart aleck," she whispered back.

"I heard that."

She swallowed the comment that sprang to her lips, something about how, if he'd heard her, he must have cleaned his ears recently. Another sarcastic zinger, tossed in his direction, probably wouldn't really help her case: proving how mature, self-possessed, and all-fired tranquil she was.

He reached over and gently tousled her hair. "I think maybe we're both a bit on edge because of this parent-teacher thing," he said. "I'd bet dollars to donuts we'll both feel better once it's over with and we know what the problem is."

"Better . . . or a whole lot worse, depending."

"Let's hope for better."

As they continued down the freeway in silence, it occurred to her that, in their little exchange, Dirk had just been the optimistic one. In all the years they had been together, she couldn't recall that *ever* happening.

She had always played the Pollyanna to his Mr. Grumpy. This turnaround was disturbing. Mostly, because, if Dirk was the most upbeat person in the car at that moment, she was in desperate need of some mental health guidance.

Or at the very least, a chocolate bar.

Her phone began to jingle with Alma's new, wedding march ringtone. She answered as quickly as possible as she vowed to change it as soon as possible.

That has to be the most irritating song ever written in the history of the world, she thought as she punched the wrong button and hung up on her sister before even speaking to her.

"Dadgum it!" she said, as she redialed. "I hate it when that happens!"

"Mellow, peaceful, calm and relaxed . . ." Dirk mumbled.

"Aw, shut up. No! Not you, Alma. I was talking to Dirk."

"You sound really annoyed," was Alma's response, spoken with a softer, sweeter version of Savannah's own Southern drawl.

"Nope. I am not," Savannah shot back. "Not one bit. I'm as relaxed as a Jell-O salad, left out in the sunshine at a Fourth of July picnic."

She heard Alma chuckle, and the sound went straight to her heart. Of Savannah's eight siblings, she had always favored Waycross and little Alma. A diminutive version of Savannah, Alma had the Reid women's black curls, sapphire eyes, and peaches-and-cream complexion.

Unlike the other Reid women, she had maintained a slender figure. She had curves, but not nearly as voluptuous as Savannah's.

So far, Alma had spent most of her life in the various shadows cast by her sisters, all of whom seemed to be smarter, sexier, stronger, more talented, and just plain luckier than she had been.

But once in a while, the Wheel of Fortune took a turn for the better and good people were unexpectedly blessed.

That had happened when Ethan Malloy and Alma Reid had attended one of Savannah's parties and danced, whirling across her backyard lawn in a scene that looked like it was straight from one of his movies.

Hero Ethan Malloy had caught the girl again, and this time she really was a princess. Beautiful, yes, but simple, kind, wise, and loving. Just the kind of woman he'd been looking for. And little Alma from the tiny town of McGill, Georgia, was going to become Mrs. Alma Malloy in only a couple of weeks.

But today, in typical bride fashion, she sounded a bit discombobulated as she said, "I don't mean to be bugging you, sis. I know you've got a lot on your mind. But the shoe place called, and they said you still haven't—"

"Oh, darn! I knew I was forgetting something. I was going over there this afternoon and then . . ." She hesitated, weighing the decision to tell anyone in the family about this unexpected school meeting or not. In the end, she chose not to, at least, not until she had more details. "Then," she continued, "some stuff came up, and I didn't get over there. I will though. Tomorrow for sure. I promise."

"It's okay, really," Alma replied. "I just thought I'd remind you, so I can scratch it off my list."

"I'm so sorry, honey. I shouldn't be on your list at all. I'm your maid of honor. I should be making that list of yours shorter, not longer."

"Don't give it another thought. Let's just relax and enjoy ourselves tonight."

"Tonight?"

Half a second later, Savannah wished she had only thought the word and not spoken it out loud. There was no way to back out of this one. She had forgotten something. Probably something very important. If she could only remember what the heck it was.

"The tasting tonight at ReJuvene," Alma told her. "Ryan and John are cooking the wedding dinner choices for us, so that we can—"

"Of course! Of course! The tasting! Oh, my goodness! I've been looking forward to it for weeks. Haven't eaten all day so that I'll be rip-roaring hungry! It's going to be so much fun!"

You're overdoing it, ol' girl, she told herself. *The jig's up. You forgot, and she knows it.*

"I'm really sorry, sweetie," she said, fighting back tears. "You know this wedding is so important to me, too. You and Ethan mean the world to me."

"Of course I know that, and I would never, ever forget it. Please don't give it a second thought. Pick up your shoes sometime in the next few days, and we'll see you at the restaurant tonight. Love you!"

"I love you, too, sweetheart."

Savannah could hardly get the phone turned off before the sobs burst from deep inside her, and in seconds she was blubbering worse than when she watched the Olympic athletes stand on the tri-level podium to receive their medals and see their countries' flags raised.

"I forgot the shoes!" she wailed. "I totally forgot to go get the dadgum shoes! The store called Alma and ratted me out!"

"Which shoes? What the hell are you talking about?"

"The yellow shoes! The ones that were dyed to match our bridesmaid gowns."

"But you're the maid of honor."

"I still have to have shoes that match my dress." She gulped, choked on her own saliva, and sobbed anew. "Now my sister thinks I don't love her. That I don't care that she's getting married to the handsomest man in the world."

Dirk pulled into the school's parking lot but drove around to the side of the building where it was more private.

Then he stopped the car, turned off the key, and gathered his weeping wife into his arms. "Honey," he said, kissing the top of her hair, "this is sorta the point I was trying to make earlier."

"Wha-wha-what point?"

He placed his hand under her chin and coaxed her to look up at him. When she finally did, he said, "Van, think about it. You're sitting in a car, sobbing your face off over yellow shoes."

"Maid-of-honor shoes. Dyed special and real expensive shoes."

"Shoes. Your long dress will probably cover them. Knowing you, you'll probably kick them off as soon as the church business is over and run around barefoot the rest of the night."

She gave him a little push and tried not to smile. "You don't understand about such things. You're a . . . guy."

"Guilty as charged. But the fact is, you are taking this whole thing way too seriously."

"But it's my sister's wedding! My favorite sister!"

"I don't mean you're taking the wedding too seriously."

"Then what?"

"Life, darlin'. You are taking life way too seriously. Sometimes you've just gotta let it happen."

"Let what happen?"

"Whatever. Whatever happens. Let it go. You can't control everything you know. You're gonna make yourself sick tryin'."

"I don't know if I can, just let go like you said."

"I don't know if you can either. But you really, really need to try. 'Cause if you don't, I think you're gonna blow a gasket."

Chapter 22

As Savannah and Dirk hurried down the hallway toward Brody's classroom, she wiped away her remaining tears and noticed a smear of her "waterproof" mascara on her fingertips.

"Do I look like I've been crying?" she asked him with a sniff.

He turned, looked her over for a moment, as though seriously considering her question. Then he said, "You look fine, darlin'. Don't sweat it."

She groaned. "Reckon that's a 'Yes,' if I ever heard one."

"If she asks, tell her you've got allergies."

"You want me to lie to Brody's teacher?"

He shrugged. "If she's rude enough to ask you why your eyes are red and swollen, she's rude enough to be lied to."

"What sort of Code of Ethics rule is that?"

"One I wouldn't share with Granny."

"I agree. She has strong opinions on lying and isn't shy about sharing them."

"Even if you don't want to hear them."

"Especially if you don't want to hear them. She figures you'd be the one most in need of instruction."

"She's cool, your grandma."

"Isn't she? I want to be just like her when I grow up."

He gave her an affectionate smile and said, "Don't look now, kiddo, but you done did . . . grow up, that is. You're just like her."

She was still grinning from his compliment, when they reached the door of room number nine. She gave a soft knock, looked through the small window, and saw Ms. Pomeroy sitting at her desk.

The teacher looked up from her work and gave them a wave of her hand, inviting them inside.

Savannah was relieved to see that, other than the teacher, there was no one else in the room. She had a feeling that the discussion they were about to have might be better kept "all in the family."

"Good afternoon," Ms. Pomeroy said, as she stood, walked around her desk, and offered her hand to first Savannah and then Dirk. "I appreciate you coming in like this on such short notice. I—oh, my!"

She leaned toward Savannah, peering at her closely. "Have you been crying?" she asked. "Are you upset that you had to come see me?"

"Of course not," Savannah snapped. "Allergies."

She gave Dirk a quick sideways glance and saw him smirk. *Oh, well,* she thought. *He did have a good point about that "deserving to be lied to" business.*

Ms. Pomeroy seemed to buy the fib. She bustled about, dragging a couple of chairs closer to the desk.

"Have a seat. It's so nice to see both of you. With parents being so busy these days, I do well to get one to come in, let alone two."

"My wife got the idea from what you told her on the phone that it's important," Dirk said. "We're both pretty concerned."

As they all took their seats, the teacher behind her desk and Savannah and Dirk in the proffered guest chairs, Ms. Pomeroy said, "I don't consider the situation we have to be critical at this point. Otherwise, I would have asked the principal and school counselor to be present."

Savannah wasn't sure how to respond to that, so she simply nodded and said, "Oo-kay."

"Hopefully," Dirk said, "we can settle whatever it is among ourselves without calling in the big guns."

"I hope so, too. But I'm afraid that it might be a symptom of another problem that—"

"Ms. Pomeroy," Savannah said, as she felt one of her nerves snap. The main one leading to her Patience Control Center. "Please spit it out. We're dying here."

"Actually, I considered calling you last week, when it first started, but I hoped it would die down on its own."

"What?" Dirk barked. "What happened?"

"One of our students, a classmate of Brody's, made some rude comments during recess. The other children overheard it, and now, unfortunately, it's become common knowledge."

Savannah cringed, anticipating the answer to her next question. "What 'knowledge' are we talking about?"

"The sad fact that Brody's biological mother is in prison."

Savannah gulped and looked at Dirk. His face darkened as the words sank deep into both of their hearts.

Of course, they had always assumed this could happen, would happen, sooner or later. But they'd been hoping for later—after Brody had gotten settled into his new school and made a few good friends.

"Yes, it is sad," Savannah said, choosing her words carefully. "The worst thing about it is that Brody is now two hundred miles away from the woman who treated him terribly, and he shouldn't have to worry about her. Especially at school, where he's trying to learn and enjoy just being a regular child for the first time in his life."

"What exactly did that kid say?" Dirk asked. "How much does everyone know?"

"Just that she's in prison, serving a pretty long term." Ms. Pomeroy glanced down at her fingernails and studied her manicure a while before adding, "Also, they know she's there because she hurt him."

"Do they know how? Specifically?" Savannah asked, feeling tears well up in her eyes again.

"No. They don't know the particulars of his abuse. Of course, being kids, they were coming up with their own stories, one tall tale worse than the last, but when I heard them doing it, I put a stop to it."

"Will that be enough?" Dirk asked. "Will you really be able to control what they say to him, around him?"

She sighed. "Not completely. You know how children are."

"Yes, they're cruel little bastards," Dirk muttered under his breath.

Unfortunately, Ms. Pomeroy heard him and gave a little, disapproving gasp.

Savannah hurried to rescue the moment. "He just means they can do a lot of damage to tender hearts."

"That's true," she replied, somewhat mollified.

"How did he take it?" Dirk asked.

When the teacher didn't reply right away, he added, "When the kids teased Brody about it, what did he do?"

"He threatened to, well, I believe his exact words to the other kid were, 'Say that again and I'll knock your teeth so far down your throat that you'll have to sit on a plate of spaghetti to eat your dinner.' "

"Oh, dear," Savannah said. "I have no idea where he might have heard such a dreadful, coarse thing."

She cast a nervous, guilty glance toward Dirk and saw he was smirking. Again.

They both knew that Savannah, with all of her down-in-Dixie charm, had spoken those exact words. Though her version included a "bologna sandwich" rather than "a plate of spaghetti."

Brody didn't like bologna and must have adapted the threat to satisfy his own taste.

"So, when he got teased about his mother, he reacted more with anger than sadness?" Savannah asked.

"I wouldn't say those emotions are mutually exclusive," Ms. Pomeroy replied. "But yes. He stood up for himself and told them that saying stuff like that would give them dog poop breath."

"That one is definitely *not* something he heard at home," Savannah rushed to say.

"No, I figured that was a Brody original. He comes up with a lot of them, actually. Quite an entertaining little boy."

"He is." Savannah felt the need to hold the child close to her at that moment. So tightly that he would most certainly object. She couldn't imagine how bad he must have felt to have his story told and shared among all of his schoolmates.

Yet . . .

"He's seemed okay lately," Dirk observed. "If you hadn't told us about this, we'd figured he was doin' fine here at school."

"That's true," Savannah agreed. "I ask him every day how his day was and he says, 'Fine.' He tells me all the silly stuff that he and the other kids said and did. I thought he was adjusting well."

"How is he sleeping?" Ms. Pomcroy asked.

Savannah flashed back on a few nights ago, when she had awoke to sounds coming from his room. She had gone into his bedroom and found him thrashing around on his bed, as though in the midst of a particularly disturbing nightmare.

Although he wouldn't tell her what it was about, she had sat on the bed next to him and read one of his favorite books until he dropped off again.

The incident hadn't been repeated, so, she figured everything was fine.

"Once in a while, he has a bad dream," Dirk answered. "But no more than any other kid, I'd say."

"Why do you ask?" Savannah wanted to know.

"I was wondering because, well, he drew a picture today that looks like it's something from a very disturbing nightmare. When I saw it, I decided to call you and ask you to come in and see it."

She reached into her top drawer and pulled out a sheet of red construction paper with stick figures drawn on it.

Handing it to Savannah, she said, "I see a lot of stuff that's violent. With so much of it on television and in video games, children can't avoid it. But knowing Brody's history, I found this one particularly troublesome."

Savannah looked down at the picture in her hand and instantly her pulse rate began to climb.

She certainly didn't need the young artist present to explain the meaning of the primitive, but effective, artwork.

"Wow," Dirk said softly, looking over her shoulder. "That's some scary sh—stuff."

Instantly, Savannah knew the five individuals depicted in the child's drawing.

The burly, musclebound guy, wearing a blue Dodgers baseball cap with a white *L* and *A* on the front, had to be Dirk. He was enormous compared to the others and had an angry snarl on his face and something that looked like a billy club in his raised hand.

Next to Dirk was a well-rounded female with black curly hair and bright blue eyes. She, too, appeared furious and ready to do battle, her arms outstretched, desperately grasping—for the small, blond boy in the center of the picture.

The child's eyes were wide with fear and his mouth was a large O, as though he was screaming.

The artist had given him a speech bubble that contained the words, *"NO NO GO AWAY."*

On the other side of the paper, opposite the portrayals of Savannah and Dirk was a stick figure of a woman with short, yellow hair that stuck out in all directions. She had a downturned mouth and frown lines on her forehead, showing she was as angry and ready to fight as the cartoon Savannah and Dirk. In her upraised hand, she held a large loop, which Savannah decided was a folded belt, and her other hand was clasped tightly around the boy's upper arm.

Savannah couldn't decide if the woman was going to hit him, drag him away with her, or both.

A chill ran through Savannah as she read the woman's speech bubble. *"You can't get away your MINE MINE MINE."*

Fastened to the woman's skinny ankle was a large, red dog with long ears, bared teeth, and his own bubble with *"GRRR"* inside.

"I guess we don't need your fancy-dandy school counselor to interpret that one," Dirk said, settling back into his chair.

"No, not at all," Ms. Pomeroy said. "Children are wonderful. They're like clear, mountain spring water. They haven't learned yet how to hide who they are."

But as Savannah sat there and looked at her new son's heartbreaking drawing and compared the child depicted in the picture to the sweet, carefree boy who lived in her house and frolicked in her backyard with an old but frisky bloodhound, she had to disagree with his teacher.

Apparently, their Brody had things on his mind, terrifying things, that he was keeping from them.

"I'm glad you asked us to come in," she told the teacher. "I'm grateful to you for calling this to our attention."

"Of course," Ms. Pomeroy replied warmly. "I can tell how much you care for Brody. I knew you'd want to know."

As she walked them to the door, she said, "If there's anything I can do to help him or you, please don't hesitate to ask."

"Same here," Dirk said, his tone far more congenial than his usual.

But the moment they had left the teacher's presence and were walking down the hallway toward the exit, they instinctively reached for each other's hand.

"That was even worse than I expected," Dirk admitted. "I thought maybe he'd wrestled some kid and got his clothes dirty, or pulled some girl's ponytail, or said a cuss word."

"Well, there *was* that 'knock your teeth down your throat' business. I don't recall ever saying that in front of Brody. Did I?"

"I don't know. I don't remember it either, but you must have."

"Oh, Lord've mercy. That's awful. I'm a rotten mother."

"You're a wonderful mother. You and me, we're just learning what you can and can't say in front of a kid."

"Basically, you can't say anything you don't want to hear coming out of their mouths. In public. To people you'd like to impress."

"You wanna impress Ms. Pomeroy?"

She shrugged. "I guess. She's my kid's teacher. I don't want her thinking I'm a bum."

He slipped his arm around her shoulders. "I'm quite sure she doesn't think that. Although your nose did grow a couple of times when you lied. She might have noticed that."

"Really? You think she knew it wasn't allergies?"

"Naw, you had her fooled with that one."

"Oh, good. That's a relief."

"But I'm pretty sure she suspects you're the source of that 'teeth down the throat' thing. Us Yankees just aren't that colorful."

Savannah looked down at the drawing in her hand and her heart sank a bit further.

"We're going to have to talk to him about this," Dirk said. "Anything bothering him that much, it needs to be discussed."

"Yes, but I don't think we should tell him that his teacher called us in and showed the picture to us. With the kids hassling him about his mother, I don't want him to think he's catching flak both at school *and* at home."

Dirk nodded. "Yeah. You're probably right. At least at first, let's not make too big a deal about it."

"If he thinks we're worried, too, he might get even more upset than he already is."

Savannah felt her throat tighten when she took another glance at the picture. "I know we aren't supposed to hate anybody. Granny taught all of us kids how important that is. But I swear, when I think of that woman hurting that child . . . let's just say it brings out the worst in my character."

"Mine, too. But then, I think about the fact that he's going to be a teenager by the time she gets out. The little boy she abused will be at least a head taller than her."

"Plus, we're going to teach him not to take any crap off anybody."

"That's right, and if worse comes to worse, I'm pretty sure the three of us can take her."

"The *four* of us."

"Oh, right. I forgot about the Colonel. That scrawny, nasty gal doesn't stand a chance."

Chapter 23

Other than her own home or her grandmother's, ReJuvene was Savannah's favorite place on Earth. Her friends Ryan Stone and John Gibson had conceived the dream of such a place many years ago, early in their relationship, while they were still agents of the FBI. It had taken a long time, both of their savings, and a tremendous effort to bring the restaurant into being, but they had done so. Now they were the proud owners of the county's finest eating establishment.

As she and Dirk walked beneath the crimson awning with its white, scrolled letters *RJ*, and through the heavy door with its sparkling, beveled glass and freshly polished, brass hardware, she felt like a queen. A queen who was about to be served an array of delectable delicacies that she could otherwise only dream about.

Ryan and John were not only gorgeous, but they were amazing cooks. Between their skills and those of the restaurant's chef, Francia Fortun, and her sous-chef, Carlos Ortez, the food at ReJuvene lured the most discriminating palates from as far away as San Francisco, Las Vegas, and Phoenix, not to mention the locals from Los Angeles.

Procuring a reservation was not only a feat but a status symbol among the rich and famous fortunate enough to live within driving distance or a short trip by private plane.

So, Savannah was surprised when she walked through the door and saw that the restaurant was nearly empty. The waiting room, which usually was filled with diners sipping predinner drinks and socializing while waiting for their table, had no one at all in it.

Savannah could see through the glass doors into the main dining room, where Alma and Ethan sat with a high chair beside them, that held Ethan's three-year-old son, Freddy. Next to Freddy's chair was another high chair with Vanna Rose securely strapped in. Both little ones were looking at books and jabbering to each other in a language only they seemed to understand.

Waycross sat next to his daughter and beside him was Tammy. Granny and Brody were situated nearest the fireplace.

Other than her family, sitting at that one table, there was no one else in the room.

"We get the whole place to ourselves?" she whispered to Dirk.

"Seems so," Dirk replied. "But then, there's the other reason why nobody's here."

"What's that?" she asked, although she had a feeling she wasn't going to like the answer.

"The Dodgers are playing the Giants tonight. Right now, in fact."

She looked his way and saw a little-boy scowl on his grown-up, craggy man-face. "By that," she said, "I suppose you mean that all the other *nice* wives in California let their husbands stay home and watch the game, instead of dragging them, kicking and screaming, to a nasty ol' five-star restaurant for a free meal that will probably be the best food they've ever eaten in their lives? Is that what you wanna say to me, darlin' husband of mine?"

"Somethin' like that." He took a sniff of the air that was filled with the aroma of all sorts of exotic spices, meat searing, breads baking, and his face lit up. "I might forgive ya for it. Later."

"I have a feeling you'll not only forgive me but thank me with a nice, long foot massage."

"I'd give you a foot massage even if I was mad at you."

She giggled. "I know. You've got a thing for feet."

"*Your* feet." He thought about it a minute, then leaned down and whispered, "Actually, I think it's the red toenail polish."

She stopped in midstride, looked up at him and said, "Are you telling me that, if I stick to my Crimson Passion polish, you'll give me even more foot massages?"

"I'll be your foot rub slave forever."

"Good to know! *Very* good to know!"

They passed through the waiting area with its wall of green slate where a sheet of sparkling water flowed from the top to the bottom and into a line of flame. The room's soft, leather club chairs were drawn close to a fireplace, set in a wall of antique, reclaimed brick. Mahogany bookshelves on either side held leather-bound classics and mementos that Ryan and John had collected from all over the world on their extensive travels.

"Coming into this place always feels like getting a nice, big hug from both of them," she said, more to herself than Dirk. "It's just so . . . them."

He grunted.

Savannah mentally slapped herself on the forehead. When would she learn to keep her glowing, over-the-top, schoolgirl crush comments to herself about her drop-dead gorgeous, brilliant, and charming friends?

For years, she had thought Dirk disliked Ryan and John. But over time, the three men had developed a somewhat tenuous friendship, based upon respect and trust—the result of them having worked various difficult cases together.

Although Ryan and John had absolutely nothing in common with Dirk when it came to politics, philosophy, background, or recreational interests, they all three shared a passion for investigation and a deep, abiding love for Savannah.

That seemed strong enough, as a bond, to hold them together. Or at least to ensure civil discourse when they were in each other's company.

Savannah and Dirk walked into the main dining room, where they were greeted by a lovely, young woman named Maria. As hostess, Maria was the first to welcome diners to this place of relaxation and rejuvenation. Her dark eyes lit up when she saw Savannah, and she hurried across the room to meet them.

Although Maria offered her hand to shake, Savannah grabbed her and enfolded her in a warm hug. "I'm so glad to see you," Savannah said. "Are you going to be with us on the wedding day, too?"

"I am! I wouldn't miss it for anything." Maria looked back over her shoulder at the main table where Alma sat next to Ethan, holding his hand and gazing up into his eyes like any other love-besotted fiancée. "She is so sweet, and he's, he's . . . you know."

"Yes, I know," Savannah said softly, as she edited the rest of her statement to omit certain adjectives like "dreamy" and "set-your-knickers-aquiver stunning."

If Dirk felt he had to compete with Ryan and John, he was bound to suffer some pangs of insecurity having a filthy rich and fabulously famous brother-in-law entering the family. Who wouldn't?

As Maria led Savannah and Dirk into the dining room, the rest of the family saw that they had arrived and jumped up from their chairs to greet them.

"Everybody's here already! I'm sorry. Are we late?" Savannah glanced at her watch and saw that it was seven o'clock sharp.

"No. You're right on time," Alma said, standing on tiptoe to give her big sister a kiss on the cheek.

"We were just early," Ethan added as he hugged Savannah and gave Dirk a hearty handshake.

"Yeah, we're starvin'!" Brody piped up. "I'm hungry as a tick on a teddy bear."

Savannah ruffled his hair and said, "Tammy said she was going to take you over to Granny's for the afternoon."

He gave her a half-sheepish grin. "Yeah. So?"

"Don't tell me that Gran starved you plumb to death, because I won't believe it. Nobody goes hungry on Granny's watch."

"That's for sure," Alma said. "Suffering a hunger pang just ain't allowed in our family."

Ethan groaned. "I guess I'd better start looking for roles like 'Overweight Gladiator' or 'Pudgy Secret Agent.' "

"Reckon you're a bit eager to get this big ol' shindig

under way." Granny said, taking Ethan by the hand. She grabbed Alma with her other and led them back to the table.

"I wish it was today," Ethan said, glancing over at his bride-to-be and giving her a wink. "But not just to have it over with. All this planning and stuff is kinda fun, but I wish we were already married."

As the others gathered around the table and began to take their seats, Savannah glanced toward the kitchen and saw Ryan and John emerging, wearing food-soiled aprons and happy, satisfied faces.

They hurried to the table and, once again, Savannah was enveloped in more welcoming hugs.

How good to be so loved, she thought, as Ryan pulled out her chair for her and John made a slight adjustment to her cutlery. Surely, time spent with family in a beautiful place, enjoying delicious food, had to be one of life's greatest gifts.

She looked up at Ryan and stifled a chuckle. Normally, both he and John were *GQ* cover-ready, impeccably dressed and meticulously coiffed, from their every-hair-in-place heads to their professionally manicured fingertips.

But tonight, they were cooking, which meant that John's silver-fox mane was standing on end, his lush mustache uncombed, and a large smudge of flour adorned his left cheek.

Ryan's dark hair hung down into his eyes, stringy, wet strands, stuck to his sweaty forehead. He had red stains on his hands that she hoped were from something like beet juice and not blood.

"I'm surprised you two are cooking tonight," she told them. "Did Francia and Carlos call in sick?"

"No, love," John said with his posh, British accent.

"They're back there, making magic. Knowing this is for your family, they wouldn't miss it for the world. Carlos is putting the finishing touches on your appetizers, and Francia is preparing the entrées. We've added a couple of new items to the menu, dishes that none of you have ever tried."

"To be honest," Ryan said, "we hadn't tried them either. But they look and smell good."

"I'm sure they'll be plumb fit to eat," Granny said. "Everything here is like heaven in your mouth."

"We want you to have plenty of choices," Ryan said, "and we didn't want Francia and Carlos to have all the fun. So here we are." He held up his stained hand and pointed to his streaked apron. "Looking like a couple of short-order cooks in an all-night Brooklyn diner."

"The messier the apron, the better the food, I've always said," Ethan told them.

"Let's hope your theory proves true." Ryan glanced around the table, then turned to Maria. "Could you please refresh everyone's beverage and then the fun will begin!"

A cheer went up around the table, the loudest roar coming from Brody.

A few minutes later, everyone had settled down and were focusing on the charcuterie tray with its exotic cheeses, cured meats, fresh berries, olives, and buttery crackers.

They dug in, *ooo*ing and *ahh*ing about how nicely the smoked provolone complemented the rosemary and juniper prosciutto.

"I had fun at Granny's today," Brody announced as he spread a bit of jalapeño jelly on a cracker and popped it into his mouth.

"Hey, watch it there, kiddo," Savannah told him. "That jelly's hot. It'll burn your whiskers off!"

She handed him her napkin, anticipating his need to clear his mouth. But to her surprise, he toughed it out, chewed briefly, and gulped it down.

"I can handle it," he said, belying the tears that had sprung to his eyes. Grabbing a glass of water, he downed half of it before stopping.

"Here," Dirk said, handing him a cracker. "When you've got a fire in your mouth, something like this works better than water."

"I'm glad you had a good time with Gran," Savannah told him. "Sorry we couldn't pick you up the way we usually do."

"No problem. I like it when different folks pick me up in front of the other kids."

"Why is that?" Alma asked him.

"Because then they know I've got a lot of people who like me."

Savannah saw something that looked like a flash of sadness cross his face for a moment, then it was gone, and he was nudging the tray closer to Granny, so she could reach some of the jelly he'd just sampled.

"There ya go, Gran," he said. "You like hot stuff."

"No, thank you. You've still got steam shootin' outta your ears, and I try to learn from the mistakes of others."

Brody grabbed a couple of olives and said, "I guess you two had something pretty important to do, since you couldn't pick me up."

Savannah glanced at Dirk, who was studying a slice of salami with more intensity than even gourmet cured meat deserved. "Um, yeah," he said. "She helped me out with a case I'm working on."

"Dr. Carolyn's case?" Brody asked with an interest so keen that, watching the glow in his eyes, Savannah was taken aback.

But then she recalled how fascinated she had been by all things relating to law enforcement and criminality, even at his young age.

"Yes, it's Dr. Carolyn's case," she told him, deciding to be as open and honest with him as possible, considering his youth, that it was murder, and the fact that he knew the victim personally.

"Somebody bumped him off, right?"

Everyone at the table turned to look at the boy who asked the question as though he was inquiring about tomorrow's weather, then popped an olive into his mouth.

Savannah drew a deep breath and said, "Dr. Liu examined the body today and ruled it a homicide."

Brody turned to Granny and nodded knowingly. "Them two's the same thing," he told her. "Gettin' bumped off or havin' somebody homicide ya—either way, you're a goner."

She stared at him for a while, then nodded slowly and said, "Yes, I reckon you'd be toes up for good, whichever way."

Savannah looked over at the blushing bride-to-be and her fiancé. "What's going on with you two? Did you meet with the florist yet?"

Alma and Ethan turned to each other, whispered something between them, and Ethan said, "If it's all the same to you, we'd rather talk about the case than flowers."

Alma nodded vigorously. "It's way more interesting."

Savannah glanced around the table, pausing on Brody, wondering how to handle this novel situation.

Normally, when members of the Moonlight Magnolia team got together, all they did was discuss whatever case was pending. Had they been honest, they would have admitted that those discussions were more fascinating and satisfying than any food a chef could prepare. Even amazing cooks like Savannah, Ryan, and John.

But Brody.

This new addition complicated things—a youngster who, unlike tiny Vanna Rose, was old enough to understand most of what they were saying and its significance.

Not only did they need to guard his innocence, but since he knew the parties involved, he might spill the beans and mention something they'd said to someone who shouldn't hear it.

Savannah decided the answer to the problem lay in what she would call "Grown-Up Code." She might need to start carrying a thesaurus in her purse, but that was a small price to pay for being able to discuss adult topics at the dinner table.

"While experiencing a lengthy, meaningful discourse with the M.E.," she began, "we discovered that the MOD was determined to be homicide and the COD was cardiac arrest precipitated by ingestion of a highly toxic substance," she said, quite proud of herself.

Brody scowled at her, as one by one, the adults at the table gave Savannah a slight, knowing nod.

"Toxin in question is pentobarbital," Tammy added. "I was researching it all afternoon. Surprisingly, considering its potential to, um, cause a cessation of respiration and cardiac failure, it's a fairly common pharmaceutical."

Ethan tapped his forehead with his finger, concentrating, then said, "I remember that drug now. Sometimes they use it for"—he looked over at Brody—"to, well, deliberately cause that cessation and failure you were just mentioning."

"Right!" Alma piped up. "When they're administering the ultimate chastisement to a . . . detainee of the penal system."

Everyone snuck a look at Brody, who appeared uninterested as he decided which cheese to pair with which salami on the cracker of his choice. This time he was avoiding the jalapeño jelly.

Savannah turned to Tammy. "You say it's fairly common. Could you make a list for us of all the places that stock it?"

"They also use it to put pets to sleep," Brody casually mentioned as he continued to build his cheese and cracker sandwich.

The adults sat motionless at the table, their mouths slightly open, staring at the child.

So much for Grown-Up Code, Savannah told herself, when she finally recovered her ability to think.

She saw the twinkle in Granny's eyes as they exchanged glances across the table, and Savannah knew exactly what her grandmother was thinking.

"You were just like him." Savannah could hear the words as clearly as if they had been spoken. "You put me through my paces back in the day, and what goes around comes around."

"Yes, Brody," Savannah said. "I do believe it's used for that purpose, too."

"It is. I know. I saw it before myself."

"You saw an animal put to sleep?"

Brody nodded. "Don't tell Dr. Carolyn though. She thought I was still cleanin' cages. But I heard her saying some words, bad ones, loud. So, I came back inside to see if something was wrong, if she needed my help."

"What was going on?" Savannah said.

"She was having a hard time gettin' Loki to go to sleep. Well, die. You know that's what they really mean."

"Yes. I know."

Dirk leaned toward the boy, his expression serious, his voice low as he said, "What do you mean, son, having a hard time with the dog?"

"He wouldn't go down. She'd done give him a big ol' honkin' dose of that pento-stuff, 'cause he was a big dog, a Great Dane, who weighed a lot. How much they weigh is a big deal at a time like that. You don't give a chihuahua a monster shot like you would a Great Dane."

"I reckon that's true," Granny said, reaching over and placing her hand on Brody's shoulder. "What exactly did you hear her say?"

"Well, some of it was cussin' and you probably don't want me to say that part."

"Tell us what you can, darlin'," Savannah told him. "Apparently, you're a lot better with words than we thought."

"Okay." He finished swallowing his enormous bite, drew a deep breath, and said, "She was saying stuff like, 'That was twice as much as he should need! Something's wrong here!' She got all upset; I thought she was gonna cry. She said, 'This poor dog's had a rough life. He's suffered so damn much. You'd think the least we could do is give him a gentle passin'.' "

"Carolyn mentioned something to me about losing a Great Dane named Loki, how upsetting it was."

"Naw, she didn't lose him. He was there the whole

time. We knew where he was. But he sure didn't wanna go down, and she sure weren't happy about it neither."

Before anyone could comment on Brody's eyewitness account, the appetizer course arrived and was laid out before them. Thai minced turkey lettuce cups and pan seared scallops with peach salsa caught the ladies' attention, while the men nabbed the bacon jam with onions, served on Parmesan crisps, and the shaved beef on crostini with a spicy horseradish sauce. Everyone grabbed the tiny, wild mushroom soufflés, which disappeared almost instantly.

The rest of the meal unfolded splendidly. The BLT salad with avocado and feta and the heirloom tomato with balsamic vinaigrette were the winners of the salad category. Wild-caught salmon with a tropical salsa, marinated flank steak, and Cuban style roasted pork were the entrées of choice.

Although the official wedding dessert would be the cake, Ryan and John wanted their special guests to have a final treat.

The dessert cart they wheeled out carried temptations galore, including: triple-berry ricotta cake, pear-walnut upside-down cake, and Savannah's personal favorite, the dark chocolate bread pudding.

"You were right," Dirk mumbled to Savannah as he gnawed on a leftover mahogany chicken drumette. "This *is* better than staying home and watching the game."

"Even if the Dodgers beat the Giants?"

"Whaddya mean *if*? It's in the bag."

"Yeah. Right. The only bag I'm counting on is the doggy bag we get to take home with us tonight. We'll be eating high on the hog for the rest of the week."

Dirk laughed. So did Tammy, who had overheard her comment.

But Savannah wasn't laughing. For all the joy of the evening, the pleasure of her family's company, and the delicious food, she couldn't stop thinking about the Great Dane named Loki.

The one who, for some reason that she could only speculate about, had simply refused to "go down."

Chapter 24

Later, when dinner was finished, Ryan and John removed their aprons, changed their shirts, combed their hair, and joined the Reid clan in the waiting area for coffee, a hot chocolate for Brody, and fresh-squeezed orange juices for Vanna Rose and Freddy.

Tammy and Waycross were playing with the children, Alma and Ethan were snuggling on a love seat near the fireplace, and Dirk was playing with his phone, pretending not to be checking the baseball game scores. So, Ryan and John joined Savannah and Granny, who were sitting on a leather sofa, perusing a picture album that had been on one of the shelves.

The photobook contained snapshots of Morocco and a younger Ryan and John by at least ten years. They were shopping in the main square of Marrakesh, having a drink at night by the pool of the lavish hotel, La Maison Arabe, with all its Moorish splendor.

Looking up at her friends, who were walking toward her, it occurred to Savannah that the two had aged most graciously.

She had a theory that the kindness they showed to their fellow human beings made a circle, returned to them, and kept them youthful.

As she patted her tummy, she said, "Lads, you outdid yourselves tonight. Absolutely splendid! I'm so full, I swear I'll never eat again."

Ryan slipped into a chair next to her and said, "You feed us all the time. Wonderful dishes. It felt nice to return the favor for a change."

John sat on the ottoman next to Ryan's chair and glanced around the room at their now fully sated guests, who seemed to be savoring the last moments of the evening and each other's company before going their separate ways.

"That's one of the finer aspects of owning an eatery," Ryan said. "It's such an easy and pleasant place to entertain your best mates."

Ryan looked down at John, and a look was exchanged between them.

It was subtle, but Savannah saw it and wondered what they had on their minds.

She didn't have long to wonder.

Ryan glanced around and, seeing that everyone else in the room was occupied, he leaned closer to Savannah and Granny and said, "When we were changing clothes, cleaning up to come out here and visit with you, we remembered something."

"Oh?" Instantly, Savannah felt a tingling in her body that had nothing to do with the sugar high from the dark chocolate bread pudding. "What sort of thing did you guys recall?"

"We met your victim, Dr. Stephen Erling, at a party last year," Ryan said. "It was a fundraiser, hosted by Dr. Harold Weinberg, the Chief of Staff at Community General Hospital."

"You've met Dr. Weinberg, love," John told Savannah. "He's the tall, stately fellow who made sure you were well-tended when you went in that time for a cracked head."

Subconsciously, Savannah put her hand to the back of her hair and recalled the pain that particular encounter with a perpetrator had caused her. She also remembered spending a long time in the ER, being totally neglected, until John and Ryan had intervened on her behalf by calling their close friend, the chief of staff.

"Of course I remember him. I never got treated like royalty before in a hospital, until that night. Not something a gal forgets."

Impatient with the walks down Yesteryear Road, Granny set the photo album aside, leaned closer to John, and said, "What'd y'all think of him, that Dr. Stephen fella, when you met 'im at the party?"

"Let's just say I wasn't impressed with the lad," John replied. "Mostly because he seemed so very impressed with himself."

"That was what Savannah thought, too," Granny told them. "Plus you three are good judges of character, so I reckon he wuddin' worth spit."

Ryan chuckled. "I'm not exactly sure how much spit he might have been worth. I understand he was an extremely talented surgeon. But that night, he'd had quite a lot to drink and was acting inappropriately with a young woman there."

"He most certainly was," John agreed. "At one point I

thought her husband might challenge him to engage in fisticuffs before all was said and done. But the lady encouraged her fellow to take her home, and eventually, he did."

"You sound a mite disappointed there, John," Granny said, giving him a wink.

"I hate to admit it, since I claim to be a peace-loving man, but after seeing how uncomfortable he'd made her, I thought someone should administer a thorough trouncing, just to teach him not to behave like a boor."

"Lordy, I wish you had," Granny said. "I'd have paid good money to've seen that!"

"What exactly did he do to the woman or say to her that would warrant a trouncing?" Savannah wanted to know.

"Let's just say he was determined that she spend some 'quality' time with him upstairs in one of the bedrooms," Ryan said. "He continued to make his suggestions, which were loud, lewd, and often."

John reached for a coffeepot on a nearby table and refilled Savannah's and Granny's cups. "Several men, including myself, Ryan, and Dr. Weinberg spoke to him, at first suggesting, then demanding that he leave her alone. Dr. Weinberg eventually had him escorted off the property."

"Do you have any idea who that couple was?" Savannah asked.

"No. We'd never met them before," Ryan replied, "and we haven't seen them since."

"But we do know their names," John added. "We heard them spoken several times amid the arguments. Hers was Lissa."

Savannah's pulse quickened.

Ryan added, "And his was—"

"Jerry."

Both men looked at Savannah, surprised.

"How do you know that?" Ryan asked. "Have you met them?"

"Not yet. I just recently heard of them. Dr. Liu told me that Erling often attended, shall we say, sexually adventurous gatherings, always accompanied by the same woman. A gal named Lissa. This woman was at least involved with, if not married to, a fellow named Jerry. How much do you want to bet they're one and the same?"

"Jerry's a common enough name," Granny offered. "You can't shake out your dust mop without hittin' one of 'em. But you don't run into a Lissa every day of the week."

"We have to find out who they are," Savannah said. "Either one of them makes a good suspect. Maybe even both of them. Stranger things have happened."

Gran reached over and patted her granddaughter's hand. "You really don't want it to be Carolyn that done it, do ya, darlin'?"

"No, I really don't want it to be her." Savannah looked over at the cheerful gang on the other side of the room.

Ethan was on his hands and knees. Brody was trying to lift Freddy up onto Ethan's back, so he could enjoy a "horsey ride" at his father's expense.

Once the little bronco buster was in place, Ethan began to "buck" and neigh loudly enough to make it exciting for the youngster.

Then it was Vanna Rose's turn. Brody held on to her throughout her ride, so she didn't slide off.

Of the group, Brody seemed to be enjoying the playing the most, and Savannah knew it was because he loved giving the little ones joy.

Why wouldn't she want the killer to be someone other than one of his very best friends, one of the people he admired most in the world?

Savannah thought of how the kids at school had said such ugly, hurtful things to him. Yes, their statements had been true, but that only made the pain worse.

She recalled the dark, frightening picture the boy had drawn, a representation of the fear he hid deep inside.

Let it be someone other than Carolyn, she heard herself silently pray. *And while you're at it, please help me catch him!*

Chapter 25

"Where do you think? In his room or down here?" Dirk asked Savannah later that evening after they and Brody had returned from ReJuvene and were getting ready to retire for the night.

"I don't know," Savannah replied. She looked down at her lap, where Diamante was stretched out, purring with ecstasy as Savannah scratched behind her ears. "I'm even neglecting my own cats these days," she said, more to herself than to him.

But since she was sitting in her comfy chair, and he was stretched out on the sofa with his head a mere three feet from her, he had heard.

"The cats are fine, Van. We're all fine."

"Then why are we sitting here trying to decide where's the best place to talk to our kid about something so awful that his teacher called us on the carpet about it?"

"Because we're being overly conscientious about this parenting business."

Savannah sat up straighter in her chair. "Do you really believe that?"

He shrugged. "I don't know. But it's possible. We both had a rough time growing up, thanks to the adults who were supposed to be taking care of us and weren't."

"Weren't . . . and worse than weren't."

"That's what I mean. We might be overdoing it, trying to go too far the other way."

Savannah thought it over, while listening for Brody to finish brushing his teeth upstairs. He'd be downstairs in a minute, ready to be tucked in. They had to decide. Now.

"Do you really think something as serious as parenting can be overdone?" she said.

"Absolutely. I see kids all the time whose parents spoiled them rotten and let them do whatever they damned well wanted to. Surprise, surprise! They grew up to be adults who expect the world to carry them for the rest of their lives and grant their every wish, like their parents did."

"We don't want to do that to him."

"We won't."

"There has to be a happy medium between spoiling and neglecting."

"There is. We'll find it."

"Might take some practice."

"He's six. I figure we've got about twelve to fourteen years to figure it out."

Savannah heard the water turn off in the upstairs bathroom. "He's done. Let's do it upstairs in his room. He probably feels safer there than anywhere else."

"Okay. Let's go on up then."

"Keep it as lighthearted as possible, like we discussed."

"We'll do our best. It's not exactly a jolly topic."

They stood and headed for the stairs, hoping to intercept him before he came down.

The three met in the hallway beside Brody's bedroom door.

"Oh, hi," he said, as he reached down to scoop Diamante, who had followed Savannah, into his arms. "I was going to come down to get her, but she came up to me."

He looked so pleased that Savannah's heart hurt. Every day she saw signs of how much this child needed love. It seemed no one and nothing would ever be able to truly fill a hole so deep, so longstanding.

But she had every intention of trying, and if she erred on the side of spoiling him a bit, then so be it.

Granny had given Savannah and her eight siblings infinite, unconditional love when they had been taken from her negligent mother and given to their grandmother. If what Gran had done was considered "spoiling," then she had every intention of spoiling the child in her care as much as she could.

"We're going to both tuck you in tonight, if that's all right with you," she told him.

Instead of looking suspicious about this change in protocol, he beamed with pleasure at the idea. "Cool," he said, tucking the cat under his arm and heading into his bedroom.

Savannah and Dirk followed the boy into the blue and white, baseball-themed room.

She pulled back the covers and got him and the cat situated in bed and sufficiently tucked in.

Meanwhile, Dirk turned on an LED night-light that

beamed a bright and intricate night sky, including the constellations, across the ceiling and walls.

Brody had seen the light advertised on television and had begged for it with an intensity that had surprised Savannah. Now, seeing how much it illuminated the room and how effectively it dispelled the darkness, she wondered if the gadget provided more comfort than entertainment for the child.

Considering what he had drawn on that picture, she could understand why he might prefer to sleep in a well-lit room than a dark one.

She sat down on one side of his bed, near the foot, and Dirk did the same on the other side. They had discussed the importance of giving him some space, even actual physical space, when they first broached the topic, until they saw what his reaction would be.

She gave Dirk a questioning look, to see if he was ready. He gave his customary nod of agreement, and she began.

"Brody, we want to ask you a couple of questions, and what we really want, more than anything, is for you to just tell us what you think is true. There isn't any right or wrong answer. Nothing you say will get you in trouble. So, just tell us whatever comes to your mind. Okay?"

He shrugged, reached down, and stroked Diamante's back. "Okay. Right now what's true is, I'm wondering what you guys are up to. I'm wondering if I'm in trouble and how bad."

Dirk laughed. "You aren't in any trouble at all, son. Promise. Like she said, there's no right or wrong answers here. Just say whatever you want to."

He grinned. Far too broadly. "Even if it's a cuss word?"

Savannah raised one eyebrow, thought about it, and said, "This one time, if you really can't think of a better word to use, I suppose so."

"Cool. Shoot."

"Okay." She drew a deep breath. "First of all, we'd like to know how it's going at school so far."

He thought carefully, then said, "I like the lunches you send me. I like my teacher. I like my classroom, even though it smells like tuna fish and bananas at lunchtime, 'cause that's what we're all eating, and it ain't the greatest combination, smell-wise."

"How about the kids?" Dirk asked. "Made any friends?"

"Yeah, a couple. We hang out at recess. There's a girl who likes me, but yuck."

"Is she cute?" Dirk asked.

"I guess. But she makes me all these love notes, a new one every day, with hearts and stuff on it, and gives them to me. Asks me if we can go together. I don't know why she asks me that. Like where are we gonna go? We're six!"

"Yeah. I'd save that 'going together' stuff until you're older," Savannah said, "when you're both more mature and know what you want out of life."

"Like when I'm eight?"

Dirk nodded. "Yeah, that sounds about right."

"Do you have any other problems at school, other than this lovesick, but artistically inclined, girl who's determined to win your heart?" Savannah asked.

A slight shadow crossed his face, then quickly disappeared. "Not really," he said. "Some of them say some dumb stuff to make me mad. But they're just a bunch of monkey fudge nuggets, so I don't pay 'em no mind. That way I don't have to hit 'em and get in trouble."

Savannah stifled a laugh and nodded solemnly. "Excellent choice. A wise and mature decision."

"Not mature enough to go out with a girl though. I might not ever be mature enough to do that."

"You'll know when the time comes," Dirk said. "Believe me, you'll know."

Savannah steeled herself as she prepared to steer the conversation down a rockier road. "How about outside of school?" she asked gently.

"You mean, like here?"

"Yes. Like here at home."

"Oh, I like here! It's the best. I got you guys and the Colonel and Di and Cleo and even Vanna and Freddy and all the grown-ups. They're all cool, but especially Granny. I had so much fun with her at the park today. The one by the pier. Do you know she's got a red swimsuit, and she wears it, too, there at the beach? She doesn't even care if she's, you know, old. She went swimming with me and the hound dog, like she was a kid, too."

"Gran's awesome," Dirk said. "We're all hoping to be like her when we grow up someday."

Brody snickered. "If you grow up any more than you already are, you won't fit in your car or your clothes or Savannah's comfy chair!"

Savannah reached over and put her hand on the little foot that was sticking up beneath the blanket. She found his toes and gave them a gentle squeeze.

"If something, anything at all, was bothering you, Brody," she said softly, "I hope you know that you can talk to us about it. Any time. But now's an especially good time. You know, if there was anything in particular."

Suddenly, his bright smile disappeared. Tears sprang to his eyes and his lower lip began to tremble.

"What is it, son?" Dirk asked, moving up the bed so that he could take him in his arms. "Tell us what it is."

"I shouldn't oughta say," he replied, choking on the words, as he laid his head on Dirk's shoulder and snuggled in.

"Are you afraid you'll get in trouble?" Savannah asked. "Because if you are, you don't need to be. We'd be really glad if you told us what's bothering you."

"I know." He sniffed. "I know you won't get mad at me. That's not what I'm afraid of."

"Are you afraid we'll tell someone else?"

Brody thought that over a moment, then said, "No. Not really. You don't talk to her."

Savannah and Dirk exchanged a loaded look. They were getting somewhere.

"You mean your mom," Savannah said. It was more of a statement than a question.

Brody nodded. "Yeah. I mean her."

Dirk wrapped his arm more tightly around the child and said, "You know where she is, right?"

"Yeah. In a jail."

"Not just in a jail, darlin'," Savannah replied. "She's in prison."

Brody looked up at Dirk. "What's the difference?"

"Well, you don't want to wind up in either place. But prisons are way more serious. They're bigger and the bars are a whole lot stronger. There're tons of big prison guards who mean business, and they make sure that nobody can ever get out of there. Not until they've served all of their sentence."

He brightened a bit. "Nobody ever got out of a prison before they were supposed to?"

Savannah searched for comforting words that wouldn't be a lie. "Brody," she said. "Your mother absolutely cannot get out of the prison she's in. There is *no* way. She's going to be in there for a long time."

"I know, 'cause she hurt a kid. Me." He looked down at Diamante, who was rubbing her face on the back of his hand. He pulled her closer and said, "I heard that she's gotta stay there a long, long time because of what she did to me. But I didn't ask the judge to do that, to make it longer. I hope she doesn't think I'm to blame for her gettin' stuck in there so long."

"She's in there for a lot of stuff she did, son," Dirk said. "She also sold a bunch of really bad drugs to a lot of people. She attacked me and the policemen who arrested her. You saw that yourself. Plus she'd committed lot of crimes before, for years, and she didn't seem to be learning her lesson."

Brody looked up at Dirk, a half grin on his face. "That was me that gave you the black eye when you arrested her. You didn't put *me* in prison."

Savannah laughed. "You got a pass, kid, because of your tender years. A one-time pass."

"Next time, it's San Quentin for you," Dirk told him as he ruffled his hair and kissed the top of his head.

Savannah wanted to move to the child's other side and hug him, too. But when she made a slight movement toward him, she saw him flinch. So, she pulled back and tried not to take it personally.

Though she couldn't help it.

"You don't ever have to be afraid of her," she told

him. "By the time she gets out of there, you're going to be a tall, grown-up man. She wouldn't even think of raising a hand to you then."

"You mean she'd be afraid of me?" He seemed enchanted by the idea.

"I think you being bigger than her and stronger would make all the difference in the world in how she treats you. Besides, you won't even have to see her or talk to her again, unless you choose to."

"I won't choose to. I sure as shootin' won't ever choose to."

"I understand, Brody."

"Do you think she'd understand?"

Savannah shrugged. "She doesn't have to understand. You aren't responsible for her. She is. Maybe she'll learn that while she's sitting in prison and maybe she won't. But it's not anything for you to concern yourself about."

He sighed. "I wish I didn't worry about her."

"You don't have to, sweetie." Savannah squeezed his toes again. "Those guards are going to make sure she doesn't get out, and here at home, you've got a real, live, police officer right here to protect you."

"You was one, too," he piped up.

"I sure was, and I haven't forgotten how it's done."

"Plus you've got the Colonel," Dirk added. "He's a ferocious watchdog."

Brody rolled his eyes. "What's he gonna do? Howl or sniff a bad guy to death?" They laughed together. "He could bite her ankle though, if he had to in a pinch."

"I'm sure he would." Savannah gave him her most reassuring smile. "You are about as safe as any kid in the world could be, Mr. Brody Greyson. You have about a dozen capable people and critters around you who would fight with all their might to keep her or anybody else from harming one hair on your head."

He giggled, and Savannah saw the first glimmer of an upper front tooth, breaking through the gum.

"Reckon I'm a pretty lucky kid, then," he said.

"I'd say everybody in this household is lucky," she told him, "because we have each other and *you!*"

Chapter 26

The next morning, Savannah was so exhausted that she slept nearly an hour later than usual. When she finally woke, she realized that Dirk had turned off the alarm, and next to the clock on her nightstand was a note, scribbled on a sheet of Brody's lined notebook paper.

It read: *Hi, Babe. Us guys are off to school and work. Sleep some more. xox*

She looked down and saw that both cats had joined her. A rare occurrence these days. Diamante was draped across her feet, and Cleopatra was snuggled against her tummy.

With all the chores on the day's calendar, Savannah knew she should jump out of bed and get going. But the allure of warm kitties, their gentle purring, and soft pillows was too strong.

She snuggled deeper into the bed and pulled Granny's quilt up to her chin. Just fifteen minutes more.

An hour later, she woke to the sound of voices in her house. She couldn't tell whose voices or what they were saying, but she figured she should roll out of bed and find out.

As she was slipping into a pair of jeans, she heard a child's gleeful squeal and realized that at least one of the visitors down below was her sweet Vanna Rose.

So, she wasn't surprised when she exited the bedroom, mostly dressed, and heard Tammy's cheerful chirping, as well.

It took her a bit longer to recognize Carolyn Erling's voice.

What the heck is Dr. Carolyn doing here? she wondered. *Did her new roommate kick her out already? They seemed to be getting along so well there at the clinic.*

As she hurried down the stairs, running her fingers through her hair to try to give her curls some sense of order, she heard Carolyn say, "I so hope she'll be willing to do it. I'm sure she'd be the best to—"

Carolyn spotted Savannah the moment she stepped from the foyer into the living room and jumped up from the sofa to greet her. "Oh, I hope we didn't wake you," she said. "I should have called first."

"No, not at all." Savannah gave Carolyn a quick hug, then reached down to scoop up the squealing toddler at her feet, who was demanding to be held. "I'm usually up and about at this hour. It's just . . ."

"It's been a hard couple of days," Carolyn said.

"Yes. It has. But not as bad as yours."

"Let me go get you both some coffee," Tammy said, scurrying toward the kitchen.

"Thank you, Tamitha. I've got the kiddo here." Savannah motioned for Carolyn to have a seat, and she took Vanna with her and sat in her chair.

As she pulled a children's book from the stack beneath her end table and gave it to the girl, Savannah waited for Carolyn to explain the reason for her unexpected visit.

When she wasn't forthcoming, Savannah decided to ask her outright. With absolutely no caffeine in her system, "patience" wasn't an option.

"How can I help you?" she said.

"I beg your pardon?" Carolyn replied.

"When I was coming down the staircase just now, I overheard you say you hoped someone would be able to help you with something. Am I wrong to think you were referring to me?"

"No, not at all. I was talking about you, and I do have a big favor to ask you."

Savannah hoped it wasn't going to be a huge favor, because at the moment, she was pretty sure that she wasn't going to be able to hold a baby and drink a cup of coffee at the same time.

It just wasn't one of those "multitasking" kind of days.

"I don't know how much help I'll be, but please feel free to ask," she said as graciously as she could manage.

"I don't know how one goes about hiring a private detective. I've never done that before. But I'd like to hire you."

"Oh. I . . . okay."

Savannah couldn't help but be surprised. Until this moment, Carolyn hadn't expressed any overwhelming desire to find out who might have murdered her husband. In fact, Savannah had thought more than once that Carolyn probably knew already. Or at least strongly suspected.

But Savannah also couldn't help being pleased. It had been months since she'd had a paying job and her savings account had dwindled considerably.

Plus, she was dying to get back to work again, and not just lurking around her husband while he solved his case.

"Sure," she heard herself say far too eagerly. "I happen to be available at the moment."

Except for being the maid of honor at my sister's fancy wedding, she silently added. *Not to mention trying to raise a troubled child, give my husband the attention he deserves, be a loving granddaughter and a good cat mommy, and wonder how I'm going to make ends meet with a sporadic income. Yes, I'm pretty much footloose and fancy-free.*

"Do we sign papers? Do I pay you now?" Carolyn asked, reaching for her purse that lay beside her on the sofa.

"Tammy takes care of all that," Savannah said. "She can fill you in on the particulars later. But like I said, there's not much to it. Just tell me what you want me to investigate."

Savannah assumed it was Stephen's murder, but she'd learned long ago not to assume anything, either in law enforcement or the private detection business.

"I want you to find out who killed my husband," Carolyn said. "I need to know."

"Of course you do. But the police are investigating it now. You must be aware that it's my husband who's leading the investigation."

Savannah didn't bother to mention that San Carmelita's city budget was so tight and their police force so small that Dirk would not only be leading the investigation, but he would be the only one doing any investigating.

Unless her Moonlight Magnolia team lent a hand, as they frequently did—as much for the love of "sleuthing" as out of affection and consideration for Dirk.

"I would just feel better if you were working the case, too. I have a feeling that you're very capable, Savannah."

"I appreciate your faith in me, and if you really want to hire me, I'd be happy to have you as a client," Savannah assured her. "But I feel I should be honest and tell you that I'm not sure the outcome will be much different, whether my husband works the case alone or if my team and I conduct our own investigation."

"You think, either way, in the end we'll know who killed him?"

"I do. Dirk is very good at his job. Thorough. Determined. A bit like an alligator with a Christmas ham in its jaws."

Carolyn glanced away and seemed uneasy with what she'd just heard.

Savannah wondered if it was because of the too-graphic imagery or because she'd just been assured the murderer would be caught.

Savannah had to be equally honest with herself and admit that she wasn't absolutely certain that Dirk was wrong.

Stephen Erling's killer might be sitting on her sofa at that moment. For all Savannah knew, Carolyn simply wanted to hire her in hopes that, through Savannah, Carolyn could keep tabs on Dirk's progress.

Or maybe even influence the investigation.

On the other hand, she appeared sincere.

"I still want to hire you and your agency," Carolyn assured her. "I've read so many good things about you in the papers over the years. I need to do something. I need to do this."

"Then you've got yourself a private detective," Savannah told her, as Tammy brought a tray loaded with Savannah's Old Country Roses coffeepot, matching cups, creamer, and sugar bowl into the living room and set it on the coffee table.

Turning to Savannah, she held out her arms and said, "Vanna and I have things to do in the backyard. I'll take the phone outside with me, so you won't be disturbed if anyone calls."

"Thank you, Tammy," Savannah said, handing over her precious burden. "Dr. Erling here is going to be a client of ours. I assured her that you can walk her through the less glamorous aspects of our little business—payment, contract, etc."

"I'd be happy to. Anytime." With her daughter on her hip, Tammy walked to the rolltop desk in the corner and picked up the business phone and her own electronic tablet.

As she sauntered out of the house, Savannah knew that what Tammy intended to do in the backyard was Internet research.

Savannah also knew that Tammy would have done the same thing whether Carolyn had hired them or not.

The kid had a calling. Though some might call it an obsession.

Savannah poured them each a cup of coffee and pushed the cream and sugar closer to her guest.

They both took a long drink, savoring the experience, much as they had enjoyed the hot toddies beneath the arbor in the moonlight.

Then Savannah turned in her chair to face her new client. Her dark blue eyes had the same predatory intensity as Dirk's when he was about to "squeeze" somebody. Hard.

"First question," she said. "Who's Lissa?"

Chapter 27

"This is a really special occasion," Savannah said as she looked around Granny's dining table at the illustrious company gathered there. "It's the first meeting of the Moonlight Magnolia Detective Agency in a month of Sundays, and the first one *ever* in Granny's new home."

"Hear, hear," John said, raising his teacup in a toast to their hostess. "A lovely home it is, too. I can hear the ocean waves from here!"

Granny chuckled. "I have to be careful not to go sleepwalkin' or I could end up in the brink! Them waves is practically outside my door!"

"I'm very happy for you, Mrs. Reid," Ryan added. "Beach living has to be the best."

"I sure enjoy it," Granny said solemnly. "It was my lifelong dream. I knew it was comin', one way or another. I just didn't know how."

Savannah looked around the interior of the luxury mobile home with its cathedral ceilings, skylights, and stone fireplace. The contemporary kitchen had every convenience, even ones her grandmother had never dreamed of, and so did the bathrooms, three bedrooms, and the formal dining room where they were sitting.

When Savannah thought of the run-down old shotgun shack in Georgia, where Granny had spent most of the years of her long life and compared it to the lifestyle her grandmother was now enjoying, she felt enormously grateful.

Grateful to a certain highly successful actor, who was about to join their family.

The depth of his generosity was hard for Savannah to comprehend or even accept. Though she realized that with so much wealth, it was likely that he barely even felt any sort of financial impact when he gave them a gift. But to them, who had been raised far poorer than most, it felt like a king had handed them the keys to his castle.

Savannah and Granny exchanged glances across the table. Only the two of them—and Dirk, because Savannah had told him—knew that this beautiful home on the sea had been paid for with money that Ethan had given Savannah.

Thanks to him, Granny no longer lived in Dirk's old trailer, sitting in a park that was rapidly becoming the drug capital of the county.

Savannah's only concern was that Ethan might think these gifts were expected of him or that they valued him more because he gave them. She wanted her soon-to-be brother-in-law to know that he was welcomed and loved only for himself and for the joy that he brought their little Alma.

Granny rose and walked around the table, making sure that Savannah, Dirk, and Ryan had coffee, John his Earl Grey tea, Tammy her mineral spring water, Waycross his root beer, and sippy juice boxes for Brody and Vanna Rose.

She replenished the platter of warm-from-the-oven chocolate-chip cookies, then turned to Brody and said, "How's about you and me take the Colonel for his sundown walk on the beach?"

"You betcha!" Brody sprang up from his seat on the floor near the fireplace, where he had been drawing pictures. As he scrambled to put the paper and crayons away, he said, "I was hopin' you'd offer, Granny. Do you think we'll see the lighthouse come on again, like we did before?"

"Most likely," she said. "It comes on ever' single night and has since many years before I was born."

"They had lighthouses before *you* were born?" Brody was amazed.

"They surely did. Most of 'em was run by dinosaurs. It was hard for 'em, climbin' up them windin' stairs, but if the light went out, they were good at relightin' it. They'd just give it a blast with their fiery breath and git 'er goin' again."

Brody gave her a doubtful look. "I think you're mixing up dinosaurs with dragons."

"I am?"

"Afraid so."

"Okay. Either way, let's get goin' before that sun sets. We wanna see all them fancy boats comin' back home to roost for the night."

Brody snickered. "Now I think you're mixing up boats with chickens."

Savannah decided to intervene. "Brody, we don't contradict Granny. She's earned the right to have every word that comes out of her mouth accepted as gospel."

"Don't tell the child that," Granny told her. "He's gotta learn to trust himself before he can trust what other folks say. I don't mind being told when I've spoken amiss." She turned back to Brody. "Long as you don't make a habit of it."

"I won't. Just if it's dinosaur stuff, 'cause I'm pretty much an expert on them guys. I read a book about 'em."

"See there," Gran said. "He read a book, and now he's an expert." She walked over to Tammy, who was holding Vanna Rose on her lap, and said, "Can I take your little darlin' out for a sundown walk on the beach, too? We'd be happy to have her."

Tammy looked down at the tiny girl in her lap. The child's head was on Tammy's chest and her eyes half-closed.

"Thank you, Granny, but I think she'll be asleep in three minutes. You and Brody go ahead and have a nice time."

Gran checked once again to see that the beverages were flowing, the platter had plenty of cookies, and everyone appeared comfortable. "Okay, then you guys get down to business with your mystery solving. When we get back, I wanna hear who it was that done it."

"No problem, Gran," Dirk told her. "We'll have them behind bars before that lighthouse comes on."

Thirty seconds later, Granny, Brody, and Colonel Beauregard were gone and the group at the table turned to the business at hand.

The most somber business of all.

"As you know," Savannah began, "we have a new client. An unexpected one. Dr. Carolyn Erling. I'll tell you now that she is Dirk's number one suspect."

Everyone turned to look at Dirk, and he nodded.

"As you may or may not know," Savannah continued, "Carolyn's husband, our victim, was held in very low esteem by those who knew him, even though he was a world-famous surgeon. We may have a hard time finding someone who *isn't* glad he's passed on."

"What a dreadful legacy to leave," John said over the rim of his teacup.

"Even if we can't take our belongings with us," Ryan added, "it's nice to think we'll leave our loved ones some good memories of us."

"Whether Dr. Erling was a nice guy or not," Savannah said, "he didn't deserve to be murdered. After talking to Carolyn this morning, I believe we have one or maybe even two more suspects that need investigating, as well as Carolyn herself."

Dirk immediately got out his pad and pencil, and Tammy took her electronic tablet from her diaper bag.

Savannah continued. "Dr. Liu told us she saw Stephen Erling at some sort of hook-up party with a gal named Lissa. They were joking about how they had gotten one over on someone named Jerry, by attending this particular get-together when he was out of town."

"Was Carolyn aware that her husband was at a party like that with another woman?" Dirk asked. "'Cause if she was, that might be another reason for her to knock him off."

"I don't believe she knew, and I didn't mention it to her today either. But I did ask her if she knew a couple named Lissa and Jerry and she immediately told me that she did. Lissa's name is actually Melissa, and she's married to Jerald Becker."

"Lissa and Jerry," Tammy said, scrolling on her tablet. "Here they are. They live in Twin Oaks. Nice place. This says he's a lawyer and she's a surgical nurse."

"She was," Savannah said. "In fact, she was Stephen Erling's surgical nurse for several years. Carolyn told me that Lissa quit abruptly a few weeks ago. Erling was furious. She left him high and dry, right before an important operation in Madrid. Apparently, he had to scramble to find and train a replacement."

Waycross nodded toward Tammy and said to Savannah, "Sounds like you need to sic my lady on those two. By this time tomorrow you'll know what color boxers Mr. Becker wears and whether Miss Lissa plucked her eyebrows this morning."

Ryan laughed. "He's right. Tammy, I wouldn't want you investigating me. I'm pretty sure you'd uncover skeletons I didn't even know were in my closet."

"Actually, I find more skeletons in basements, attics, and rose gardens than in closets," Tammy said in a most officious tone. When they all laughed, she shrugged and said, "To be honest, Savannah and Dirk may have found some actual bone skeletons, but I only find the boring kinds, like the sort of secrets you uncover in bank accounts, tax returns, credit reports, and posted messages on dating sites."

"Then you're gonna check out those two a bit more and get back to us with whatever you find?" Dirk asked Tammy.

When she nodded, he said, "Okay. Thanks. By the way, I've got a little something of my own to report. Today I went back out to the crime scene, looked around. CSU had been pretty thorough. I didn't see anything new there. But I did go next door and talk to the teenage kid and his dad."

"Shane and Dylan Keller?" Tammy said, again wearing her self-satisfied smirk. "Both of whom were arrested for assault after a road rage incident in Nevada. They weren't tried for it because the guy they beat up dropped the charges right before the trial began."

Dirk stared at her for a moment and said, "They didn't mention that today."

"No, I don't suppose they did. I doubt they shared the fact that, until eight days ago, Shane Keller was president of the H.O.A. there in Joya del Mar. He was given his walking papers after he threatened another member of the board with great physical harm. Something about stomping a mud hole in his, um, backside, then knocking him into next Monday."

Everyone at the table turned to look at Savannah.

"What?" she said. "Y'all figure, 'cause he said that, Keller's a good ol' boy from Georgia? I didn't get that impression the other day when we talked. No drawl a'-tall."

"Shane Keller struck me as a guy with a crap attitude that gets him in trouble at least seven or eight times a week," Dirk said, "and he's taught his bad manners to his kid. But I don't hold it against them that they hated their neighbor. They did mention that during that ruckus with the dog, Erling hit Dylan. Hard. They showed me a picture of the bruise on his cheekbone."

"Did Erling happen to backhand him?" Savannah asked.

Dirk nodded. "That's probably where Erling got that bruise on the back of his hand that Dr. Liu showed us."

"I didn't think that looked like a defense wound." Savannah mulled it over then shook her head. "I can't see Shane Keller going to a lot of trouble to get his hands on a deadly drug and then sneak it into Erling's birthday champagne toast. His son either. Seems like if they were going to kill him, they'd just use a tire iron or sic Webster on him or drown him out there some night in the ocean when nobody was watching. Poison just sounds too complicated for knuckleheads like those two."

"I thought the same thing when I left their house," Dirk agreed. "I think we can cross them off our list, or at least, move them down toward the bottom."

"Okay, let's divvy up the chores." Savannah turned to Tammy. "Tamitha, you did some good work, finding out that stuff about Melissa and Jerry. Anything else you can dig up would be helpful."

To Dirk, she said, "If either of those two are in town and we can find them, would you like me to go with you to question them?"

"Sure," he replied. "Twin Oaks is a bit of a drive, and I wouldn't mind some company. After we drop the kid off at school tomorrow morning?"

"That works for me." Turning to Ryan and John, she said, "We don't have any homework for you two yet. Which is a good thing, considering all you're doing with Alma and Ethan. You've got your hands full already."

"With lovely things, rather than murder," John replied. "But don't hesitate to ask us. You must know by now, we enjoy uncovering a villain as much as anyone here."

Chapter 28

At nine o'clock the next morning, Savannah and Dirk were standing at the door of Melissa and Jerald Becker's Mediterranean home in the rural community of Twin Oaks.

A few miles inland from San Carmelita, Twin Oaks provided the luxuries of beautiful desert vistas, as well as open hills and arroyos that were perfect for hiking or horseback riding.

The town's upscale homes sat on large acreage parcels and were bordered by rough-cut, post-and-rail fences.

The quaint shopping area's Rodeo Drive and Fifth Avenue-level stores reminded all passing through town that those living in Twin Oaks were hardly your average country folk.

"I don't think nurses make enough money to afford

a house like this," Savannah said as they waited for someone to answer Dirk's resounding knock. "Not even surgical nurses who work for world-famous neurosurgeons. Jerry must be a pretty successful lawyer."

"Did Tammy find out what kinda lawyer?"

"Yeah. Divorce."

Dirk grumbled something under his breath, expressing his less-than-stellar opinion of attorneys, then he knocked again, considerably harder than before.

Immediately, the door flew open, startling them both. They jumped back to avoid something large that was coming at them, fast and hard.

Savannah even saw Dirk reach inside his jacket and touch his shoulder holster where he kept his Smith & Wesson revolver.

Instead of the lady of the house or a member of the staff, they saw that the door had been thrown open by several burly workmen who were in the process of moving an extremely large, and no-doubt heavy, armoire. They grunted and swore, as they wrestled the enormous piece of furniture, trying to get it through the door.

Unfortunately for them, the armoire was rectangular, and the doorway arched.

"Like trying to get a round peg through a square hole," Savannah said as she watched them attempt what appeared to be impossible.

Dirk stepped forward. "Can I give you a hand with that?" he asked.

One gave him a curt nod, and he joined the battle.

From where Savannah stood, she knew they wouldn't make it. Not with a dozen Dirks. She wanted to tell them so and save them a lot of sweat and even blood; one of the guy's knuckles had sprung a leak after his hand was trapped between the corner of the piece and the door hardware.

"Hold on! What the hell are you guys doing there!" yelled an extremely loud and excited female voice from farther inside the house. "Wait a damn minute! You're going to break that piece or destroy my door! Stop that!"

They set the armoire down and turned toward the tiny woman with a platinum blond bob. She was practically flying down the stairs, her hands fluttering like she was trying to take flight.

Savannah wriggled past the armoire and into the room. She wanted a much better view of this new development.

"You idiots!" the blonde screamed as she ran toward them.

More specifically, toward Dirk.

"Don't you know anything at all about moving furniture?" she shouted at him, practically shaking with rage.

Dirk gave her one of his best Elvis half smirks and said calmly, "No, actually, I don't know much about furniture because I'm a—"

"That much is obvious!" She gave each of the sweaty men a nasty look, one after another, including the guy whose hand was bleeding. "You are supposed to take this piece apart before you move it! It divides into five sections, unless you're too stupid to figure out how."

The men glanced at the armoire, at each other, then at Dirk.

He threw up his hands and shook his head. "Don't look at me. I just offered to help with the 'muscle' part. If you need somebody to think, count me out."

He turned to the woman, pulled his badge from his

pocket, and flipped it open so she could read it. "I'm Detective Sergeant Dirk Coulter with the San Carmelita Police Department. Are you Melissa Becker?"

She nodded. Reluctantly. "Ye-e-s, why?"

"I can see you're busy here," he said, looking around the room that was filled with half-packed boxes and miscellaneous mess, "but I need to speak to you for a few minutes."

"What about?" she snapped.

"Murder," he replied just as curtly.

Savannah watched the woman's red face lose its rosy tone in seconds, blanching to a sickly pallor usually seen on those who were suffering the worst moments of a stomach flu.

When she didn't respond, Dirk added, "Is there someplace we could talk? Someplace a bit more private?"

That seemed to jar the woman out of her trance. She shook her head, as though coming awake, and said, "Yes. Okay. Follow me." To the workers she said, "If you can't figure out how to take that apart and move it properly, just leave it where you found it and tell Jerry I said, 'Too bad. You don't get to take *everything,* divorce attorney or not.' "

As she led Dirk and Savannah out of the entryway, into a great room and on through some large glass doors into a tropical garden, Melissa made no eye contact with them at all. Nor did she say anything. At least, not aloud. But she was mumbling to herself in tones that sounded argumentative.

To Savannah, she appeared to be practicing the responses she would soon have to give.

Although Savannah was thirsty and would have appreciated some sort of offer of refreshment, she didn't expect any displays of hospitality from Melissa Becker.

Obviously, the woman was in the midst of moving and splitting up her household with her soon-to-be ex-husband.

No one was their "gracious hostess/best self" at a time like that.

But Melissa was even less hospitable than Savannah expected. Neither she nor Dirk were even invited to have a seat.

"Okay. What?" Melissa asked as she came to a stop beside a giant bird-of-paradise plant and stood with her arms crossed over the front of her gauze tunic with its embroidered pastel flowers.

A pretty top and pretty lady, Savannah thought, noticing that, just as Dr. Liu had described, Nurse Melissa had big eyes and a Betty Boop mouth. *Too bad she's such a Miss Cranky Pants.*

Dirk crossed his own arms and said, "I'm investigating a homicide—"

"So you said, and . . . ?"

"You knew the victim."

"Stephen Erling?"

"Yes."

"Unfortunately, I knew him, and I also worked for him."

"Yes, I know." Dirk gave her a dark look. "In fact, Mrs. Becker, we know quite a bit about your relationship with Dr. Erling. You two were very close, both in the operating room and, well, elsewhere, too."

For the first time, Melissa seemed to notice Savannah.

She wasn't pleased.

"Who is she? Is she the one who told you that crap? It's not true. Not at all."

"This is Savannah Reid. She's assisting me today, and the people who told us all about you and Erling are extremely reliable. I believe every word they said."

"Who? Who told you that?"

"You don't know their names," Savannah told her. "But they're professional people who have no reason to lie or speak badly of you. They just told us what they saw."

"Which is what?"

Savannah could swear she could hear Melissa's voice shaking. But her stance was just as belligerent and her tone just as nasty.

"They saw it all, Mrs. Becker," Dirk said in his exasperated voice. "So, let's drop the innocent maiden routine here and get down to brass tacks. I couldn't care less what you and Erling were up to. That was between the two of you and maybe your mates. None of my business. But somebody murdered him, and that *is* my business."

She didn't reply, other than to glare at him.

He continued. "We know that you accompanied Dr. Erling to a number of parties, gatherings where everyone there knew that he was married to Dr. Carolyn Erling."

"She was busy and couldn't go with him. I attended strictly in a business capacity."

"Was it business when you accompanied him, his steady partner no less, to private sex clubs?"

Melissa gasped, and for a moment, Savannah thought she might faint and got ready to catch her, if necessary, before she hit the ground.

"Yeah, we know about that stuff," Dirk replied, sounding pretty pleased with himself.

Savannah spoke up. "Seriously. We don't give a hoot what you and Erling did in those clubs. We're just trying to solve a murder."

"If I did that sort of thing," Dirk said, "my wife could kill me. But hey, if you, Erling, his wife, and your husband were all fine with it . . ."

Her silence confirmed everything Savannah suspected. She decided to press on. "But maybe your husband *wasn't* very happy about it. We hear he got mad as hell about the way Erling was acting toward you at a certain, high-society fundraiser."

"Was that the night Jerry figured out what was between you?" Dirk asked.

Melissa gave a small nod, and her large eyes grew misty.

"Is that why he's got those guys moving stuff out of here?" Savannah suggested.

"Yes." Melissa took a couple of faltering steps toward a chaise and collapsed onto it. Every trace of her former bravado gone. "That was the night he found out, and that was the beginning of the end."

Savannah pulled a chair close to the chaise and sat down. "I'm sorry," she told Melissa as she handed her a tissue. "I've heard that Stephen Erling was a hard guy to say no to. With him being your boss—"

"That made it impossible. Stephen wasn't all that charming. But he did have a way of getting what he wanted. He was relentless."

"Tell me about it," Savannah said. "We want to hear your side."

"There isn't all that much to it." She sniffed and

wiped her eyes. "Only a few weeks after he hired me, Stephen made it clear he wanted to be with me. You know, intimately."

Savannah gave her a knowing, sympathetic nod. "Gotcha. Go on."

"At first it was kinda flattering, him being so good-looking, superrich, powerful, and all that. But he was no fun at all to be with. In any way, in any situation."

"I can imagine that."

"But when I tried to break it off, at least the, um, sexual part, he let me know in no uncertain terms that he'd make up some excuse and fire me."

"You should've sued him before he died."

"I wouldn't have done that to Jerry. He's been through enough because of me and that guy already."

"Did your husband make you quit your job?" Dirk asked.

She seemed surprised that he had guessed, then said, "Yes. He told me, if I wanted to stay married to him, I'd never be in the same room with Stephen again. He said I was such a good nurse that I'd find another position right away. But of course, I didn't. I had to use Stephen as a reference, and he told them he'd fired me for being drunk on the job. He blamed me for the lawsuit that's being brought against him right now."

She paused, then added, "Well, it was in the works. Now that he's dead, I don't know if Mr. Willis will continue with the case. But if Stephen had lived, he probably would have lost his practice over it."

"Who's Mr. Willis?" Dirk asked, taking out his notebook and pencil.

"Mr. James Willis. He lives in Santa Barbara."

"Why was Mr. Willis suing Erling?" Savannah asked.

"Because Stephen made a bad error while performing a craniotomy on Grace Willis. His wife. The surgery wasn't a complicated one. At least, not as brain surgeries go. A small brain tumor, within easy reach, benign. But Stephen had a few drinks before, and I believe they affected his dexterity and his judgment. Poor Grace was far worse after the surgery than before."

"I can understand why Mr. Willis was seeking some sort of compensation," Savannah said.

"I guess Willis was pretty mad at your former boss," Dirk said. "If he'd done that to my wife, I'd be wanting to take him apart at the seams."

"Oh, Mr. Willis made plenty of threats like that, too. In fact, Stephen got a restraining order against him."

"Really?" Savannah perked up. "The judge must have thought Willis was a genuine threat to Erling, to have given him an R.O."

"Yes. I do believe Mr. Willis would have hurt Stephen if he could have." She thought for a moment then locked eyes with Savannah. "You don't think Mr. Willis might have been the one who murdered Stephen, do you?"

Dirk was scribbling, but he answered, "Don't know yet. Right now, I'm just finding out where everybody was the night the doctor died." He looked up from his writing and watched her closely as he asked, "Where were you and Jerry?"

"We had dinner with friends at The Oyster Shell, then we went to their house for the evening. Played card games. Listened to their golden oldies music collection."

"What are their names?" Dirk asked.

"Maggie and Ralph Johnson. They live two doors down, if you want to ask them."

When Dirk had finished writing, he said, "Okay, so you were with the Johnsons on Wednesday. How about two Wednesdays before that, the evening of the fifth?"

Melissa didn't take long to answer. "We went to dinner and then to a movie."

Her response was so fast that Savannah wondered if it was because she was telling the simple truth, and had a great mental calendar, or because she had her reply all prepared.

"Which movie?" Dirk asked.

"*The Lady in the Fog.*"

Again, Savannah thought the response a bit too quick. Or maybe not. It was hard to tell. She said, "Was it any good?"

"What?"

"The movie. I thought I might go see it. Should I?"

Melissa shrugged. "It was so-so. I wasn't feeling well that night, and I went to sleep during it. Ask my husband. He stayed awake for it all."

"We will," Dirk said. "Which theater?"

"The multiplex next to the mall."

"Which showing?"

Melissa thought for a moment. "We went to dinner around seven o'clock, so it was probably the nine o'clock viewing."

"Would you happen to have your ticket stubs? Did you keep them?"

"They might be in my purse. Would you like me to look?"

"Yes," Dirk told her. He glanced at Savannah and added, "Please."

Melissa rose from her chair, and they followed her back into the house.

Once inside, Melissa saw two movers carrying an enormous mirror. A third worker bopped around a corner and nearly fell right into the center of the glass, missing by an inch at best.

"That's it! Get out of my house!" she screamed. "Now! You're all fired."

"But, but," one of them stammered, "you aren't the one paying us. *He* is."

"Ou-u-u-ut!"

They laid the mirror on the floor and ran for the door.

Not for the first time, Savannah wondered at the power of diminutive people. Maybe because of their size, they learned early to use their voices and the force of their personality to get what they wanted and needed from a world that might, otherwise, ignore them.

She decided to take a lesson from Lissa aka Melissa Becker.

The now surprisingly calm lady of the house walked over to a coat closet, opened the door, and reached inside.

A moment later, she had opened her Louis Vuitton bag and pulled out a couple of movie theater admission tickets.

"Good thing I hadn't cleaned out my purse yet, huh?" she said as she proudly handed them over to Dirk.

Savannah could see over his shoulder that they were, indeed, for that multiplex theater near the mall, *The Lady in the Fog*, at nine P.M., on the night the drugs were stolen from Carolyn's clinic.

Both Melissa and Jerald Becker had solid alibis for both nights.

Just peachy, she thought. *Reckon we're back to "Carolyn must've done it."*

She looked ovcr at Dirk and could see the frustration in his eyes.

She knew he was thinking the exact same thing.

Chapter 29

After leaving the Beckers' home and driving back to San Carmelita, Savannah and Dirk stopped at their favorite fish restaurant which also happened to be situated on one of their favorite places—San Carmelita's pier.

Over baskets of fish and chips, disturbed only occasionally by the odd seagull bombing their table and snatching their french fries, they discussed their conversation with Melissa.

"They may have the perfect alibis for both nights in question," Dirk said, "but she's hiding something. I can tell."

"With her complicated lifestyle, I suspect she's been hiding a lot for a long time. Maybe she'll have to practice 'open and honest' awhile before she gets the knack of it."

"No." He shook his head as he dragged several fries through an enormous puddle of ketchup and popped them into his mouth. "She had her alibi answers right there, on the tip of her tongue, and she wasted no time pulling those tickets out and flashing them under my nose. I could swear she was humming, 'Nanny, nanny, boo, boo' under her breath when she did it, too."

"Yes," Savannah agreed. "I sensed a bit of a 'Gotcha' attitude in play, too."

"She or he or both of them could've gone over there and bought the tickets. Nothing says they stayed for the show. She couldn't even tell you if the movie was good or not."

"That occurred to me, too."

They both looked at each other, swatted away a gull, and said, "Security video."

"I'll take you back home, then go to the theater and check out their footage if they still have it," he told her.

"I'll ask Tammy to get a good photo of Jerry Becker and text it to you first—something better than his DMV shot—so you'll know who you're looking for."

"Okay. Thanks." He downed the last of his root beer float and reached over to nab some of her fries. "I'm hopin' I can get hold of that James Willis guy and have him come down to the station for a chat. I need to see for myself what sorta dude he is, and whether he's got an alibi all ready for me like that Lissa gal."

"Good idea. At least one judge thought he was a threat, so it's worth looking into."

He reached for another fry, a big, long, perfectly cooked one, that she'd been saving for her last. She grabbed it before he could and shoved it into her mouth. "Once you drop me off," she said, "I'm going to drive over to see Carolyn and give her an update."

"Another interrogation disguised as an update?"

She shrugged. "That makes me feel like the world's shadiest and least client-loyal P.I. in the world, but yes. She's probably at the clinic."

"Actually, she's probably home."

"Home? In Joya del Mar?"

"Yeah, CSU was done, so I cleared her to go back. I called her first thing this morning, before you got up."

"I have to stop sleeping in. I miss too much."

"Sleep all you need to, darlin'," he told her with a concerned look on his face. "You're burning your firecracker at both ends, and you're likely to either explode or fizzle out before your time."

"I thought it was a candle that gets burned at both ends."

"Some gals are candles. Most, I'd say. But I got lucky. I've got myself a firecracker!"

When Savannah pulled her Mustang into the driveway of Carolyn's seaside home, the first thing she noticed was that the Lamborghini was gone.

Probably in the garage, she thought.

She wouldn't help wondering if, at that moment, Carolyn was loading Stephen Erling's knickers into plastic donation bags.

Savannah wouldn't blame her. If he'd been her husband, Savannah would have been quite happy to haul everything he owned and anything that reminded her of him to the curb on garbage day.

Maybe even his cremains, if there wasn't some sort of ordinance against it.

As she got out of the Mustang, she glanced around, half expecting to see Dylan or Shane walking Webster.

She was glad not to. Just the brief talk she'd had with Shane the other day had been enough. Maybe, with any luck, she could avoid him for the rest of her life.

Long ago, Savannah had learned the wisdom of limiting those she allowed to breathe the same oxygen as her. Meanness was contagious. So was negativity and anxiety. Why expose yourself if you could possibly avoid it? She'd discovered that, with practice, it became easier and easier to avoid those folks, and life became far more pleasant and peaceful for having done so.

As she walked over the bridge and looked down at the koi, Savannah wished for a moment she had Brody with her. Funny, how seeing things through a little boy's eyes made one's world so much brighter. Even down to the color of the fins on an exotic fish.

As she walked up to the door, Savannah couldn't resist a glance through the floor-to-ceiling windows. It made her feel a bit like a Peeping Tom, but not enough for her to resist the urge.

She was surprised to see Carolyn standing in the middle of the room, vacuuming the floor with an oversized upright cleaner. Her pixie hair was pulled back from her face with a blue kerchief, and she was wearing a simple white T-shirt and jeans.

Savannah thought she looked more like the weekly cleaning lady than the mistress of a fine house.

Patiently, Savannah waited at the front door until she heard the vacuum stop, then she knocked.

I probably should've called first, she thought when Carolyn didn't answer right away. But she quickly dismissed the notion. She'd discovered, years ago, that if you wanted truthful answers from someone, it was best not to give them a heads-up that you were coming. Less rehearsal time that way.

After what seemed like a long time, Savannah heard footsteps and Carolyn opened the door. She had a large, dark smudge of what looked like the CSU's latent fingerprint dust on her cheek. But she was smiling and seemed more relaxed than Savannah could recall ever seeing her.

"Savannah!" she said, as though greeting a lifelong friend, whom she hadn't seen in ages. "Come on in!"

She threw the door wide and ushered Savannah inside.

Looking around at the disarray and the dark dust all around the fireplace, its mantel, hearth, and nearby furniture, Savannah's heart sank.

"Oh, Carolyn, I'm so sorry," she said. "I hate it when they leave the families with messes like this."

"That's okay. I don't mind."

"Well, I would! I'd feel like jerking some knots in some tails if I walked in and found this in my home."

Savannah reached down and picked up a dusting cloth from an end table. "At least I can do some dusting while we talk."

"No, Savannah. Thank you, but—"

"I don't mind a bit and if both of us jump on it, we'll get 'er done in no time."

Carolyn reached over and gently pulled the cloth from Savannah's hand. "To be honest, I'm enjoying the cleaning. It feels . . . symbolic . . . somehow."

Savannah nodded, understanding. "I noticed the Lamborghini wasn't out front."

"Back to the dealership," Carolyn said, "where it belongs. We never needed a vehicle like that. It cost more than my first house!"

"Yeah, that's always been one of my personal mottos: Never buy a car that's the price of a house."

Of course, not being a famous neurosurgeon, movie star, or rock singer, Savannah had never been tempted to violate her conscience in such a way. It was easy to convince yourself that you were above all that.

Materialism.

It was easy to avoid, easy to resist.

Unless, of course, you knew all the cool stuff that money could buy out there in the world.

"I need to take a breather," Carolyn said, whipping the bandana off her head and running her fingers through her hair. "How about we go out back and have a beer?"

"Make mine a soda or tea, and you've got a deal."

A few minutes later, Savannah and Carolyn were sitting in big, comfortable, Adirondack chairs down on the beach in front of the house. Savannah had a sweetened green tea in hand. *One that Tammy might actually approve,* she thought, *since it's organic and honeyed rather than sugared.*

Carolyn had nearly drained her beer before they even started talking. She seemed so relaxed, so peaceful, that Savannah had to admit it: the young widow appeared happy to be so.

"My husband and I went to Twin Oaks today," Savannah said, throwing it out with a light tone and watching closely to see how Carolyn would react.

She didn't. Not at all. She just took another swig of beer, closed her eyes, held it in her mouth, and savored it for a long while before swallowing it.

"I spoke to Melissa Becker," Savannah added.

"Okay, and . . . ?"

"She and her husband are splitting up. He's leaving her."

Carolyn leaned down, pulled a footrest over, and propped her legs on it. "Not surprising," she said. "Stephen ruined a lot of marriages besides his own. Some guys play golf to relax. He seduced other men's women, then made sure the guys found out about it. Gave him a real thrill, being one up on them that way."

"Sounds pretty awful."

"He was."

"Also sounds dangerous."

"He got a lot of threats. Sometimes he'd come home from wherever and tell me to pack a bag, we were leaving for the Bahamas, or Paris . . . or Marrakesh, if he was *really* in trouble. At first, I thought he was impetuous, spontaneous, and romantic. Then we'd come back, he'd get some ugly phone calls at night or a subpoena server would show up at the door. Once in a while, there'd be a guy banging at the doors and windows, screaming obscenities. Stephen would tell me not to answer it and not to call the cops. He'd make me just stay in the bedroom until the man left."

"What a way to live."

"He loved it. He thrived on conflict and drama."

"Ugh. No thank you. Had enough of both to last me a lifetime."

"Me, too."

Savannah looked out across the sparkling Pacific and watched what looked like sheets of fine lace, sprinkled with diamond dust, glittering atop the waves.

"I think you're going to have some peace in your life now, Carolyn. Maybe you can find happiness just being here in this beautiful home, your home, with your animals. Maybe it will be enough for a while—home and the clinic, the animals who need you. Not a lot of pesky human beings muddying up the crystal-clear waters of your spirit."

"Wouldn't that be lovely?" she said with a sigh. "To have nothing to worry about but caring for myself and my patients. Ah-h. I could get used to that."

"I hope you will. Very soon."

Savannah thought of Dirk and wondered if he'd had any luck looking at the theater's security videos or if he'd been able to talk to James Willis.

"I suppose," she said, "that you're familiar with a fellow by the name of James Willis."

"I am now," Carolyn replied, looking annoyed. "I hadn't been home even five minutes when a process server knocked on the door. Stupid me, I answered and took the papers he held out. Apparently, this Mr. Willis is suing Stephen's estate—which, I guess, is now me—for damages. Something having to do with a surgery on his wife that went wrong."

"Then you don't know Mr. Willis personally?"

"Never laid eyes on the man. Though I do feel bad if there's any merit to his case."

"You think there might be?"

"Absolutely. Stephen was good, but he wasn't as good as he claimed to be. He thought if he said something enough times, that made it true. It was shocking to see how many people believed him."

"A forceful personality can bumfuzzle folks quicker than ducks can snap up June bugs. But back to Mr. Willis. You hadn't met him or heard about him until today, until you got that subpoena?"

"No. That was our introduction. Hopefully, by the time he's done suing me, I'll still have a home."

"The surgery was on his wife, Grace," Savannah said gently. "Apparently, Stephen operated on a small, benign, accessible tumor, and she hasn't been the same since mentally. Word is, Stephen may have been drinking when he performed the surgery."

Carolyn closed her eyes and shook her head. When she finally opened them, she said, "If Mr. Willis lost his wife because her mind was destroyed by a routine surgery, then me losing this place is nothing compared to that poor man's situation."

Chapter 30

Savannah and Dirk stood on either side of the back-yard grill, each attempting to fulfill their chosen "dinner duties."

The picnic table bore the fruits of Savannah's labors: a potato salad, a platter of thickly sliced, vine-ripened, beefsteak tomatoes drizzled with balsamic vinaigrette, and fresh onion rolls.

On the grill—and smoking so badly that Savannah half expected the fire brigade to appear at any moment—was Dirk's tri-tip. The enormous cut of meat had been marinating all night in its bath of teriyaki sauce, red wine, and Worcestershire sauce, and it had smelled divine even before Dirk put it on the fire.

Savannah glanced at her watch. Alma and Ethan could arrive at any minute, and after everyone's busy day, they were bound to be hungry.

She decided to throw the foil-wrapped corn on the cob into the coals. They and the tri-tip should be finished about the same time.

"When's that meat gonna be done?" Brody asked as he streaked by, wearing his swim trunks. He was on his way to the sprinkler that was spraying the flower garden.

"It'll be finished in about thirty minutes," she told him, "but we're waiting for company, so—"

"Yeah! Freddy's coming! Yee haw!"

"Watch out for my peonies!" she shouted as he plunged into the spray, cutting a wild Irish jig, like a tiny leprechaun who had just discovered a pot of gold.

"I will," he said. "You don't need to tell me about the dadgum peonies no more! I got it!"

"Don't get fresh there, buddy," Dirk called out to him. Then he turned to her and said, "He's got it. You don't need to nag him about it anymore. I guarantee you that he'll remember not to step on peonies for the rest of his life."

She looked at Dirk, then at the kid whose flying feet were coming perilously close to her prize blossoms. But not touching. "I'm not sure if I like this new ratio of testosterone to estrogen in this household. Before it was just me and the kitties. Girls all. Now we've got male hormones running amuck all through the place. I feel like us gals are slipping a bit."

"Bwahaha. Before you know it, we'll be scratching our butts and belching to our heart's delight."

"I could start polishing my nails when you're home, right under your overly sensitive nose, while you're trying to enjoy a game."

"Passive aggression."

"Better than active aggression."

"Yours? Yes." He shuddered. "I've seen you actively aggressive. Not a pretty sight."

"Like when we were undercover as old street people and had to take down those bank robbers?"

"Yeah. I wouldn't have thought anybody could do that much harm with a lightweight, aluminum walker."

Having situated the corn the way she wanted it, Savannah handed Dirk a beer, then sat down at the picnic table and began to drink a glass of iced tea.

"Tell me about the quality, personal time you spent with Willis," she said. "Anything good?"

"Nothing to get excited about. At all. While the Erling birthday party was going on, Willis was at a fundraiser, given by some friends of his. They were trying to help him with his wife's medical bills. One of which was Erling's bill for thirty thousand dollars. Willis didn't mind telling me how bitter he is to owe the guy anything other than maybe a bullet. He told me in no uncertain terms that he would enjoy turning Stephen Erling into the mentally diminished person his wife is now."

"That's pretty bitter. But if Grace was someone I loved, I'd probably feel the same. An accident is one thing. That can happen to anyone, even a doctor. But drunk on the job? No, that's a choice. Willis has every right to his anger."

"I agree. I don't blame him for how he feels. But if he acted on those feelings, that's another matter altogether."

"But he was at a fundraiser? That's a pretty solid alibi. There'd be a ton of witnesses. Probably photos and videos, too."

"He could've hired somebody to do it. He looks like a guy with a few shekels put away."

"Any kind of record?"

"None. A clean life. At least on paper."

Savannah thought back on her conversation with Carolyn regarding Willis. "He's suing Carolyn," she said. "The funny thing is that she doesn't seem to care. As long as she has some sort of roof over her head and her clinic, I think she'd be happy."

He sat down across the table from her and took a long drink of his beer. "Didja get anything else outta her?"

"Yes. I asked her about that gal Patrice."

"The redhead you saw at the party?"

"Yes. The one who used to work for Carolyn there in the clinic, then didn't, but does again."

"You got some weird vibes offa her, right?"

"I did. So I 'squeezed' Carolyn about her, as you would say."

"What came out?"

They both winced as a spray of water came their way, thanks to Brody rearranging a nearby sprinkler.

"Hey, noodle head!" Savannah yelled. "Knock it off! You're gonna get my food wet and put out the barbecue fire."

Brody expressed his shame with a fit of giggles while he returned the sprinkler to its original position.

Savannah grabbed a paper napkin and wiped off her face. "As I was saying before that unexpected cloudburst," she continued, "Patrice worked for Carolyn as a vet assistant for a while and both seemed to enjoy their arrangement. Then Patrice had an unpleasant run-in with Stephen, and he fired her on the spot."

"What sort of run-in?" Dirk asked.

"An honest-to-goodness, literal run-in. Carolyn said the staff was having some sort of emergency. They were scurrying around the clinic, all in a hurry. Patrice was carrying an uncovered urine specimen in a cup. She came rushing around a corner, ran right into Stephen, and spilled a large amount of Saint Bernard pee all over the front of his brand-new bespoke suit."

Dirk laughed. "Oh darn."

"Yeah. Terrible."

"But how could Erling fire Patrice? She was his wife's employee."

"I don't think he gave a hoot about such things as staying out of your spouse's personal business. Carolyn told me that she regretted not standing up for her employee. She's thrilled that Patrice agreed to come back, and any hard feelings that were between them appear to be gone."

"Then where is Patrice on our suspect list?"

"I guess close to the bottom. All I had was a weird feeling about her. But hearing what happened with Stephen, it all came together. Like why he was so mad that Patrice had dropped by his birthday party to pick up her check."

"Was Patrice working at the clinic at the time of the break-in?"

"No, she'd already been fired."

"Where was she that night?"

"Carolyn said the two of them met for a glass of wine at El Viñedo, that nice, new bar down on the beach. She said they drank and talked until the place closed at eleven."

"That's not much of an alibi for Patrice. She could have broken into the place any time after she left Carolyn and before the clinic opened the next morning. Or Carolyn could have been lying to cover for Patrice."

"Or herself or both of them," Savannah added.

He finished his beer, stood, and walked over to the grill. He opened the lid and began to baste the tri-tip with more marinade.

"How about the movie theater security videos?" she asked, watching him. "Any sign of Melissa and Jerry?"

"Both. Clear as can be. Going into the complex at ten to nine. Leaving three minutes after the movie ended at eleven-o-five."

"Darn."

"Yeah."

"What if they snuck out a back door after it started and came back before it ended?"

"I thought of that. I called Ryan and asked him if he'd pull some of his strings at the bureau and find out if their phones were there at the movie the whole time."

"Good idea."

"Hello! Hello!" shouted a deep voice as the side gate to the backyard opened and Alma, Freddy, and Ethan came through. "Ah, there you are," Ethan said.

"We just followed our noses," Alma added. "It smells like heaven back here!"

"Dirk's been working on that for half an hour," Savannah told them, pointing to the grill. "Your timing is perfect. The tri-tip's almost done."

Brody came bounding across the yard, dripping wet from his sprinkler adventures. He ran straight for Freddy and said, "Do you have your swimsuit with you, buddy? I hope so. We can run around in the rain!"

Ethan looked at Alma, who shook her head. "I'm sorry, Brody," Ethan told him. "We didn't pack a suit for him, but we've got spare diapers."

"He can play in the water in a diaper?"

"He certainly can."

Alma knelt to remove Freddy's shirt, shorts, shoes, and socks, and a moment later, the three-year-old was running with Brody to the flower garden.

"I'm going to go relocate that sprinkler," Dirk said, "before one of those boys steps on a peony and incurs my wife's wrath."

"Savannah takes her peonies very, very seriously," Alma told Ethan, who was obviously pretending to be interested.

Savannah noticed him glancing back at the gate a couple of times. She offered him one of Dirk's beers and said, "Paparazzi problems again?"

"Yeah," he said. "I don't know how they got wind of our wedding, but they did, and now they're popping up everywhere."

"Literally out of bushes!" Alma said. "I never saw the likes of it. A couple of them was hiding in our oleanders when I took some trash out this morning. I was in my robe, my hair hanging down, just minding my own business when there they were, taking my picture." She sighed and shook her head. "If I'd known they were going to be there to greet me so early in the day, I'd have at least brushed my hair and worn one of my pretty robes."

Ethan gave her a sideways hug as they settled down at the picnic table. "I'm sorry, honey. I hate it that you have to put up with this."

"It's part of the job of being Mrs. Ethan Malloy, and considering the perks, I don't mind."

Savannah slid a large bowl of tortilla chips and smaller bowls of guacamole and salsa over to them. "I hate it that either one of you has to deal with rude people. But those photographers can sell a picture of Ethan Malloy's bride-to-be for fifty thousand bucks, maybe more if she's in an unattractive bathrobe."

"Infuriating but true," Ethan said. "That's why we just came from ReJuvene. We had a really great offer from Ryan and John, and we've decided to take them up on it."

"What's that?" Dirk asked, rejoining them at the table.

"We were over there, talking about food just now, and we mentioned that the paparazzi knows we're getting married, even our venue, and they're all over us. Twenty-four-seven."

"What was the really great offer they made you?" Savannah asked, having a pretty good idea what it was, but knowing they would want to make the announcement.

"They said we could move the whole thing, the ceremony and the dinner and party afterward, to their place."

"The restaurant?" Dirk asked.

"No," Alma replied. "That gorgeous old mansion they've been restoring."

"Yuck." Dirk shuddered. "That place was a junkyard, the world's worst hoard when that old gal died. Don't tell me they've got it cleaned out already."

"Cleaned out, refurbished, and refurnished. It's absolutely breathtaking," Ethan said. "The perfect place for a wedding."

"The paparazzi have no idea that you're changing venues," Savannah said. "Brilliant! I love it!"

"I like the idea of us marrying in a friend's house rather than a chapel-for-hire," Ethan continued, "and having our reception in our friends' home instead of a sterile, soulless catering hall. I'm very happy about the change, and more importantly, the bride is, too."

Savannah had been wondering about something, but she'd been afraid to ask. Something told her she shouldn't, but her curiosity often triumphed over her virtue.

"Ethan," she began, "are your parents going to be able to join us for the wedding?"

He looked a bit sad, and for a moment she regretted that she had brought it up.

"No," he said. "They aren't in very good health, and flying is such a miserable experience these days. Needless to say, driving from Texas would be an ordeal for them, too. We'll go there and visit soon."

"Oh, I'm so sorry," Savannah said. What she didn't say was that she'd seen pictures of Ethan's parents, and they didn't look old or particularly infirm. She was sure that, if they really wanted to fly, Ethan would arrange luxurious transportation for them. Either first-class accommodation on a commercial flight or even a private plane.

She recalled when she and Ethan had first met, he'd told her that he and his father had disagreed strongly about his career choice. His dad was a self-made cattle rancher, who was horrified to hear that his son wanted to be an actor rather than continue the family business.

Unfortunately, having his son win an Oscar, Emmy, and Golden Globe, not to mention become one of the highest paid actors in history, hadn't changed Dad Malloy's mind.

Savannah felt sorry for the Ethan and for the father who had chosen his own ambitions over his son's dream and lost his boy in the process.

What a loss it was, too, Savannah thought as she watched the way Ethan anticipated Alma's every desire, passing her chips, getting her a napkin, filling her glass with tea, and gazing at her lovingly between each action. She saw the way his eyes lit up when his son and Brody came running by, splashing water everywhere, laughing.

She laughed when he grabbed his boy, hugged him, and got soaked for his troubles.

Ethan Malloy was a true family man. If his own family had been foolish enough to turn their backs on him, then their loss was the Reid clan's gain.

"By the way," Ethan said, turning to Dirk, "we have an important message to give you from Ryan."

"What's that?"

"It doesn't make a lot of sense to me, but he said you'd understand."

"Shoot."

"He said to tell you, 'Both phones were inside the theater the whole time the movie was playing.' "

"Oh. Okay. Gotcha."

"Is that code?" Alma asked. "Like 'the fox has now entered the chicken coop' or 'Red Bear has engaged—most meaningfully—with Blue Eagle'?"

"We're cops," Dirk told her. "Not spies. We've got 10-codes when we want to say something sneaky."

"Ten-four, good buddy!" Brody shouted as he sailed by in pursuit of his younger friend, who was on his way back to the sprinklers for another dousing.

"We've gotta watch what we say a little closer," Savannah said. "That kid doesn't miss a thing."

Chapter 31

After their company had left and the kitchen was cleaned, Savannah, Dirk, and Brody settled down for a quick Disney film before bed.

As usual, Savannah was in her chair with Diamante, and the "boys" were sprawled on the sofa with Cleo.

Usually, this was one of Brody's favorite times of the day. But tonight he seemed subdued and thoughtful.

Finally, Savannah paused the video and said, "Is there anything I can get you guys before we hit the sheets? Some hot chocolate or . . . ?"

"No, thank you," Brody said. "I'm okay."

He wasn't okay. Savannah knew that. Mr. Brody Greyson never refused food and especially anything with chocolate in it.

She liked to think he took after her side of the family in that respect.

"Is somethin' up, son?" Dirk asked, obviously as aware as she was of the change in the child's mood.

"Yeah. I like this show, but . . ."

"But what?" Savannah prompted.

"Remember when you guys told me before that if I wanted to ask you something I could?"

"Sure. That's one of those forever offers," she assured him. "It never expires."

"Good, 'cause I wanna ask you something about Ethan and Alma."

"All right." Dirk nudged him in the ribs with his elbow. "Speak up. Whaddya wanna know?"

"Ethan said his parents aren't coming to the wedding."

"That's true. They aren't," Savannah admitted, though she warned herself that anything she told the boy about the situation might be repeated. Loudly. At the wedding. Little-boy candor might be fun most of the time, but not in the middle of a marriage ceremony with witnesses and videos galore being recorded.

"Why not?" Brody wanted to know. "Isn't it a rule that parents have to be at their kids' weddings?"

"Most do it that way," Dirk told him. "But there's no set rules. It's not always possible."

"I think Ethan's folks could've come. If they'd really wanted to. If I was Ethan, I'd be mad."

"Whatever's going on with Ethan and his parents, that's between him and them," she told him. "It isn't our business."

"I'm just wonderin'," Brody protested.

Dirk gave him a hug. "The less you worry about other people's business, Mr. Brody, the happier you're gonna be in life. I guarantee you."

"How about Alma?" he asked, undeterred. "Is her dad gonna walk her down the aisle?"

"No," Savannah said, her heart sinking by the minute. "He's not really . . . around."

"If my daughter was getting married, I'd be around, for sure!"

"I know you would," Savannah said. "You'll be a wonderful father someday."

"Is Alma's mom coming? Hey, wait a minute. Her mom is your mom!" he said to Savannah, proud of himself for having figured out the family tree. "Is your mom gonna come?"

"No," Savannah replied.

"She didn't want to come either?"

Savannah hesitated, wondering whether to be open or to guard painful family secrets from the boy. At least a bit longer.

Then she thought about their admonition to him about being honest and speaking the truth at all times.

She had to practice what she preached. Kids noticed such things and held it against their elders if they caught them doing a no-no they had forbidden them to do.

"I don't know if she wanted to come or not," Savannah said. "I suspect that Shirley doesn't even know about the wedding, and that's probably for the best."

"Shirley? You call your mom by her name?"

"Yes. She prefers it that way."

"Why isn't anybody telling her about the wedding?"

Savannah took a deep breath, held it, and let it out slowly. Then she said, "Brody, my mother has an illness called alcoholism."

"I know about that. She drinks too much booze."

"Yes. She does. She drinks so much that it changes who she is. It makes her into a person who's very hard to be around. Even for those who love her."

"What does she do? Does she hit people?"

"She has. But mostly she says terrible, hurtful things to people and ruins special occasions."

"That's not good. Special occasions are, you know, special. You have fun at them and then you have fun again later when you remember them."

"True. Like Alma and Ethan's wedding. That's going to be one of the most important and happiest days of their lives. We wouldn't want anything or anybody to ruin it for them. They deserve to have a good time and make good memories to enjoy for the rest of their lives."

"Then you don't have to invite your mom to your wedding if you don't want to?" he asked.

"I didn't," Savannah told him.

Brody turned to Dirk. "Did you invite your mom?"

"I didn't know her then. I was given up for adoption. I didn't meet my real mom and dad until last year."

"Then does that mean when I grow up and get married, I don't have to invite my mother either?"

"No," Savannah told him. "You don't. Like we told you, when we had our talk upstairs, you can choose not to ever see her again if you want."

"That's what I want!"

"I understand," Savannah said. "Believe me, I do."

Dirk tightened his arm around him. "Savannah's mom was a whole lot like yours."

"She was?"

Savannah nodded. "She had to go to prison, too."

"Was she mean to you guys?"

"Yes. Not like your mom, but . . ."

"Did she hit you?"

"Yes. But mostly, she was just really not good at taking care of kids, and that was because of the alcohol."

"She shoulda learned how to take care of you guys the right way. You can watch videos on the computer that show you how to do almost everything."

Savannah chuckled. "That's true. Unfortunately, we didn't have Internet back then, you know, when dragons were in charge of lighthouses."

Dirk reached for the remote. "Is that all?" he asked. "Wanna get back to the show?"

"There's one more thing. Remember when you guys told me that I had to tell you guys the truth. The whole truth and all that stuff?"

"Yes, we remember," she told him.

"I reckon there's some true stuff I need to tell y'all, 'cause somebody else didn't tell you the truth, like she should've, and I think it might be important."

Dirk sat up to attention, and so did Savannah. "Okay, kiddo. Let 'er rip. Let's hear it all."

"In the backyard, you guys were talking about Dr. Carolyn and Patrice, and when Patrice spilled pee all over Dr. Erling."

"Yes . . ."

"That wasn't an accident."

"Really?" Savannah felt her own pulse quickening. She suspected Dirk's was, too, by the flush of his face. "How do you know?"

"I was there. I saw it."

"You saw Patrice spill the urine on Dr. Erling?"

"No. I saw her throw it on him. The whole big cupful. She threw it on his face, and it got all over his clothes, too."

Dirk said, "Tell us what you saw, son. Everything you remember."

"I remember it all. It happened quick, so there isn't much to remember. Me and Dr. Carolyn were checking on a puppy who'd been sick, but he was getting better, and we heard some people arguing really loud in another room. Dr. Carolyn told me to stay there with the puppy, and she took off to find out what was going wrong."

"Let me guess," Savannah said. "You didn't wait. You followed her."

"Sure I did! I thought if they were bad people who were yelling at each other, then she might need help."

"You followed her and what did you see?" Dirk asked.

"I heard Patrice yell at Dr. Erling and say, 'I hope you rot in . . . um, H-E-double hockey sticks.' 'Cept she didn't say hockey sticks or spell it out. If you know what I mean."

"I know what you mean, Brody," Savannah said. "You heard her say that and then . . . ?"

"Then Dr. Carolyn ran in the room where they were, and I ran in after her and that was when Patrice threw that pee all over Dr. Erling. He was really surprised at first but once it sunk in on him—the Saint Bernard pee, that is—then, whoa, he was madder than the snake that married the garden hose."

"Must have been awful," Savannah said, trying not to laugh.

"Oh, it was! Terrible! It was all in his eyes and nose and ever'where."

The three sat in silence for a moment as Savannah and Dirk considered what they'd just heard, and Brody, having unburdened himself, relaxed.

Finally, Savannah said, "I want a root beer float. Can I make one for anybody else."

Hands shot into the air as both guys said, "Me! Me! Me!"

Savannah went into the kitchen, got out the glass mugs, then called, "Dirk. Could you come give me a hand?"

"Sure" was the speedy reply.

A second later, she heard Dirk walking toward her and Brody say, "She don't need no help makin' floats. She just wants to talk to you behind my back."

Dirk walked into the kitchen, shaking his head. "That kid's too smart for our own good."

"No kidding."

She glanced toward the living room and lowered her voice. "You know what this means, don't you?" she said, all levity aside.

"Yes. Carolyn was right there in the room when it happened, just like Brody. If he heard what he heard and saw what he saw, so did she."

"Carolyn lied to me. She outright lied."

She waited for him to say, "I told you so," or to give her that annoying, knowing look that he assumed at times like this.

But he didn't, and she thanked him for it, because she really wasn't in the mood.

It really hurt to be lied to, especially by someone you trusted.

Chapter 32

The next morning, Savannah had taken Brody to school and returned home to find Dirk on the phone in the kitchen, looking excited. Or, at least as excited as Dirk ever looked that early in the morning.

She gave him a questioning glance and received a thumbs-up.

"Are you absolutely sure?" he asked the person on the other end.

Savannah wasn't certain what the person replied, but she heard the tone of voice, loud and brusque, and recognized it as belonging to Eileen, the cantankerous head of the county CSU lab. Whatever Eileen was saying to Dirk, it wasn't even civil, let alone cordial.

"Okay, bye," he replied, equally curt, when she was done. He hung up the phone and told Savannah, "Hey, hey! Good news."

"Not for Eileen, apparently."

"That woman's a nuisance. Gets all miffed over nothin'."

"Nothing . . . as in . . . 'Are you sure you did your job correctly?' "

"I never said that to her."

"Subtext, darlin'. Subtext. What's the good news?"

"They found pentobarbital on that fancy green glass that was broken there by the hearth."

"That *is* good news! Any prints?"

"No-o-o. Don't rain on my parade here. I haven't finished celebrating about the pento on the glass."

"Sorry. Far be it from me to—"

There was a knock on the door followed by the sound of a key in the lock.

"Tammy," they said together.

As Savannah's assistant, Tammy had been given a set of house keys and told to come and go as she pleased. After all, the house doubled as a home and an office for the detective agency.

"And Waycross!" they heard him yell. "I'm here, too!"

Savannah and Dirk looked at each other, surprised. Since when did Waycross, who worked at a specialty garage, wonderfully restoring old classic vehicles, go anywhere other than his job at this hour of the morning?

"We're in the kitchen," Savannah called out. "Come on back."

"You guys come in here!" Tammy said. "Hurry! We've got some good stuff to show you."

Their enthusiasm was contagious, and Savannah and Dirk hurried into the living room. Dirk scooped Vanna Rose into his arms, as Tammy and Waycross began to pull three of Savannah's dining chairs up to the desk.

"I'm so glad you forwarded me those videos from the movie theater," Tammy said. "Last night, Baby Boo-Boo was teething again, so we didn't get a lot of sleep. But since we were awake anyway, we got to work on the case, and we found awesome stuff!"

Savannah and Dirk sat in the extra chairs, as Tammy directed them, and Waycross squeezed into the chair between Tammy and the wall.

Tammy flipped on the desktop computer and said, "Waycross spent hours looking at the videos that the security lady at the theater gave you."

"Hours?" Dirk was confused. "Why would it take hours? They went in and watched the movie and came back out when it was over."

"That's true, guys," Savannah told them, "and that's not all. Ryan got somebody at the bureau to check their cell phone records, and they were both in there the whole time."

"Their phones were there," Tammy said. "Maybe you should have the jury re-examine the evidence as to determine whether both Melissa and Jerry were there the whole time."

Tammy brought the selection of videos up on the screen. Waycross pointed to one that covered the parking lot.

"Okay," he said. "This is them arriving in the big Beamer."

The group watched as a man and woman got out of the luxury vehicle and walked up to the front of the complex.

Once the lighting became brighter, they could see that the woman had Melissa's distinctive, platinum blond bob.

As soon as the couple entered the front door,

Tammy switched videos to show the interior of the lobby.

"Here's them coming in," Waycross said, pointing to the screen and the two entering the complex. Now it was quite clear that the woman was Melissa. She was wearing a sequin-spangled T-shirt, tight jeans, and knee-high boots, and she carried a large tote that seemed oversized for her petite body.

The man beside her matched the DMV picture of Jerry Becker, as well as the additional photos that Tammy had downloaded.

Waycross followed them across the screen with his finger, as they bought tickets, popcorn, and sodas. Then they briefly stood in a short line, displayed their tickets to the security guard at the end of the queue, and continued on, out of sight.

"Okay, Tams," Waycross said, "bring 'em up on that hallway camera."

Tammy did as he said, and once again, Waycross followed their brief journey down a passageway and into one of the multiplex's six theaters.

"There ya go," Dirk said. "They've got their munchies and drinks. They're about to settle in for the long haul."

"So you'd figure," Waycross replied. "But watch this." He tapped on Tammy's shoulder. "Fast forward it for us, sweetie, all the way up to nine-o-seven."

She did, and at first, all they saw was an empty hallway. But as Tammy advanced the video to the spot Waycross had indicated, he pointed excitedly to the screen and said, "See there! She's coming out of the theater and into the hall. All by herself."

"Maybe she needs to use the can," Dirk said, obviously bored and unconvinced of anything.

They sat and watched as she strolled down the hallway and disappeared through a doorway with a female restroom symbol above it.

"What did I tell ya?" Dirk said. "Potty break. That's all it is. Did you see the size of those sodas they bought? Big enough to take a Jacuzzi in. No wonder she has to go."

"Would ya please fast forward it to nine-o-nine, darlin'?" Waycross asked his wife. "Get ready to freeze it, too."

Tammy did as he directed. When he yelled, "There!" she stopped it.

Savannah and Dirk leaned forward to get a better look at the figure on the screen.

Someone had just exited the restroom. This woman was dressed in jeans, short booties, and a black hoodie, which she'd pulled over her head.

"Okay. Who's that?" Dirk asked.

Savannah caught her breath. "It's her. It's Melissa."

"No way," he said. "Our gal's wearing a sparkly T-shirt and those up-to-the-knee boots."

"Those are the same boots," Tammy said. "You recognize them, don't you, Savannah? Didn't you tell me you like Antonette Lillyan boots?"

"I love them, and I've been wanting a pair of those fold-down ones for ages!"

Savannah turned to Dirk. "Seriously, honey. Listen. Us girls know our boots and those are the same ones. The hoodie covers the rhinestone shirt and the hood covers her hair. Plus she's got dark glasses on now. Who'd wear sunglasses in a movie theater at night?"

Waycross intervened. "If you need further proof," he told Dirk, "watch this."

He instructed Tammy to go back to the lobby cam, and sure enough, only a few seconds later, the hooded woman walked through the room and out the front door.

"Now back to the parking lot!" Waycross pointed to the woman with the black hoodie getting into the same BMW that the Beckers had just arrived in.

This time, even Dirk was on board. "Don't tell me. Later, she returns in the same car, probably a few minutes before the movie ends."

"She sure does. Comes sidlin' back in ten minutes before it's over. He gave Tammy a little nudge. "Show it to 'em, darlin'."

Tammy complied, and they were able to see the hooded woman return, go inside, show her ticket to the guard, hurry into the bathroom, and re-emerge dressed in her glittering T-shirt, with something black rolled up and stashed beneath her arm.

"Her boots are pulled back up again, see?" Savannah said. Then, to Tammy she added, "They really are the greatest design, don't you think? So versatile and—"

"Do you mind?" Dirk snapped. "People workin' here."

"Sorry. Continue."

Dirk turned to Waycross. "I assume you actually sat there last night and watched every minute of that hallway video to make absolutely sure that the Melissa Becker, who was dressed in the gaudy T-shirt, did not come out of that bathroom until the very end there."

"Nope. Other than her going in, the hooded lady coming out, the hooded lady going in and sparkly gal coming back out, there was no one in or out of that restroom." Waycross leaned back in his chair and locked his fingers behind his head. "Not bad for a cotton picker from McGill, huh?"

"Not bad at all," Savannah said, excited.

Dirk seemed less excited. In fact, he looked downright put out.

That boy sure can't stand to be wrong, she told herself.

"But Ryan said their phones show they were there the whole time," he grumbled.

"Duh, sugar," Savannah said. "You must be dog-tired and not thinking straight. She handed her husband her phone and left without it."

"Do you really think that little tiny gal left her husband in that theater, got in the car, drove to the clinic and burgled it, then drove back?"

"I most certainly do! It's the only thing that makes sense."

He growled.

"Then how do you explain what you just saw on that video?"

Dirk thought it over, stopped grimacing, and said, "No way a man's wife gets up to go to the bathroom in a movie theater and doesn't come back for two hours, without him getting up and finding out why. He knew exactly what she was doing. He was in on it, too."

"Don't be surprised if we find out that he coerced her to do it," Savannah said. "He was extremely jealous of Stephen and furious because he seduced his wife. He made her quit her job so that she wouldn't be seeing Stephen anymore. Maybe that wasn't enough to satisfy him. Perhaps he didn't want *anybody* to see Stephen Erling ever again."

Ten minutes later, the four of them and Vanna Rose had relocated to the dining room. Fresh coffee was flowing, and cinnamon rolls were in the oven.

Thinking was hard work, and Savannah wanted to

make sure that everyone had plenty of carb/caffeine energy on board and were up to the task.

"That only gives you a momentary boost you know," Tammy told her. "A quality, vegetable-based protein and a high-complex, high-fiber carb would energize you for hours."

"Okay," Savannah said, resisting the temptation to get into a discussion with Tammy about how the quality-of-life factor should be considered when choosing one's diet.

There was a good reason why nobody made chocolate Easter bunnies stuffed with kale or Christmas fudge with liver sauce.

Case closed.

"I hope you don't mind me showing you these printouts I made instead of sitting at the computer," Tammy said as she walked over to the table and began to spread papers all over it. "But between not sleeping and staring at a screen all night, my eyes just need a break."

"No problem, Tams," Dirk said, looking over the array. "What are these anyway?"

"Social media pages. You can learn almost everything you'd ever want to know about someone—and a lot of stuff you'd rather not know—on social media sites. I studied Melissa Becker's page to get a view into what makes her tick. Then I checked out Patrice Conway's for the same reason. I discovered . . . drumroll, please . . . they're friends."

"Friends?!" Savannah was flabbergasted. "Those two?"

"How?" Dirk said. "Melissa worked for Stephen, Patrice for Carolyn. Did they meet at a party or something?"

"Actually, I was able to hack into Patrice's account and use her password to read her private messages. I printed them out." She looked around the table and picked up a certain stack. "A lot of it is just boring nothingness. But read the exchanges between her and Melissa, starting several months ago, when they were both still working for the Erlings."

Savannah sat down and began to read. "Oh, wow!" she said. "In these messages, Patrice is furious at Melissa. She's accusing her of being the 'other woman,' of causing Stephen to end it with her."

"If Patrice had only known. Melissa was like the other, other, other woman," Dirk grumbled. He picked up some of the papers. "Look at this one. They seem to be friends now. Laughing about what they'd like to do to him. Hmm . . . colorful stuff here."

"Do they mention feeding him poison?" Savannah asked, half joking.

"Not for a few more weeks," Tammy said, quite full of herself as she pointed to some more printouts. "They're actually discussing an 'old mongrel' that they want to put down. Debating how much pentobarbital it would take and where to get it."

"I see it here," Savannah said. "Patrice says, 'I can get some at work. They won't miss it.' "

Dirk leaned over her shoulder and read, " 'Even if C asks about it, I think I could tell her what we need it for, and she'd give us all we want. She said last night she's sick of him, wants to be rid of him.' "

Dirk looked up at Tammy. "From reading all of this stuff, could you tell if Carolyn's involved?"

"I don't think she is. She could have said something like that to Patrice over drinks, girl-to-girl, but it certainly doesn't mean that she wanted anybody to knock off her husband for her."

"They killed a man because he fooled around on them both . . . with the other one?" Savannah asked her.

"I think that was Patrice's attitude. Throughout their correspondence, you could see that she started off furious at Melissa, then after they shared back and forth, she realized what a jerk he was and wanted him dead."

"How about Melissa?" Dirk asked.

"She talks a lot about Jerry. How mad he is. How he can't stand the idea that she might hook up with Stephen again someway, somewhere. At some point she must have told Jerry what she and Patrice were considering, and he latched on to it."

"Hence his cooperation in producing the fake movie alibi," Savannah said. "That had already occurred to me. Melissa wouldn't be the only wayward spouse or lover who killed her former sneak-around-squeeze to pacify her real one-true-love and keep him home."

"He's leaving her anyway," Dirk said. "She commits murder for him, and it's all for nothing."

"I don't understand something," Waycross said. "If Patrice stole the pentobarbital from the clinic when she was working there, why did Melissa break into the place two weeks before the murder?"

Tammy reached for another stack of printouts. "It's all right here," she said. "These are links they sent to each other. Articles about narcissists, serial cheaters, how they never change. Then they progress to sharing links about pentobarbital and executions."

Tammy found the one she'd been looking for and pulled it out. "Patrice sent this one to Melissa just a few days before the break-in. It's a link to a story about a nurse who found out she had cancer and tried to end her life with pentobarbital. She failed to use enough, and she survived. If you call being on permanent life support without hope of meaningful recovery 'surviving.' "

"They were afraid they didn't have enough and wanted more," Dirk said, reading on. "But Patrice had gotten fired, so she couldn't easily sneak back in and get it."

Waycross waved another sheet around. "Here's your proof that the husband, Becker, was determined they'd do it. Patrice tells Melissa she thinks they should call a halt to it, that the pentobarbital is too risky, too unreliable if it isn't injected. She's nervous about him drinking it and it not taking effect quick enough and doing the job. But Melissa tells Patrice they have to go through with it. Jerry wants her to do it to prove her love."

They all sat quietly for a while, reading more of the papers, underlining passages, clipping relevant stuff together.

"This is great, Tammy," Dirk said. "Excellent work on those videos, Waycross."

"But there's a problem, isn't there, with the printouts?" Tammy said. "We can't use the social media stuff, at least not the private messages, in a court of law, because we aren't supposed to have them."

"There are disadvantages to breaking the law while making a case," Dirk said. "It'll come back and bite you on the ass every time."

"If you aren't careful," Savannah said under her breath.

"I didn't hear that." Dirk thought for a moment. "The movie videos are enough to get a search warrant on the Beckers. We'll take their computers and tablets. I'll hire you as a freelancer, Tammy, on the county's dime. Then you can 'rediscover' everything you've got here. Okay?"

Tammy cackled with glee and rubbed her hands together. "I can't wait! Maybe I'll find even more!"

Savannah looked at her brother and his wife and felt a flood of pride rising in her. "You two are amazing!" she said. "You did all of this in the wee hours of the morning with a fussy, teething child."

They all turned and looked down at the little red-haired fairy princess, who was stretched across her uncle Dirk's lap, sound asleep.

"She's resting," Dirk said. "Regaining her strength."

"For all the shrieking she's going to do tonight," Waycross said.

Tammy just groaned.

Chapter 33

It took Dirk two hours to get his search warrant. Another hour for him and two uniforms to show up at Melissa Becker's house, then Patrice's, and take their electronic communication devices. They also seized the clothing that Melissa had worn to the theater the night of the burglary, the crowbar from her BMW's trunk, and some gloves that had been tucked into the wheel well. With the gloves they found a plastic grocery bag, containing a small box of assorted food color dyes, and a half-full, disposable, water bottle.

Once Tammy had the computers and tablets in hand, she needed only thirty minutes to "regather" the nails-in-their-coffins messages that they had been too foolish to delete.

By noon, Dirk had three arrest warrants in his hand and joy in his heart.

"Wanna come along?" he asked Savannah as he prepared to go to the station house to interview the three suspects who had been detained for questioning.

He didn't have to ask twice.

"Patrice first," Dirk told Savannah as they walked down the hall toward the interrogation rooms.

"Good choice," she replied. "We've already spent enough time with Melissa to know she isn't likely to fold easily."

"More like an iron rod than a cheap lawn chair in that regard." Dirk paused outside the door, his hand on the knob. "Wish me luck," he said.

Savannah was taken aback. Cocky Dirk was proud of his well-earned reputation for being the quintessential interrogator. He managed to get suspects to confess who hadn't spoken a word to others who had questioned them. Since when did he think he needed luck?

"You got this, darlin'," she said. "If there's anything you know how to do, it's squeeze somebody and get them to confess to their evil deeds. I'm glad you didn't become a priest. You'd have been a terror in a confessional."

He gave her a quick, lusty look up and down. "I'm glad I didn't become a priest either," he said and gave a little growl.

He punched in the door's combination, opened it, and stepped inside with Savannah. The room was only a bit bigger than a broom closet with torn gray padding on the walls, a utilitarian steel table in the center with four folding, metal chairs around it.

Patrice Conway sat on one of them, her head down, and her beautiful, red hair flowing around her shoulders.

When she looked up at them, Savannah saw none of the anger she had felt coming from the young woman, as she had when she'd seen her at the clinic.

No, this Patrice reminded Savannah of the one she had seen fleeing the party in Joya del Mar. Frightened, sad, with tear-reddened eyes.

"Hello, Ms. Conway," Dirk said as he took a seat across the table from her. "Thank you for waiting to speak to me."

"I was told I didn't have a choice," she replied.

"That's true. But thank you anyway."

Savannah sat down next to Dirk. "Hi, Patrice. We've been running into each other a lot lately," she said. "Not under very nice circumstances though."

"Are you a police officer, too?" Patrice asked her.

"No. Not anymore. I'm married to Detective Coulter here. I'm just along for the ride." When Patrice didn't respond, Savannah added, "Is it okay with you if I sit in? I can leave if you'd prefer."

Patrice shrugged. "I guess it's okay. Probably won't matter much either way."

Dirk laid a large folder on the table. Savannah could see it contained the printout sheets that Tammy had given him.

"Ms. Conway," he began, "I assume you know why you're here, or at least have a good idea."

"Not really," she replied, unconvincingly.

"We're investigating the homicide of Stephen Erling."

"I don't know anything about that," she instantly shot back.

"Oh, but you do, Ms. Connelly. You know al-l-l about it."

"No! I don't. I—"

"Patrice, I know that you poisoned him with a drug

called pentobarbital. I know that you put it in a pretty, antique, green crystal glass."

Savannah watched her carefully and saw a look of panic cross her eyes. She glanced toward the door, as though wishing she could run through it and never stop running.

"Would you like to know what else I know?" Dirk asked.

All he received was a weak nod.

He picked up the folder, opened it, and started laying the papers side by side in front of her.

"These are from your social media pages. Some are private messages between you and Melissa Becker."

Patrice looked at the papers and gagged. Savannah got ready to move aside with haste, if Patrice looked like she was going to throw up and direct it toward her.

"How did you get those?" she asked, breathing heavily. "Those are private!"

"I had a subpoena to search your house. That included your computer. A computer specialist was able to pull all these pages up for us and print them out."

Patrice covered her face with her hands and started to cry.

Dirk leaned across the table, closer to her, and said, "I just want to hear your side of it, Patrice. You seem like a nice lady, and I doubt you'd do a thing like that unless you had a really good reason."

Patrice dropped her hands from her face and stared across the table at him with something that looked like eternal gratitude on her face. "I did!" she exclaimed, nodding vigorously. "I never would have even *thought* about doing something like that to a regular person. But Stephen wasn't regular. He was evil, that guy. Pure evil!"

If Savannah had been chewing gum, she would have swallowed it and choked on it. A confession? Already? Wow! After only maybe thirty seconds into the interview!

This had to be a record, even for Dirk!

"I believe you," Dirk told her with what appeared to be total sincerity and deep-seated compassion. "I know enough about Stephen Erling to understand why you did it. Extenuating circumstances and all that."

She just nodded, so he continued to press her. "I might be able to help you if you just tell me why," he continued. "He really hurt you, didn't he?"

"He hurt a lot of people. Especially women. He used us, then threw us away."

"I know the type," Savannah said. "They think they're God's gift to us gals, and they're actually a curse."

"He was!" Patrice's tearful, green eyes had the look of someone who was experiencing much-needed validation after a long, dry spell. "He just didn't care about anybody but himself."

"I can't stand guys like that," Savannah told her. "They cause so much damage. Narcissists." She glanced down at the folder. "You had some links about narcissists on your page. I looked at them and instantly thought of Stephen. He ticked every box. A total narcissist. Don't you think?"

"I *know* he was. He was so selfish. So hurtful."

"You loved him at one time," Dirk told her. "I could tell by what you said to Melissa in those private messages. Nobody hates a rival that much unless you're really in love."

"I fall in love way too easily," Patrice admitted. "Always have. I can't believe I betrayed a good friend like Carolyn for a dirtbag like him. Yes, I hated the 'other woman,' until I realized she was just another one of his victims."

"But eventually," Savannah said, "you and Melissa became close."

"We did," Patrice admitted. "Once we started sharing what it was like to be used by that bastard, we sort of bonded over it. He hurt us both in the same way. It helped a lot to know I wasn't the only woman in the world stupid enough to believe in him, to let him into my heart."

"Whose idea was it to kill him?" Dirk asked. "Yours, Melissa's, Carolyn's?"

"I don't remember. We were just joking about different awful things we wished we could do to him. I don't think we meant any of it. We were just blowing off steam. You know?"

"Yes, I know," Savannah tried to sound convincing, and Patrice seemed to be convinced. "It's easy to talk about something and not realize that your words are actually leading you down a destructive road. All of a sudden, you realize that your words became actual plans and plans became actions. Then you're sunk."

"Are you telling me," Dirk asked, "that you didn't actually intend to murder Stephen Erling?"

"Yes! That's what I'm saying. I didn't want to. After I read about that nurse botching her suicide with the pentobarbital, I chickened out. What if we just made him sick? He would have figured out it was us, and he'd have killed us."

"Was he that bad a dude?" Dirk asked.

"Worse. The worst person I ever met."

"The poison," Savannah said. "How much of it was your idea and how much was Melissa's?"

"I thought of it. I knew about pentobarbital because I've helped Carolyn administer it to animals when necessary there in the clinic. I was joking with Melissa about what a nasty guy Stephen was and how Carolyn had told me she was thinking of getting rid of him. At the time Carolyn told me, I thought she was serious, like she was actually thinking of killing him. Later, I realized she was just a depressed, abused wife talking. When she'd said she needed to 'get rid of him,' she just meant divorce him. She never would have killed him. She wasn't strong enough."

"You thought you were helping your friend?" Savannah said, pouring on the so-sweet sympathy.

"I was helping all three of us. Carolyn, Melissa, myself, and who knows how many others?"

"I understand," Savannah told her. "You really didn't feel like you had a choice."

"That's exactly right!"

"You had so many reasons to hate him on so many levels. Anyone would have, after him betraying you like that."

"Yes! It *was* a betrayal, too. He told me he was going to ask Carolyn for a divorce so he could marry me. I bought it all. But even the ring he gave me was fake. Told me it was a pre-engagement ring. I found out he bought mine and two others at the same time. I know he gave Melissa one. Who knows who received the third one?"

"Let me get this straight, Patrice," Dirk said thoughtfully. "You were the one who stole the pentobarbital out of the clinic's medicine chest the first time. But it was Melissa who stole even more when she faked the break-in."

"I really shouldn't speak for them."

Dirk gave an airy wave of his hand. "That's okay. I've talked to them, and they told me all about it."

"They did?"

"Sure," Savannah said. "They told us all about how they staged the movie theater alibi, how Melissa changed clothes in the bathroom, then left, did the burglary, and came back."

Having been raised by Granny, Savannah felt a rib-jab from her conscience as the lie tumbled out of her mouth. They hadn't spoken to Melissa or Jerry yet, figuring Patrice would be the softest egg to crack.

They were right. She was swallowing it all in one big gulp.

"They told you!" she gasped. "I can't believe they told you! They kept telling *me* not to say a word and then they . . . Wow!"

"They spilled their guts," Dirk said, leaning back in his chair with his hands behind his head in his most pseudo-casual pose. "We even know about how they put red food coloring and water into the half-empty bottle of pentobarbital to make it look full again."

"Man, they really did blab!" Patrice shook her head in amazement.

"Did you hear what happened to Loki, the Great Dane you guys loved so much there at the clinic?" Savannah asked in a less friendly tone.

Patrice cringed. "I heard. Poor dog. I feel really bad about that. In fact, that's part of why I tried to pull the plug, talk Melissa and Jerry out of it. It just didn't feel right anymore. I told them I was having second thoughts. Big-time. That it wasn't as easy to administer a fatal dose as I'd thought. But Jerry threw a fit. Wanted Melissa to demonstrate her love to him by killing Stephen. She really wanted to work things out with Jerry. God only knows why, because he's a loser, too, but she wanted him. No accounting for taste, I guess."

Savannah thought that any woman who had fallen so deeply in love with a jerk like Stephen, and her friend's husband to boot, shouldn't talk about anyone else having bad taste in men. But she kept her opinion to herself. The interview was going swimmingly. She didn't want to flub it now.

"I believe you when you say that you didn't want to go through with it, Patrice," Savannah told her in her most comforting voice. "I remember the way you looked the day of the party, when you and I ran into each other in front of the Erling mansion. I saw the tears in your eyes. You weren't some gleeful murderer, running from the scene of your crime. You felt bad about what you'd just done."

"I did! I felt terrible. I was worried someone else might drink it, even though Melissa assured me that Stephen never let anybody drink from that green glass. He even took it with him in his suitcase when he traveled."

"How did you get the pento-stuff into the glass without anybody noticing?" Dirk said.

"The funny thing is, I never really thought I'd get the opportunity to do it. Such a big crowd! People everywhere. The kitchen was full of cooks and waiters. I just stayed in the background and watched. I saw them fill up the glasses on a big tray, and one of them was the green one. I couldn't believe my luck when everyone just sorta walked away from that tray and left it on a sideboard for a minute. It didn't take long to dump a little of the champagne out of his glass and into the others, then put the drug in."

"Girl, you have got nerves of steel." Savannah said cheerfully, as though congratulating her.

"Not really. I was worried and so nervous, I was shaking. I was afraid he'd see the pinkish tint in the medicine. But with the champagne diluting it, and the glass being green, it wasn't that obvious."

"Why were you the one stuck doing the actual deed, if Melissa and Jerry were the ones who were actually insisting on following through with it?" Savannah asked.

"Because, if they'd shown up there, Stephen would have had a fit! He was beside himself just seeing me. Plus, Jerry wouldn't have been caught dead in the house of the man who seduced his wife. Stephen hated me, too, but at least I had an excuse to be there. To pick up my check."

"Did Carolyn know you were going to do it?" Dirk asked, his face hard, his eyes inscrutable.

"No. She didn't know before. Later, I think she figured out that it had been either me or Melissa."

"Carolyn didn't ask you to do it for her?" Dirk pressed again.

"No. Not at all. I keep telling you, she didn't know. Carolyn is a wonderful person. I love her. She was another one of his victims. But an innocent one."

Savannah felt a knot in her throat, one that had been tightening more and more over the last couple of days, loosen and release. Brody's friend wasn't a murderer. The boy could continue to visit the clinic and do the work he loved with someone he loved and respected.

What a wonderful turn of events, a great way to close a case.

But Dirk wasn't finished yet. "One more thing, Patrice.

I've just gotta know. Why did you throw the Saint Bernard's urine in his face?"

"Because I confronted him about Melissa. I told him that he'd led me on, gave me reason to believe I was his one and only. He'd told me he was crazy about me and wanted a future with me. Finally, I realized the only person Stephen Erling was crazy about was himself."

Savannah couldn't maintain the pretense any longer. "Yeah, Stephen was a jackass's hind quarters. No doubt about it. But killing a man? Your dear friend's husband? Premeditated murder?" She shook her head and gave a *tsk-tsk.* "Really, Patrice? You should've been satisfied with the dog pee."

Chapter 34

If anyone deserves a perfect wedding day, it's my little Alma, Savannah thought as Dirk parked the Buick on the brick driveway in front of Ryan and John's magnificent Moroccan-style castle, situated on one of the highest mountain peaks in the county.

The glorious old place once known as Qamar Damun—Arabic for "Blood Moon"—was new only to Ryan and John, as it had been built in the 1920s. During Prohibition, it had been a glittering mecca, attracting the brightest stars of the silver screen, the most influential politicians of the day, and members of European royalty, as well as the most feared and revered mob bosses.

In spite of its beauty, Qamar Damun had been notorious as the ideal place for decadent parties and corrupt dealing of all sorts. A glamorous and glittering venue for the intermingling of all the vices known to humankind and humans who were obsessed with practicing them.

But today, Qamar Damun had been transformed. After yet another murder had occurred there, Ryan and John had taken pity on the old place, purchased, and lovingly restored her.

They had even given her a new name, Qamar Jadid, which meant "New Moon."

"What better place for Alma and Ethan to get their new start in life," Savannah said as she picked up her beaded bag, took out her compact, and checked her mascara.

Surprisingly, it was still on her lashes and not under her eyes or running down her cheeks. But that was bound to change before the day was over. "Waterproof" or not.

"You look fine," she heard Dirk say. "Beautiful, in fact."

Savannah looked down at the bright yellow sheath dress and shuddered. "Thank you. But I don't feel beautiful. I look like a giant daffodil."

"No, you don't," Brody said, leaning over her shoulder and looking down at her dress. "You look pretty."

"Why, thank you, Brody! What a sweet thing to say."

"Yeah. Like a big ol' lemon Popsicle."

"Oh."

Dirk looked back at the boy and said, "You came close, dude. So-o-o close. Only to fumble at the one-yard line."

Brody reconsidered and tried again. "A Popsicle with matching yellow shoes?"

"Seriously, son. Stop while you're ahead."

Savannah glanced back at Brody, who looked like a mini Robert Redford in his black tuxedo with a bright yellow vest and tie. His blond hair had been heavily gelled and carefully sculpted into a coiffure worthy of a gentleman of the Roaring Twenties.

He was adorable.

He also meant well. He loved Popsicles.

She turned to Dirk and enjoyed the sight of him for a moment, as well. He was wearing a tuxedo, too. He hadn't been thrilled at the prospect, until he'd found out that he was being asked to do so because he had been assigned a most prestigious honor. One he had not been expecting.

Alma asked him to honor her by walking her "down the aisle." Or down the staircase leading into the ballroom, where the ceremony was to be performed.

Dirk had gotten teary-eyed and choked up a bit when he accepted—most graciously and gratefully.

He had balked at the yellow vest and, like the rest of the males in the wedding party, conceded to a yellow rose boutonniere.

Savannah looked him over and thought she had never seen him more handsome. She was looking forward to this evening for more reasons than one. The best thing about attending weddings and parties with Dirk was that he loved to ballroom dance. Much to the surprise of those who knew him, he was quite good at it. She couldn't wait for their first waltz.

But while Savannah was looking Dirk over and approving of his appearance, Brody was studying him, as well. "I'm sorry they didn't give you a cool vest, too," the boy told him, genuinely concerned about the injustice of the situation.

Dirk shrugged. "I know, huh? My feelings were plumb hurt."

Dirk turned to Savannah and rolled his eyes. She gave him an air kiss.

"Let's get going," she said, reaching for the gift bag on the floor. "I'm supposed to be helping the bride put on her veil or garter or something."

"What's a garter?" Brody asked. Then his eyes grew large, "Oh, wait. I know. It's one of those things that ladies put around their legs and . . . never mind. Yuck."

They got out of the Buick and walked toward the massive, arched entryway with all of its intricate brickwork. Brody craned his neck to look up the entire height of the four-story building with its marble façade, decorated with bands of complicated geometric patterns, and lit with Moroccan lanterns, their stained-glass panels casting their jewel-toned glow on the stone and masonry.

"This is so, so cool!" he exclaimed. "It's like a castle where Aladdin would live. Maybe the genie, too!"

When they arrived at the door, Brody asked if he could do the knocking, and Dirk gave him a boost so he could reach the large, brass hand affixed to the center of the door. No sooner had Brody used it to rap as loudly as he could, than someone answered.

In fact, it wasn't a person, but a crowd consisting of the seven people Savannah loved most in the world: Granny, Waycross, Tammy, Ryan, John, and little Vanna Rose and Freddy.

The munchkins were dressed as befitted their royal titles of "Flower Girl" and "Ring Bearer," with Vanna in a frilly, yellow dress that reached down to her beloved penguin slippers. For the occasion, the birds were adorned with yellow daisies on their heads instead of the usual bells.

"Hey! He got a cool yellow vest, too!" Brody said, pointing to Freddy's outfit, which was as festive as his own. "I guess those tuxedo folks like kids more than grown-ups."

The quintessential hosts, Ryan and John, greeted Savannah and her fellows warmly and coaxed everyone to pass through to the parlor for refreshments.

Savannah took Tammy's hand, looked her up and down, and said, "You look especially stunning in that shade of yellow."

Tammy ducked her head and blushed, which was most becoming on a goddess who was unaware of her unearthly beauty. "I'm so pleased she asked me. I mean, with all of her sisters—"

"—her sisters, her real sisters, are gonna be standin' right there with her," Granny piped up, slipping between the two. She grabbed Savannah's hand, then Tammy's. "You two were the ones her heart chose. I believe she picked well. It takes more than being born to the same parents to be a sister, and you two have been the best sisters in the world to her. Accept the honor and hug it to your hearts. You deserve it."

Savannah looked down into her grandmother's blue eyes, so like her own, and thought how much she loved this lady with the silver halo of hair, looking so lovely in her dress of pale aqua lace.

"Thank you, Granny," Savannah said. "We'll do just that. But where *is* the special couple?"

"Ethan's in one of the guest rooms, gettin' hisself dressed. Alma's in the master bedroom. Ryan and John were set on her havin' the fanciest."

"Of course they did. When it comes to heart-adopted brothers, they're the best. Good restorer/decorators, too."

She looked around the glorious foyer, large enough to be the lobby of a fine hotel or theater. Light from the stained-glass windows streamed in, setting the marble walls aflame with shades of ruby, emerald, sapphire, and amethyst.

More exotic Moroccan lanterns, like the ones outside, lined the walls, lending their gleaming warmth to the embossed bronze friezes.

To her left, Savannah could see the ballroom, and she was floored by the difference in the place from the last time she had seen it.

Back then it had been a terrible hoard, head high and packed from wall to wall. The owner had died there in that mess, under terrible circumstances. Savannah would never have guessed, standing in that same spot last year, what the place could look like.

At that moment, Ryan walked by, also decked out in a tux, looking far too good.

Before Savannah had met Ethan, Savannah had considered Ryan to be the most gorgeous male she had ever seen. Tonight, he was simply stunning in his evening wear, and in spite of his hosting responsibilities, he was relaxed and obviously enjoying himself.

But handsome as he was, Savannah had found Dirk to be a better dancer, and along with that was the fact that he was hers and appeared to want to remain so. Those things put him at the top of the list of men in her life. Forever.

"You and John did an amazing job on this place,

Ryan," she said. "You took it from a nightmare to simply stunning."

"Thank you." He beamed at the praise. "I won't say it was easy. There were times we thought we were crazy to have even tried to do it. But we're very happy with the results. Do you think she would have approved?"

Savannah didn't have to ask who "she" was. He meant the elderly, former silver screen actress who had lived in the house from the time she was young, beautiful, and the toast of old Hollywood—until she died inside it, lying amid the clutter of a life lived, sometimes without conscience, but always with gusto.

"She absolutely would have approved," Savannah told him. "She would have loved to see it like this, restored to its original grandeur and with modern plumbing."

He laughed, leaned down, and kissed her cheek. "Thank you. That means a lot to me, and it will to John, too, when I tell him."

Savannah looked around to see what everyone was doing. Dirk, Waycross, Brody, Freddy, and Vanna Rose had left the parlor and gone into the ballroom. The little ones were toddling about, taking full advantage of the vastness of the gigantic room.

She couldn't help noticing the glistening parquet floor and the stately floor-to-ceiling, marble fireplace. Neither of which had been visible before because of the hoard. The massive crystal chandelier hanging in the center of the coffered ceiling now sparkled like ones in the palaces Savannah could only imagine as a child.

"This is so special," she told Ryan, "such a gift to our family, you hosting us here in your home. Far away from paparazzi eyes. A beautiful setting with just friends and family. It doesn't get better than this, Ryan."

"Yes, it does," he said with a smile. "You haven't seen your little sister on her wedding day yet. She is *gorgeous!*" He offered his arm. "May I have the honor of escorting the maid of honor to our lovely bride?"

"Sure!" Savannah turned to Granny and Tammy. "Would you two like to go up with me? I'm sure the master bedroom in this place is large enough to accommodate the bride's entire entourage."

Granny glanced down at the gift bag in Savannah's hand and said, "That's okay, darlin'. We were just up there with her for a long time while she was getting her face done. I know you've got something in that bag you want to discuss with her. Go on ahead and have some private time with your sister."

"Good idea," Tammy said. "We're going to go check out the ballroom."

Savannah passed her hand through Ryan's arm. "Thank you, kind sir," she said, giving him a dimpled smile. "Lead on."

The moment Savannah stepped into the magnificent bedroom, she saw a scene that would be a forever, lifelong memory. One of her favorites.

She saw her precious little Alma Joy, the quiet one in the family, gentle but brave, always there when you needed her, compassionate and understanding Alma.

But at that moment, she didn't look like their Alma, the plain little girl who had grown up on the wrong side of the tracks in a one-flashing-light town in rural Georgia.

Sitting on a chair in front of a dresser, checking her makeup in the mirror, her white lace gown and its train cascading down her lithe body and onto the floor around her, she looked like a glamorous, silver screen actress from the Roaring Twenties.

She also looked like a heroine from one of Ethan Malloy's romantic movies.

But mostly, she looked happy. Ecstatically happy.

More important than her glossy, raven's wing black hair, her perfect skin, and her sapphire blue eyes, her joy was what illuminated her and made her seem to literally shine.

Alma saw Savannah in the mirror, turned, and said shyly, "Hi."

"Hi? You're sitting there looking like an oil painting on a castle wall and all you have to say is, 'Hi'?"

Savannah hurried over to her, started to hug her, then said, "You're so perfect, I don't want to mess you up."

"Aw, let's risk it," Alma said, as she gathered Savannah into a tight embrace and held on for a long time before releasing her with a satisfied sigh. "I needed that," she said, sinking back onto the chair.

"Are you okay?" Savannah asked, concerned.

"Oh, I'm so okay I can hardly stay inside my own skin. I'm so happy, I feel like I'm going to just float away!"

"Good. That's the way a gal should feel on her wedding day, if she's marrying the right guy."

"Ethan's the right guy. For me, anyway."

"I know, sugar."

"Were you this happy the day you married Dirk?"

"I was. We were older than you and had known each other way longer than you and Ethan have, but we were still excited about starting our lives together. Being a couple. All that good stuff."

Savannah leaned down to study Alma's makeup more carefully. It was exquisitely done, subtle, gentle colors that suited her creamy complexion and accentuated her eyes, making them sparkle all the more.

"You did an amazing job on your makeup, kiddo," she told her. "I wish I could do mine like that."

Alma laughed. "I wish I could, too."

"You didn't do it?"

"No. My makeup was a present to me, a surprise. A few weeks ago, I was watching one of Ethan's older movies, and I told him I thought the heroine's makeup was really pretty. I said I was going to try to do mine like that for the wedding. So this morning, we get here, and what has he done? He got the exact same makeup artist that worked on that actress to fly here all the way from New York and do mine for me this morning."

"Wow! He's even more perfect that I thought. What a guy!"

"I know. He's so good to me, Sis. I just hope I can make him happy. That's what I want, more than anything."

"You will. I know you, Miss Alma Joy. You were appropriately named. You make people happy everywhere you go. He's blessed to have you, and I'm quite sure he knows it, too."

Savannah looked down at the gift bag in her hand. "I have something to give Ethan, something I made especially for him in honor of his wedding day. But before I give it to him, I want you to see it. I won't let him have it without your blessing."

Alma glanced down at the bag, smiled, and said, "If you made it, I'm sure it's wonderful and you have my blessing to give it to him. But I'd sure like to see it, just for curiosity sake."

Savannah took the gift from the bag, placed it in her sister's hands, and waited to see what she would do.

She cried.

But thankfully, not enough to mess up her makeup, that had been applied so perfectly, so professionally, by the lady from New York.

Chapter 35

When Savannah knocked on the door of the guest bedroom, it opened almost immediately, and she found herself facing a disheveled and nerve-frazzled groom, who fortunately had his pants on but was still in his undershirt.

"Oh, Savannah. Hi," he said. "I'm, I'm trying to . . . Do you know anything about those stupid tuxedo shirt stud things. I hate them, and the shirt I've got has white buttons on it and . . ."

"Sh-h-h," she said. "Don't fret. You don't wanna get all in a tizzy over buttons on your wedding day."

"I hate to sound spoiled, but the few times a year I wear a tux, there's usually somebody around who does that stuff for me."

"You're in luck because I'm an expert when it comes to tuxedo shirt studs."

"You are?"

"I am now. I just helped my husband and son with theirs not an hour ago. I do believe I still recall how they work."

She looked over at the dresser and saw a bunch of black studs and some cufflinks scattered across a baroque, antique jewelry tray. "Tell you what," she said. "I'll get you into that shirt, if you can give me two minutes afterward. There's something I want to give you."

"Sure!" He rushed over to the bed, picked up the shirt, hurried back to her, and shoved it into her hands. "There you go. I'm all yours."

As Savannah slipped the shirt onto her soon-to-be brother-in-law's back, turned him around, and started to slip the studs through the small holes above each white button, she couldn't help thinking she must be the envy of all womanhood at that moment. Ethan Malloy himself had just told her, "I'm all yours," which, of course, meant nothing at all. Especially since it was his wedding day and his bride was her little sister. But still.

Better yet, she was actually dressing Ethan Malloy.

Considering how outrageously popular the actor was, if she sat down later in the evening and wrote a one-page book, detailing the experience, she could publish it tomorrow, and it would be a best seller.

Well, maybe not a New York Times *best seller,* she thought. For it to hit the top of the charts, she'd have to be *un*-dressing Ethan Malloy.

But there wasn't time for that. He was marrying her sister in half an hour.

Not to mention the fact that she already had a man of her own, and he was an excellent dancer.

In no time, she had Ethan's shirt buttoned and

cuffed. Helped him into his vest and had adjusted his tie.

Once he was dressed, he seemed to calm down considerably. "I won't put on the coat until I get ready to go down," he told her. "Thank you so much!"

"No problem. Really. Happy to help."

She picked a tiny bit of lint off the coat and laid it carefully on the bed.

"Have you seen Alma?" he asked.

"Just left her. She's still in the bedroom, happier than I've ever seen her. Or anybody else for that matter."

"Good." He grinned and, for a moment, the world-renowned actor looked like a shy little boy experiencing his first crush. "I'm glad. I'm happy, too. Oh, what was it you wanted me to do for you?"

"I want you to sit over there in that chair for a minute. I made something for you, and I'd like to give it to you before the ceremony, if that's okay."

"Okay? Of course it's okay. That's so kind of you, Savannah, especially with all that you've had going on."

She followed him over to the chair she had indicated, where he sat down. She placed the gift bag in his hand and sat on another chair next to him.

"A present just from you to me? This is so special," he said.

He reached into the bag, brushed away the copious yellow tissue paper she had stuffed inside, and pulled out the gift—a rosewood memory box. She had sanded, stained, and polished the finish to a soft shine, then added a gold-leafed, ornate letter *A* to the top.

"How beautiful!" he said, running his fingers over the smooth surface. "You made this?"

"I did. But the box isn't important. The gift is what's in it."

He opened it slowly, then peered inside at the strange assortment of objects. A stack of photos, some old and faded, tied together with a frayed red ribbon. A small lozenge tin that had been painted white with a large red cross on the lid. A necklace of glittery plastic, pop-together beads. And four blue ribbons printed with the words *1st Place Winner, McGill Spelling Bee.*

"These are some of Alma's treasures," Savannah told him. "I have her blessing to give them to you."

"Really?" He stared down into the box. "Wow. Tell me about them."

She picked up the lozenge tin and opened it. "This is her own first-aid kit. She used to try to 'doctor' every hurt animal or person she could find," she told him, showing him the bandages, tape, tiny scissors, and a thermometer. "She never could get the animals to hold still long enough to take their temperatures, but she certainly tried hard enough."

He laughed. "That's sweet."

"It could be annoying at times, depending on what she brought home and whether it was venomous or not, but yes, very sweet."

She pointed to the plastic necklace. "Santa brought her that when she was just an itty-bitty thing. She loved it. Thought it was the most beautiful jewelry in the world." A wave of sadness swept through Savannah as she remembered. "I'm glad she loved it so much, because that was before we went to live with Granny, and it's the only thing Santa brought Alma that year. She was lucky. If I hadn't shoplifted it from our local five-and-dime store, she wouldn't have gotten that."

Ethan picked up the necklace and ran it slowly through his fingers, touching each glittery bead. Then he kissed it, like it was a rosary, and said, his voice trembling, "She told me that things were rough for you guys. She didn't say how rough."

"She wouldn't. Alma's never been one to complain about anything. But we had some very bad times, Ethan. The little girl Alma was, she suffered, and that wounded child is still inside her. Always will be. You need to know that, or you won't understand some of the things you'll see in her, hear from her."

He nodded and solemnly placed the necklace back in the box.

Savannah pointed to the blue ribbons. "You have an extremely good speller at your beck and call now. Better than a walking dictionary. There is nothing that gal can't spell."

"Good to know, 'cause I'm a pretty lousy speller myself."

Savannah picked up the stack of photos and untied the red ribbon from around them. "This ribbon was a cherished adornment in our household. Marietta and Vidalia drew blood, fighting over who was going to wear it every morning. By the time it got passed down to poor little Alma, well, you can see the condition it was in. But she loved it all the same. It looked so pretty on her with her black curls."

She slipped a photo into his hands, "This is her with an alley cat she nursed back to health. This one is her with the cast on her hand after the truck accident that almost killed us all."

She showed him another picture of a rundown, shotgun house, sitting in the middle of nowhere with Granny as a younger woman sitting on its rickety step, her "grand-angels" gathered around her. "This is the house we were raised in, once the courts gave us to Granny," she told him. "Not really much more than a shack, but that's where Gran lived for most of her life. See why she adores that beautiful new beach home you bought her? Why it's such a dream come true for her?"

He nodded and whispered, "I'm so glad."

She chose one more photo from the stack, a picture of a burned heap and a little girl standing next to a fire truck. A firefighter had placed his hat on her and was kneeling beside her, his arm around her shoulders.

"This was taken the night our mom's rented house burned down. I was with Granny that night, and Shirley had left the little ones alone to go to the tavern. Cordelia set the house on fire, and Alma was the one who made sure they all got out, including the youngest, who was asleep in the bathtub on a pile of dirty clothes. Alma saved her siblings' lives when she was only eight years old."

She placed the photos back in the box and closed it. "It's about time for you go to downstairs and make that remarkable woman your wife, Ethan, but I just wanted you to know where she came from. You're going to have to embrace who she was, along with who she is and who she will be."

"I will, Savannah. I promise. I'll also cherish this box and what it represents for the rest of my life. Thank you."

A knock sounded on the door. Then Ryan called, "Mr. Malloy, five minutes to curtain."

Savannah stood and pulled him to his feet.

"Enough walks down Memory Lane," she said. "You've gotta get downstairs so you can make some new ones with your beautiful bride. Beautiful memories! The first of many!"

"I can hardly wait," he said.

She could tell he meant it.

Chapter 36

Savannah, Tammy, Vanna Rose, and Freddy stood at the back of the ballroom, waiting for the pianist to begin the wedding march. Savannah stole a glance at Ethan and Waycross standing near the marble fireplace with the clergyman in his white robe and scarlet sash. Ethan looked as radiant as Alma had, and Savannah was both happy and relieved that he had accepted her gift so graciously.

He was a good man. He loved Alma. He was kind to her family. What more could one ask for in a brother-in-law?

Savannah stepped aside and allowed Granny to enter first, arm in arm with an extremely happy six-year-old. Brody couldn't have been more excited or taken his job more seriously if he had been escorting a queen.

What a pair they make, Savannah thought, grateful to

have four generations of her family enjoying the blessed occasion together.

She heard the pianist pause, then the old traditional tune began, and her heart started to race. This was it.

Tammy corralled both Freddy and Vanna Rose, making sure that he was holding the ring pillow and she a basket of petals. Gently, she guided them down the aisle toward the fireplace and the waiting groom and groomsmen.

Other than Vanna trying to eat some of the flowers and Freddy tossing the pillow into the air a few times—fortunately with the ring tied on securely with ribbons—all went well.

Savannah was next to walk across the enormous room to the small gathering near the fireplace. The guests were few. Very few. But Ethan and Alma had wanted a quiet, intimate wedding, and that's what it was.

She stood next to Tammy, turned a bit, and smiled down at Granny, who had taken her seat next to Brody in the front row. Together they were holding the youngsters by their hands to keep them from running away or engaging in an impromptu basket/pillow fight.

A moment later, a new verse of the song began, the music swelled, and they all turned to the staircase, where Alma was floating down, step by graceful step, holding on to Dirk's arm.

Savannah's eyes filled with tears and her heart with joy. Looking at the two of them, she knew she had never loved them more. Her sister. Her man taking care of her sister, stepping in to fill the traditional role, and hopefully, a bit of the vacancy in the bride's heart as well.

As Dirk guided Alma to her groom and placed her

hand in his, he glanced over at Savannah and gave her a smile. She blew him a discreet kiss as he slipped into place next to Ethan.

"Dearly beloved," the minister began, and they listened to the traditional words, the admonishments and encouragements spoken for as long as couples have chosen to join their lives together in the sight of the Almighty and those they love.

The usual pledges followed, and all went as expected.

Until it was Ethan's time to speak his vows, and he decided to go "off script."

"I, Ethan Malloy," he said, "take you, Alma Joy Reid to be my lawfully wedded wife. I promise to love you, to honor you, and protect you. I will cherish the precious child you were in your past, the beautiful woman you are at this present moment, and lovely person you will be as we spend our years together, till death do us part. So help me God."

Savannah reached up, touched her cheek, then looked at her fingertips.

Waterproof mascara? No. Not even close, she thought. *But in a few minutes, I get to dance with my husband, maybe even my son. And Alma looks like she's going to be dancing on Cloud Nine for the rest of her days with her Prince Charming, so . . . all is well.*

Yes. Very well, indeed.

Visit us online at
KensingtonBooks.com
to read more from your favorite authors,
see books by series, view reading
group guides, and more!

BOOK CLUB
BETWEEN THE CHAPTERS

Visit us online for sneak peeks, exclusive
giveaways, special discounts, author content,
and engaging discussions with your fellow readers.

Betweenthechapters.net

Sign up for our newsletters and be the first
to get exciting news and announcements about
your favorite authors!
Kensingtonbooks.com/newsletter